His name is Thomas.
Thomas Cavendish.
And he is the Duke of Wyndham . . .
Maybe.

Her name is Amelia.
Lady Amelia Willoughby.
And she's engaged
to the Duke of Wyndham . . .
Whomever that might be.

Mr. Cavendish, I Presume

by

Julia Quinn

By Julia Quinn

JULIA QUINN

Mr. Cavendish, I Presume

AVON

An Imprint of HarperCollinsPublishers

This is a work of fiction. Names, characters, places, and incidents are products of the author's imagination or are used fictitiously and are not to be construed as real. Any resemblance to actual events, locales, organizations, or persons, living or dead, is entirely coincidental.

AVON BOOKS
An Imprint of HarperCollins*Publishers*
10 East 53rd Street
New York, New York 10022-5299

Copyright © 2008 by Julie Cotler Pottinger
ISBN 978-0-06-087611-1
www.avonromance.com

First Avon Books paperback printing: October 2008

Avon Trademark Reg. U.S. Pat. Off. and in Other Countries, Marca Registrada, Hecho en U.S.A.
HarperCollins® is a registered trademark of HarperCollins Publishers.

Printed in the U.S.A.

10 9 8 7 6 5 4 3 2 1

Mr. Cavendish, I Presume

Chapter 1

$\mathcal{I}$t was a *crime* that Amelia Willoughby was not married.

At least that was what her mother said. Amelia—or more correctly, Lady Amelia—was the second daughter of the Earl of Crowland, so no one could fault her bloodlines. Her appearance was more than passable, if one's taste ran toward wholesome English roses, which, fortunately for Amelia, most of the ton's did.

Her hair was a respectable shade of medium blond, her eyes a grayish sort of greenish color, and her skin clear and even, so long as she remembered to stay out of the sun. (Freckles were not Lady Amelia's friend.)

She was also, as her mother liked to catalogue, of adequate intelligence, able to play the pianoforte and paint watercolors, *and* (and here was where her mother punctuated the speech with an enthusiastic flourish) in possession of all of her teeth.

Even better, the aforementioned teeth were perfectly straight, which could not be said of Jacinda Lennox, who had made *the* match of 1818, neatly landing the Marquis of Beresford. (But not, as frequently reported by Jacinda Lennox's mother, before turning down two viscounts and an earl.)

But all of those attributes paled next to what was certainly the most pertinent and overreaching aspect of Amelia Willoughby's life, and that was her longstanding engagement to the Duke of Wyndham.

Had Amelia not been betrothed in the cradle to Thomas Cavendish (who was at the time the Heir Apparent to the dukedom and barely out of leading strings himself), she certainly would not have reached the unappealing age of one-and-twenty as an unmarried maiden.

She had spent one season back in Lincolnshire, because no one thought she'd need to bother with London, then she'd spent the next in the capital, because her elder sister's also-betrothed-in-the-cradle fiancé had the misfortune of contracting a fever at the age of twelve, leaving his family heirless and Elizabeth Willoughby unattached.

And as for the next season—Elizabeth was almost, practically, we're-sure-it-is-forthcoming-at-any moment engaged by then, and Amelia was, as ever, still engaged to the duke, but they went to London anyway, because by then it would have been embarrassing to remain in the country.

Amelia rather liked town. She enjoyed conversation, and she very much enjoyed dancing, and, if one spoke with her mother for more than five minutes, one would have learned that had Amelia been free to marry, there would have been a half-dozen offers, at least.

Which meant that Jacinda Lennox would still have been Jacinda Lennox and not the Marchioness of Beresford. And more importantly, Lady Crowland and all of her daughters would still outrank the annoying little chit.

But then, as Amelia's father was often heard to say— life wasn't always fair. In fact, it rarely was. Just look at him, for the love of heaven. Five daughters. Five! And now the earldom, which had descended neatly from father to son since there were princes in the tower, would revert to the Crown, with nary a long-lost cousin in sight to lay claim upon it.

And, he frequently reminded his wife, it was thanks to his early maneuverings that one of his five daughters was already settled, and they need only fret about the other four, so would she *please* stop yammering on about the poor Duke of Wyndham and his slow progress to the altar.

Lord Crowland treasured peace and quiet above all else, which was something he really ought to have considered before taking the former Anthea Grantham as his bride.

It wasn't that anyone thought that the duke would renege on his promise to Amelia and her family. On the contrary, it was well-known that the Duke of Wyndham was a man of his word, and if he said he would marry Amelia Willoughby, then as God was anyone's witness, he would.

It was just that he intended to do so when it was convenient to *him*. Which wasn't necessarily when it would be convenient to her. Or more to the point, her mother.

And so here she was, back in Lincolnshire.

And she was still Lady Amelia Willoughby.

"And I don't mind it at all," she declared, when Grace Eversleigh brought up the matter at the Lincolnshire Dance and Assembly. Aside from being the closest friend of Amelia's sister Elizabeth, Grace Eversleigh was the companion to the dowager Duchess of Wyndham, and thus in far closer contact with Amelia's affianced husband than Amelia ever had occasion to be.

"Oh, no," Grace quickly assured her. "I did not mean to imply that you did."

"All she said," Elizabeth put in, giving Amelia a queer look, "was that his grace plans to remain at Belgrave for six months at least. And then *you* said—"

"I know what I said," Amelia bit off, feeling her skin flush. Which wasn't precisely true. She could not have repeated her speech word for word, but she had a sneaking suspicion that if she tried, it would come out something like:

Well, that's certainly lovely, but I shouldn't read anything into it, and in any case Elizabeth's wedding is next month so I certainly could not dream of finalizing anything anytime soon, and regardless of what anyone says, I am in no great rush to marry him. Something something something. I barely know the man. Something something more, still Amelia Willoughby. And I don't mind it at all.

Which was not the sort of speech one generally wished to relive in one's head.

There was an awkward, empty moment, and then Grace cleared her throat and said, "He said he would be here this evening."

"He did?" Amelia asked, her eyes flying to Grace's.

Grace nodded. "I saw him at supper. Or rather, I saw him as he walked through the room as we were taking supper. He chose not to dine with us. I think he and his grandmother are quarreling," she added as an aside. "They frequently do."

Amelia felt the corners of her mouth tighten. Not in anger. Not even in irritation. It was resignation, really, more than anything else. "I suppose the dowager pestered him about me," she said.

Grace looked as if she did not wish to answer, but finally she said, "Well, yes."

Which was to be expected. It was well-known that the dowager Duchess of Wyndham was even more eager to see the marriage take place than Amelia's own mother. It was also well-known that the duke found his grandmother vexing at best, and Amelia was not at all surprised that he would agree to attend the assembly just to get her to leave him alone.

As it was *also* well-known that the duke did not make promises lightly, Amelia was quite certain that he would indeed make an appearance at the assembly. Which meant that the remainder of the evening would follow a well-worn path:

The duke would arrive, everyone would look at him, then everyone would look at her, and then he would approach, they would share several minutes of awkward conversation, he would ask her to dance, she would accept, and when they were done, he would kiss her hand and depart.

Presumably to seek the attentions of another woman. A different kind of woman.

The sort one did not marry.

It was not something Amelia cared to ponder, not that that ever stopped her from doing so. But truly, could one expect fidelity from a man *before* marriage? It was a discussion she and her sister had had any number of times, and the answer was always depressingly the same:

No. Not when the gentleman in question had been betrothed as a child. It was not fair to expect him to forgo all of the entertainments in which his friends partook, just because his father had signed a contract a few decades earlier. Once the date was set, however, *that* was a different story.

Or rather, it would be, if the Willoughbys ever managed to get Wyndham to set a date.

"You don't appear to be terribly excited to see him," Elizabeth remarked.

Amelia sighed. "I'm not. Truth be told, I enjoy myself far better when he stays away."

"Oh, he's not so bad," Grace assured her. "He's actually rather sweet once one gets to know him."

"Sweet?" Amelia echoed dubiously. She had seen the man smile, but never more than twice in a conversation. "Wyndham?"

"Well," Grace hedged, "perhaps I overstated. But the

duke will make you a fine husband, Amelia, I promise you. He's quite diverting when he chooses to be."

Amelia and Elizabeth stared at her with such expressions of disbelief that Grace actually laughed and added, "I do not lie! I swear! He has a devilish sense of humor."

Amelia knew that Grace meant well, but somehow this failed to reassure her. It wasn't that she was jealous. She was quite certain she was not in love with Wyndham. How could she be? She rarely had occasion to exchange more than two words with the man. Still, it was rather unsettling that Grace Eversleigh had come to know him so well.

And she could not tell this to Elizabeth, in whom she usually confided everything. Elizabeth and Grace had been fast friends since they'd met at the age of six. Elizabeth would tell her that she was being silly. Or she'd give her one of those dreadful looks that were meant to be sympathetic but instead came out as pitying.

Amelia seemed to be on the receiving end of many such glances these days. Usually whenever the topic of marriage arose. Had she been a betting woman (which she actually thought she might be, should she ever be given the opportunity to try), she would have wagered that she had received sym-pitying looks from at least half the young ladies of the ton. And all of their mothers.

"We shall make it our mission for the autumn," Grace suddenly announced, her eyes sparkling with intent. "Amelia and Wyndham shall finally become acquainted."

"Grace, don't, *please* . . . " Amelia said, flushing. Good Lord, how mortifying. To be a *project*.

"You are going to have to get to know him eventually," Elizabeth said.

"Not really," was Amelia's wry reply. "How many rooms are there at Belgrave? Two hundred?"

"Seventy-three," Grace murmured.

"I could go weeks without seeing him," Amelia responded. "Years."

"Now you're just being silly," her sister said. "Why don't you come with me to Belgrave tomorrow? I devised an excuse about Mama needing to return some of the dowager's books so that I might visit with Grace."

Grace turned to Elizabeth with mild surprise. "Did your mother borrow books from the dowager?"

"She did, actually," Elizabeth replied, then added demurely, "at my request."

Amelia raised her brows. "Mother is not much of a reader."

"I couldn't very well borrow a pianoforte," Elizabeth retorted.

It was Amelia's opinion that their mother wasn't much of a musician, either, but there seemed little reason to point it out, and besides, the conversation had been brought to an abrupt halt.

He had arrived.

Amelia might have had her back to the door, but she knew precisely the moment Thomas Cavendish walked into the assembly hall, because, drat it all, she had *done* this before.

Now was the hush.

And now—she counted to five; she'd long since learned that dukes required more than the average three seconds of hush—were the whispers.

And now Elizabeth was jabbing her in the ribs, as if she needed the alert.

And now—oh, she could see it all in her head—the crowds were doing their Red Sea imitation, and here strode the duke, his shoulders broad, his steps purposeful and proud, and here he was, almost, almost, almost—

"Lady Amelia."

She composed her face. She turned around. "Your grace," she said, with the blank smile she knew was required of her.

He took her hand and kissed it. "You look lovely this evening."

He said that every time.

Amelia murmured her thanks and then waited patiently while he complimented her sister, then said to Grace, "I see my grandmother has allowed you out of her clutches for the evening."

"Yes," Grace said with a happy sigh, "isn't it lovely?"

He smiled, and Amelia noted it was not the same sort of public-face smile he gave her. It was, she realized, a smile of friendship.

"You are nothing less than a saint, Miss Eversleigh," he said.

Amelia looked to the duke, and then to Grace, and wondered—*What was he thinking?* It was not as if

Grace had any choice in the matter. If he really thought Grace was a saint, he ought to set her up with a dowry and find her a husband so she did not have to spend the rest of her life waiting hand and foot upon his grandmother.

But of course she did not say that. Because no one said such things to a duke.

"Grace tells us that you plan to rusticate in the country for several months," Elizabeth said.

Amelia wanted to kick her. The implication had to be that if he had time to remain in the country, he must have time to finally marry her sister.

And indeed, the duke's eyes held a vaguely ironic expression as he murmured, "I do."

"I shall be quite busy until November at the earliest," Amelia blurted out, because it was suddenly imperative that he realize that she was not spending her days sitting by her window, pecking at needlework as she pined for his arrival.

"Shall you?" he murmured.

She straightened her shoulders. "I shall."

His eyes, which were a rather legendary shade of blue, narrowed a bit. In humor, not in anger, which was probably all the worse. He was *laughing* at her. Amelia did not know why it had taken her so long to realize this. All these years she'd thought he was merely ignoring her—

Oh, dear Lord.

"Lady Amelia," he said, the slight nod of his head as much of a bow as he must have felt compelled to make, "would you do me the honor of a dance?"

Elizabeth and Grace turned to her, both of them smiling serenely with expectation. They had played out this scene before, all of them. And they all knew how it was meant to unfold.

Especially Amelia.

"No," she said, before she could think the better of it.

He blinked. "No?"

"No, thank you, I should say." And she smiled prettily, because she did like to be polite.

He looked stunned. "You don't wish to dance?"

"Not tonight, I don't think, no." Amelia stole a glance at her sister and Grace. They looked aghast.

Amelia felt *wonderful*.

She felt like herself, which was something she was never allowed to feel in his presence. Or in the anticipation of his presence. Or the aftermath.

It was always about *him*. Wyndham this and Wyndham that, and oh how *lucky* she was to have snagged the most handsome duke in the land without even having to lift a finger.

The one time she allowed her rather dry humor to rise to the fore, and said, "Well, of course I had to lift my little baby rattle," she'd been rewarded with two blank stares and one mutter of "ungrateful chit."

That had been Jacinda Lennox's mother, three weeks before Jacinda had received her shower of marriage proposals.

So Amelia generally kept her mouth shut and did what was expected of her. But now . . .

Well, this wasn't London, and her mother wasn't watching, and she was just so *sick* of the way he kept her on a leash. Really, she could have found someone else by now. She could have had fun. She could have kissed a man.

Oh, very well, not *that*. She wasn't an idiot, and she did value her reputation. But she might have imagined it, which she'd certainly never bothered to do before.

And then, because she had no idea when she might feel so reckless again, she smiled up at her future husband and said, "But you should dance, if you wish it. I'm sure there are many ladies who would be happy to partner you."

"But I wish to dance with you," he ground out.

"Perhaps another time," Amelia said. She gave him her sunniest smile. "Ta!"

And she walked away.

She walked away.

She wanted to skip. In fact, she did. But only once she'd turned the corner.

Thomas Cavendish liked to think himself a reasonable man, especially since his lofty position as the seventh Duke of Wyndham would have allowed him any number of unreasonable demands. He could have gone stark raving mad, dressed all in pink, and declared the world a triangle, and the ton would still have bowed and scraped and hung on his every word.

His own father, the sixth Duke of Wyndham, had not gone stark raving mad, nor had he dressed all in pink or declared the world a triangle, but he had *certainly* been a most unreasonable man. It was for that reason that Thomas most prided himself upon the evenness of his temper, the sanctity of his word, and, although he did not choose to reveal this side of his personality to many, his ability to find humor in the absurd.

And this was definitely absurd.

But as news of Lady Amelia's departure from the assembly spread through the hall, and head after head swiveled in his direction, Thomas began to realize that the line between humor and fury was not so very much more substantial than the edge of a knife.

And twice as sharp.

Lady Elizabeth was gazing upon him with a fair dose of horror, as if he might turn into an ogre and tear someone from limb to limb. And Grace—drat the little minx—looked as if she might burst out laughing at any moment.

"Don't," he warned her.

She complied, but barely, so he turned to Lady Elizabeth and asked, "Shall I fetch her?"

She stared at him mutely.

"Your sister," he clarified.

Still nothing. Good Lord, were they even educating females these days?

"The Lady Amelia," he said, with extra enunciation. "My affianced bride. The one who just gave me the cut direct."

"I wouldn't call it *direct*," Elizabeth finally choked out.

He stared at her for a moment longer than was comfortable (for her; he was perfectly at ease with it), then turned to Grace, who was, he had long since realized, one of the only people in the world upon whom he might rely for complete honesty.

"Shall I fetch her?"

"Oh, yes," she said, her eyes shining with mischief. "Do."

His brows rose a fraction of an inch as he pondered where the dratted female might have gone off to. She couldn't actually leave the assembly; the front doors spilled right onto the main street in Stamford—certainly not an appropriate spot for an unescorted female. In the back there was a small garden. Thomas had never had occasion to inspect it personally, but he was told that many a marriage had been proposed in its leafy confines.

Proposed being something of a euphemism. Most proposals occurred in a rather more complete state of attire than those that came about in the back garden of the Lincolnshire Dance and Assembly Hall.

But Thomas didn't much worry about being caught alone with Lady Amelia Willoughby. He was already shackled to the chit, wasn't he? And he could not put off the wedding very much longer. He had informed her parents that they would wait until she was one-and-twenty, and surely she had to reach that age soon.

If she hadn't already.

"My options appear to be thus," he murmured. "I could fetch my lovely betrothed, drag her back for a dance, and demonstrate to the assembled multitudes that I have her clearly under my thumb."

Grace stared at him with amusement. Elizabeth looked somewhat green.

"But then it would look as if I cared," he continued.

"Don't you?" Grace asked.

He thought about this. His pride *was* pricked, that was true, but more than anything he was amused. "Not so very much," he answered, and then, because Elizabeth was her sister, he added, "Pardon."

She nodded weakly.

"On the other hand," he said, "I could simply remain here. Refuse to make a scene."

"Oh, I think the scene was already made," Grace murmured, giving him an arch look.

Which he returned in kind. "You're lucky that you're the only thing that makes my grandmother tolerable."

Grace turned to Elizabeth. "I am apparently unsackable."

"Much as I've been tempted," Thomas added.

Which they both knew was untrue. Thomas would have laid himself prostrate at her feet if necessary, just to get her to remain in his grandmother's employ. Luckily for him, Grace showed no inclination to leave.

Still, he would have done it. And tripled her salary at the same time. Every minute Grace spent in his grandmother's company was a minute he didn't have to, and truly, one could not put a price on something such as that.

But that was not the matter at hand. His grandmother was safely ensconced in the next room with her band of cronies, and he had every intention of being in and out of the assembly without their having to share a single word of conversation.

His fiancée, however, was another story entirely.

"I do believe I shall allow her her moment of triumph," he said, coming to this decision as the words crossed his lips. He felt no need to demonstrate his authority—really, could there be any question of it?—and he did not particularly relish the idea that the good people of Lincolnshire might imagine he was besotted with his fiancée.

Thomas did not *do* infatuation.

"That's very generous of you, I must say," Grace remarked, her smile most irritating.

He shrugged. Barely. "I'm a generous sort of man."

Elizabeth's eyes widened, and he thought he heard her breathe, but other than that, she remained mute.

A wordless female. Maybe he should marry *that* one.

"Do you depart, then?" Grace asked.

"Are you trying to be rid of me?"

"Not at all. You know I always delight in your presence."

He would have returned her sarcasm in kind, but before he could do so, he spied a head—or rather, a part of a head—peeking out from behind the curtain that separated the assembly hall and the side corridor.

Lady Amelia. She had not gone so far afield after all.

"I came to dance," he announced.

"You loathe dancing," Grace said.

"Not true. I loathe being required to dance. It is a very different endeavor."

"I can find my sister," Elizabeth said quickly.

"Don't be silly. She obviously loathes being required to dance, too. Grace shall be my partner."

"Me?" Grace looked surprised.

Thomas signaled to the small band of musicians at the front of the room. They immediately lifted their instruments.

"You," he said. "You don't imagine I would dance with anyone else here?"

"There is Elizabeth," she said as he led her to the center of the floor.

"Surely you jest," he murmured. Lady Elizabeth Willoughby's skin had not recovered any of the color that had drained from it when her sister turned her back and left the room. The exertions from dancing would probably lead her to swoon.

Besides, Elizabeth would not suit his purposes.

He glanced up at Amelia. To his surprise, she did not dart immediately behind the curtain.

He smiled. Just a little.

And then—it was most satisfying—he saw her gasp.

She ducked behind the curtain after that, but he was not concerned. She'd be watching the dance. Every last step of it.

Chapter 2

*A*melia *knew* what he was trying to do. It was clear as crystal to her, and she was quite aware that she was being manipulated, and yet, drat the man, there she was, hiding behind the curtain, watching him dance with Grace.

He was an excellent dancer. Amelia knew as much. She'd danced with him many times—quadrille, country dance, waltz—they'd done them all during her two seasons in London. Duty dances, every one of them.

And yet sometimes—*sometimes*—they had been lovely. Amelia was not immune to the thoughts of others. It was splendid to place one's hand on the arm of London's most eligible bachelor, especially when one was in possession of a binding contract declaring said bachelor hers and hers alone.

Everything about him was somehow bigger and

better than other men. He was rich! He was titled! He made the silly girls swoon!

And the ones of sturdier constitution—well, they swooned, too.

Amelia was quite certain that Thomas Cavendish would have been the catch of the decade even if he'd been born with a hunched back and two noses. Unmarried dukes were not thick on the ground, and it was well known that the Wyndhams owned enough land and money to rival most European principalities.

But his grace's back was not hunched, and his nose (of which, happily, he possessed but one), was straight and fine and rather splendidly in proportion with the rest of his face. His hair was dark and thick, his eyes riveting blue, and unless he was hiding a few spaces in the back, he had all of his teeth. Objectively speaking, it would have been quite impossible to describe his appearance as anything but handsome.

But while not unaffected by his charms, she was not blinded by them either. And despite their engagement, Amelia considered herself to be a most objective judge of him. She must have been, because she was quite able to articulate his flaws, and had on occasion entertained herself by jotting them down. Revising, to be sure, every few months.

It seemed only fair. And considering the trouble she would find herself in should anyone stumble upon the list, it really ought to be as *au courant* as possible.

Amelia did prize accuracy in all things. It was, in her estimation, a sadly underrated virtue.

But the problem with her fiancé, and, she supposed, most of humanity, was that he was so difficult to quantify. How, for example, to explain that indefinable air he had about him, as if there was something quite . . . *more* to him than the rest of society. Dukes weren't supposed to look quite so capable. They were meant to be thin and wiry, or if not, then rotund, and their voices were unpleasing and their intellect shallow, and, well . . . she had caught sight of Wyndham's hands once. He usually wore gloves when they met, but one time, she couldn't remember why, but he'd taken them off, and she'd found herself mesmerized by his hands.

His hands, for heaven's sake.

It was mad, and it was fanciful, but as she'd stood there, unspeaking and probably slack-jawed to boot, she could not help but think that those hands had done things. Mended a fence. Gripped a shovel.

If he'd been born five hundred years earlier, he would have surely been a fiercesome knight, brandishing a sword into battle (when he wasn't tenderly carrying his gentle lady off into the sunset).

And yes, she was aware that she had perhaps spent a bit more time pondering the finer points of her fiancé's personality than he had hers.

But even so, when all was said and done, she didn't know very much about him. Titled, rich, handsome— that didn't say much, really. She didn't think it was so very unreasonable for her to wish to know something more of him. And what she truly wanted—not that she could have explained precisely why—was for him to know something of *her*.

Or for him to *want* to know something of her.

To inquire.

To ask a question.

To listen to the answer, rather than nodding as he watched someone else across the room.

Since Amelia had begun keeping track of such things, her fiancé had asked her precisely eight questions. Seven pertained to her enjoyment of the evening's entertainment. The other had been about the weather.

She did not expect him to love her—she was not so fanciful as that. But she *thought* that a man of at least average intelligence would wish to know something of the woman he planned to marry.

But no, Thomas Adolphus Horatio Cavendish, the most esteemed Duke of Wyndham, Earl of Kesteven, Stowe, and Stamford, Baron Grenville de Staine, not to mention a host of other honorifics she had (blessedly) not been required to memorize, did not seem to care that his future wife fancied strawberries but could not tolerate peas. He did not know that she never sang in public, nor was he aware that she was, when she put her mind to it, a superior watercolorist.

He did not know that she had always wished to visit Amsterdam.

He did not know that she hated when her mother described her as of adequate intelligence.

He did not know that she was going to miss her sister desperately when Elizabeth married the Earl of Rothsey, who lived on the other end of the country, four days' ride away.

And he did not know that if he would simply inquire after her one day, nothing but a simple question, really, pondering her opinion on something other than the temperature of the air, her opinion of _him_ would rise immeasurably.

But that seemed to assume he cared about her opinion of him, which she was quite certain he did not. In fact, his lack of worry over her good judgment might very well be the only thing of substance she _did_ know about him.

Except . . .

She peered carefully out from behind the red velvet curtain currently acting as her shield, perfectly aware that he knew she was there.

She watched his face.

She watched the way he was looking at Grace.

The way he was smiling at Grace.

The way he was—good heavens, was he _laughing_? She had never heard him laugh, never even seen him do so from across a room.

Her lips parted with shock and perhaps just a touch of dismay. It seemed she did know something of substance about her fiancé.

He was in love with Grace Eversleigh.

Oh, wonderful.

There was no waltzing at the Lincolnshire Dance and Assembly—it was still considered "fast" by the matrons who organized the quarterly gathering. Thomas thought this a pity. He had no interest in the seductive nature of the dance—he never had occasion to waltz with anyone he intended to seduce. But waltzing did afford the opportunity to converse with one's partner. Which would have been a damned sight easier than a word here and a sentence there as he and Grace went through the convoluted motions of the country dance.

"Are you trying to make her jealous?" Grace asked, smiling in a manner that he might have considered flirtatious if he did not know her so well.

"Don't be absurd."

Except that by then she was crossing arms with a local squire. Thomas bit back an aggravated grunt and waited until she returned to his side. "Don't be absurd," he said again.

Grace cocked her head to the side. "You've never danced with me before."

This time he waited an appropriate moment before replying, "When have I had occasion to dance with you?"

Grace stepped back and bobbed, as required by the dance, but he did see her nod her head in acknowledgment. He rarely attended the local assembly, and although Grace did accompany his grandmother when she traveled to London, she was only rarely included in evening outings. Even then, she sat at the side, with the chaperones and companions.

They moved to the head of the line, he took her hand for their *olevette*, and they walked down the center aisle, the gentlemen to their right, the ladies to their left.

"You're angry," Grace said.

"Not at all."

"Pricked pride."

"Just for a moment," he admitted.

"And now?"

He did not respond. He did not have to. They had reached the end of the line and had to take their places at opposite sides of the aisle. But when they came together for a brief clap, Grace said, "You did not answer my question."

They stepped back, then together, and he leaned down and murmured, "I like to be in charge."

She looked as if she might like to laugh at that.

He gave her a lazy grin, and when he had the opportunity to speak again, asked, "Are you so very surprised?"

He bowed, she twirled, and then she said, her eyes flashing mischievously, "You never surprise me."

Thomas laughed at that, and when they met once again for a bow and twirl, he leaned in and replied, "I never try to."

Which only made Grace roll her eyes.

She was a good sport, Grace was. Thomas doubted that his grandmother had been looking for anything more than a warm body that knew how to say "Yes, ma'am" and "Of course, ma'am" when she'd hired her companion, but she had chosen well all the same. It was a bonus, too, that Grace was a daughter of the district, orphaned several years earlier when her parents had caught a fever. Her father had been a country squire, and both he and his wife were well-liked. As a result, Grace was already familiar with all of the local families, and indeed friendly with most. Which had to be an advantage in her current position.

Or at least Thomas assumed so. Most of the time he tried to stay out of his grandmother's way.

The music trickled to a close, and he allowed himself a glance at the red curtain. Either his fiancée had departed or she'd become a bit more skilled in the art of concealment.

"You should be nicer to her," Grace said as she accepted his escort from the dance floor.

"She cut me," he reminded her.

Grace merely shrugged. "You should be nicer to her," she said again. She curtsied then, and departed, leaving Thomas on his own, never an attractive prospect at a gathering such as this.

He was an affianced gentleman, and, more to the point, this was a local assembly and his intended bride was well known to all. Which *should* have meant that those who might envision their daughters (or sisters or nieces) as his duchess would leave well enough alone. But alas, Lady Amelia did not provide complete protection from his neighbors. As well as she was liked (and as best as he could tell, she was, quite), no self-respecting mama could neglect to entertain the notion that something *might* go awry with the engagement, and the duke *might* find himself unattached, and he *might* need to find himself a bride.

Or so he was told. He wasn't generally privy to such whispers. (For which he assiduously thanked his maker.)

And while there were citizens of Lincolnshire who were not in possession of an unattached daughter/sister/niece, there was always someone looking to curry his favor. It was damnably tiring. He'd have given his arm—well, maybe a toe—for just one day in which no one said something to him because it was what they *thought* he wished to hear.

There were quite a few benefits to being a duke, but honesty from one's companions was not among them.

Which was why, when Grace abandoned him at the edge of the small dance floor, he immediately strode toward the door.

A door, to be more precise. It didn't particularly matter which. He just wanted out.

Twenty seconds later he was breathing the crisp air of the Lincolnshire night, pondering the rest of the evening. He'd planned to go home; he'd actually been looking forward to a quiet evening before his grandmother ambushed him with her plans for the assembly.

But now he was thinking that a visit to Stamford might be more in order. Celeste would be there, his own private widow—very intelligent and very discreet. Their arrangement suited both of them perfectly. He brought gifts—lovely tokens that she could use to supplement the tidy house and modest income her husband had left for her. And she provided companionship with no expectation of fidelity.

Thomas paused for a moment to get his bearings. A small tree, a birdbath, and what appeared to be an overpruned rosebush . . . he'd apparently *not* exited through the door that led to the street. Ah, yes, the garden. With a slight frown, he glanced over his shoulder. He wasn't sure if one could actually reach the street without re-entering the assembly hall, but—at this point he could have sworn he heard someone shrill his name, followed by the words *daughter*, *must*, and *introduce*—by God, he was going to try.

Thomas made his way around the birdbath, intending to round the corner of the building, but just as he passed the abused rosebush, he thought he saw a movement out of the corner of his eye.

He didn't mean to look. The lord knew he didn't *want* to look. Looking could only lead to inconvenience. There was nothing more untidy than finding someone where he (or more often, *she*) was not supposed to be. But of course he looked, because that was simply how his evening was progressing.

He looked, and then he wished he hadn't.

"Your grace."

It was Lady Amelia, most assuredly where she was not supposed to be.

He stared at her forbiddingly, deciding how to approach this.

"It was stuffy inside," she said, coming to her feet. She'd been sitting on a stone bench, and her dress—well, truth be told, he couldn't recall what color her dress was, and in the moonlight he certainly couldn't tell for sure. But it seemed to blend in with the surroundings, which was probably why he hadn't noticed her right away.

But none of that mattered. What mattered was that she was outside, by herself.

And she belonged to him.

Really, this would not do.

It would have been a far grander exit had Amelia been able to sweep out of the assembly hall and leave the premises entirely, but there was the pesky matter of her sister. And her other sister. And her mother. And her father, although she was fairly certain he would have been happy to follow her right out the door, if not for those other three Willoughbys, all of whom were still having a grand time.

So Amelia had made her way to the side of the assembly hall, where she could wait for her family to tire of the festivities on a small stone bench. No one came out this way. It wasn't in the garden proper, and as the purpose of the assembly was to see and be seen—well, a dusty old bench didn't really advance the cause.

But it wasn't too chilly, and the stars were out, which at least provided something to look at, although with her abysmal talents at spotting constellations, this was only likely to keep her busy for a few minutes.

But she did find the Big Dipper, and from there the little one, or at least what she thought was the little one. She found three groupings that might have been bears—really, whoever had devised these things must have had a liking for the abstract—and over there was something she could have sworn was a church steeple.

Not that there *were* any steeply constellations. But still.

She shifted her position—better to get a look at the

sparkly blob off to the north that might, with enough imagination, prove itself an oddly shaped chamber pot—but before she could squeeze her eyes into a proper squint, she heard the unmistakable sound of someone tromping through the garden.

Coming her way.

Oh, bother. Her kingdom for a private moment. She never got any at home, and now it appeared she wasn't safe here, either.

She held herself still, waiting for her intruder to leave the area, and then—

It couldn't be.

But of course it was.

Her esteemed fiancé. In all his splendiferous glory.

What was *he* doing here? When she'd left the assembly hall, he was quite happily dancing with Grace. Even if the dance had drawn to a close, wouldn't he be required to escort her to the edge of the floor and indulge in a few minutes of useless conversation? Followed by several more minutes of being accosted by the many various members of Lincolnshire society who were hoping that their engagement might fall apart (whilst not wishing the prospective bride any ill will, to be sure, but Amelia had certainly heard more than one person ponder the possibility of her falling in love with someone else and racing off to Gretna).

Really, as if a body could escape *her* house without someone noticing.

But it seemed that his grace had managed to extricate himself with record speed, and now he was slinking through the back garden.

Oh, very well, he was walking straight and tall and insufferably proud, as always. But even so, he was definitely sneaking about, which she found worthy of a raised eyebrow. One would think a duke had enough clout to make his escape through the front door.

She would have been content to spin embarrassing stories about him in her head, but he chose that moment—because she was clearly the unluckiest girl in Lincolnshire—to turn his head. In her direction.

"Your grace," Amelia said, because there seemed little point in pretending she was not aware that he'd seen her. He did not make a verbal acknowledgment, which she found rude, but she didn't think she was in a position to abandon her own good manners, so she stood, explaining, "It was stuffy inside."

Well, it was. Even if that hadn't been her reason for leaving.

Still, he didn't say anything, just looked at her in that haughty way of his. It was difficult to hold oneself perfectly still under the weight of such a stare, which she supposed was the point. She was dying to shift her weight from foot to foot. Or clench her hands. Or clench her teeth. But she refused to offer him that satisfaction (assuming he noticed anything she did), and so she stood utterly still, save for the serene smile on her face, which she allowed to shift just a little as she tilted her head to the side.

"You are alone," he said.

"I am."

"Outside."

Amelia wasn't certain how to affirm this without making at least one of them look stupid, so she simply blinked and awaited his next statement.

"Alone."

She looked to the left, and then to the right, and then said, before she thought the better of it, "Not any longer."

His stare grew sharper, not that she'd thought that possible. "I assume," he said, "that you are aware of the potential dangers to your reputation."

This time she did clench her teeth. But just for a moment. "I wasn't expecting anyone to find me," she replied.

He did not like that answer. That much was clear.

"This is not London," she continued. "I may sit unattended on a bench outside the assembly hall for a few minutes without losing my position in society. Provided, of course, that you don't jilt me."

Oh, dear. Was that *his* jaw clenching now? They made quite a pair, the two of them.

"Nevertheless," he bit off, "such behavior is unbecoming for a future duchess."

"Your future duchess."

"Indeed."

Amelia's stomach began performing the oddest selection of flips and turns, and truly, she could not tell if she was giddy or terrified. Wyndham looked furious, coldly so, and while she did not fear for her person—he was far too much a gentleman ever to strike a woman— he could, if he so chose, turn her life into a series of breathless miseries.

As far back as her earliest memory, it had been impressed upon her that this man (boy that he was, at the time) was in charge. Her life, quite simply, and with no arguments accepted, revolved around his.

He spoke, she listened.

He beckoned, she jumped.

He entered a room, and she smiled with delight.

And, most importantly, she was glad for the opportunity. She was a *lucky* girl, because she got to agree with everything he said.

Except—and this had to be his greatest offense—he rarely spoke to her. He almost never beckoned—what could he possibly require that she could provide? And she'd given up smiling when he entered a room because he was never looking in her direction, anyway.

If he made note of her existence, it was not on a regular basis.

But right now . . .

She offered him a serene smile, gazing up at his face as if she did not realize that his eyes were the approximate temperature of ice chips.

Right now, he noticed her.

And then, inexplicably, he changed. Just like that. Something within him softened, and then his lips curved, and he was gazing down at her as if she were some priceless treasure, dropped into his lap by a benevolent god.

It was enough to make a young lady *extremely* uneasy.

"I have neglected you," he said.

She blinked. Thrice. "I beg your pardon?"

He took her hand, raising it to his mouth. "I have neglected you," he said again, his voice melting through the night. "It was not well done of me."

Amelia's lips parted, and although she ought to have done something with her arm (using it to return her hand to her own side would have been an obvious choice), she just stood there like an imbecile, slack-jawed and limp, wondering why he . . .

Well, just wondering *why*, to tell the truth.

"Shall I dance with you now?" he murmured.

She stared at him. What was he up to?

"It's not a difficult question," he said with a smile, tugging gently at her hand as he moved closer. "Yes . . . or no."

She caught her breath.

"Or yes," he said, chuckling as his free hand found its place at the small of her back. His lips approached her ear, not quite touching, but close enough so his words drifted across her skin like a kiss. "Yes is almost always the correct answer."

He exerted a bit of pressure and slowly . . . softly . . . they began to dance. "And always," he whispered, his mouth finally brushing her ear, "when you're with me."

He was seducing her. The realization washed over her with equal parts excitement and confusion. She couldn't imagine why; he had never shown the least inclination to do so before. It was deliberate, too. He was unleashing every weapon in his arsenal, or at least every one allowable in a public garden.

And he was succeeding. She knew that his aims had to be Machiavellian—she was quite certain she had not turned irresistible during the course of one evening—but still, her skin was tingling, and when she breathed (which was not as often as she ought), her body seemed to lighten and float, and maybe she did not know so very much about relations between men and women, but she knew one thing . . .

He was making her silly.

Her brain was still working, and her thoughts were mostly complete, but there was no way he'd know that, because it was all she could do to gaze at him like a lovesick calf, her eyes begging him to move his hand, press at her back.

She wanted to sink against him. She wanted to sink *into* him.

Had she uttered a word since he'd taken her hand?

"I never noticed how lovely your eyes are," he said softly, and she *wanted* to say that that was because he'd never bothered to look, and *then* she wanted to point out that he could hardly see the color in the moonlight.

But instead she smiled like a fool, and she tilted her head up toward his, because maybe . . . just maybe, he was thinking about kissing her, and maybe . . . just maybe, he would actually do it, and maybe . . . oh, definitely, she would let him.

And then he did. His lips brushed hers in what had to be the tenderest, most respectful, and romantic first kiss in history. It was everything she'd dreamed a kiss could be. It was sweet, and it was gentle, and it made her turn rather warm all over, and then, because she couldn't help it, she sighed.

"So sweet," he murmured, and she felt her arms come around his neck. He chuckled at her eagerness, and his own hands moved lower, cupping her bottom in the most scandalous fashion.

She let out a little squeak, squirming against him, and then his hands tightened, and his breathing changed.

And so did his kiss.

Chapter 3

The kiss, of course, had been intended to get her under his thumb, but *this* was a pleasant surprise.

Lady Amelia was rather delightful, and Thomas was finding her bottom to be especially enticing, so much so that his mind was already wandering far ahead, to some fuzzy and frockless place, where he could edge his hands ever so slightly down and around, past the insides of her thighs, his thumbs tickling their way up, and up, and up . . .

Good Lord, he might have to consider actually setting a date with the chit.

He deepened the kiss, enjoying her soft cry of surprise, then tugged her closer. She felt glorious against him, all soft curves and lithe muscles. She liked to ride; he'd heard that somewhere. "You're lovely," he murmured, wondering if she ever rode astride.

But this was not the time—and it was certainly not

the place—to let his imagination get ahead of him. And so, confident that he had quashed her little rebellion, he pulled back, letting one hand linger on her cheek before finally lowering it to his side.

He almost smiled. She was staring at him with a dazed expression, as if she wasn't quite certain what had just happened to her.

"Shall I escort you in?" he inquired.

She shook her head. Cleared her throat. Then finally said, "Weren't you departing?"

"I could not leave you here."

"I can go back in on my own."

He must have looked at her dubiously, because she said, "You can watch me enter the building, if you like."

"Why do you not wish to be seen with me?" he murmured. "I will be your husband before long."

"Will you?"

He wondered where that dazed creature of passion had gone, because now she was watching him with eyes that were clear and sharp. "You doubt my word?" he asked, his voice carefully impassive.

"I would never do that." She took a step away from him, but it was not a movement of retreat. It was more of a signal—he no longer held her mesmerized.

"What, then, was your intention?"

She turned and smiled. "Of course you will be my husband. It is the 'before long' part of it that I question."

He stared at her for a lengthy moment before saying, "We have never spoken frankly, you and I."

"No."

She was more intelligent than he had been led to believe. This was a good thing, he decided. Vexing at times, but overall, a benefit. "How old are you?" he demanded.

Her eyes widened. "You don't know?"

Oh, bloody hell. The things females chose to get up in arms about. "No," he said, "I don't."

"I'm twenty-one." She curtsied then, a mocking little bob. "On the shelf, really."

"Oh, please."

"My mother despairs."

He looked at her. "Impertinent baggage."

She considered this, even looked pleased by the insult. "Yes."

"I ought to kiss you again," he said, lifting one brow into a practiced, arrogant arch.

She wasn't so sophisticated that she had a ready retort for that, a circumstance with which he found himself quite satisfied. He leaned forward slightly, smirking. "You're quiet when I kiss you."

She gasped with outrage.

"You're quiet when I insult you as well," he mused, "but oddly, I don't find it quite as entertaining."

"You are insufferable," she hissed.

"And yet they arrive," he sighed. "Words. From your lips."

"I'm leaving," she declared. She turned to stalk back into the assembly hall, but he was too quick, and he slid his arm through hers before she could escape. To an onlooker, it would have seemed the most courteous of poses, but the hand that rested over hers did more than cover it.

She was locked into place.

"I'll escort you," he said with a smile.

She gave him an insolent look but did not argue. He patted her hand then, deciding to let her choose whether she found the gesture comforting or condescending. "Shall we?" he murmured, and together they strolled back in.

The night was clearly drawing to a close. Thomas noted that the musicians had set down their instruments and the crowd had thinned a bit. Grace and his grandmother were nowhere to be seen.

Amelia's parents were in the far corner, chatting with a local squire, so he steered her across the floor, nodding at those who greeted them, but not choosing to pause in his journey.

And then his future bride spoke. Softly, just for his ears. But something about the question was devastating.

"Don't you ever get tired of the world ceasing its rotation every time you enter a room?"

He felt his feet grow still, and he looked at her. Her eyes, which he could now see were somewhat green, were open wide. But he did not see sarcasm in those depths. Her query was an honest one, fueled not by spite but by quiet curiosity.

It wasn't his practice to reveal his deeper thoughts to anyone, but in that moment he grew unbearably weary, and perhaps just a little bit tired of being himself. And so he shook his head slowly, and said, "Every minute of every day."

* * *

Many hours later, Thomas was climbing the steps to his bedroom in Belgrave Castle. He was tired. And in a bad temper. Or if not bad, exactly, then certainly not good. He felt impatient, mostly with himself. He'd spent the better part of the evening ruminating on his conversation with Lady Amelia, which was annoying enough—he'd never wasted quite so much time on her before.

But instead of coming straight home from the assembly, as had been his original intention, he'd driven to Stamford to visit Celeste. Except once he'd got there, he hadn't particularly felt like knocking upon her door. All he could think was that he'd have to *talk* with her, because that was the sort of friendship they had; Celeste was not a high-stepping actress or opera singer. She was a proper widow, and he had to treat her as such, which meant conversation and other niceties, whether or not he was in the mood for words.

Or other niceties.

And so he'd sat in his curricle, parked in the street in front of her house, for at least ten minutes. Finally, feeling like a fool, he left. Drove across town. Stopped at a public inn where he was not familiar with the clientele and had a pint. Rather enjoyed it, actually—the solitude, that was. The solitude and the blessed peace of not a single person approaching him with a query or a favor or, God help him, a compliment.

He'd nursed his pint for a good hour, doing nothing but watching the people around him, and then, noticing that the hour had grown preposterously late, he went home.

He yawned. His bed was extremely comfortable, and he planned to make good use of it. Possibly until noon.

Belgrave was quiet when he let himself in. The servants had long since gone to bed, and so, apparently, had his grandmother.

Thank God.

He supposed he loved her. It was a theoretical thing, really, because he certainly did not *like* her. But then again, no one did. He supposed he owed her some fealty. She had borne a son who had then married a woman who had borne him. One had to appreciate one's own existence, if nothing else.

But beyond that, he couldn't think of any reason to hold her in any affection whatsoever. Augusta Elizabeth Candida Debenham Cavendish was, to put it politely, not a very nice person.

He'd heard stories from people who'd known her long ago, that even if she'd never been friendly, at least she had once been perhaps not so *un*friendly. But this was well before he'd been born, before two of her three sons died, the eldest of the same fever that took her husband, and the next in a shipwreck off the coast of Ireland.

Thomas's father had never expected to become the duke, not with two perfectly healthy older brothers. Fate was a fickle thing, really.

Thomas yawned, not bothering to cover his mouth, and moved quietly across the hall toward the stairs. And then, to his great surprise, he saw—

"Grace?"

She let out a little squeak of surprise and stumbled off the last step. Reflexively, he sprang forward to steady her, his hands grasping her upper arms until she found her footing.

"Your grace," she said, sounding impossibly tired.

He stepped back, eyeing her curiously. They had long since dispensed with the formalities of titles while at home. She was, in fact, one of the few people who used his given name. "What the devil are you doing awake?" he asked. "It's got to be after two."

"After three, actually," she sighed.

Thomas watched her for a moment, trying to imagine what his grandmother could possibly have done that might require her companion to be up and about at this time of night. He was almost afraid even to ponder it; the devil only knew what she might have come up with. "Grace?" he asked gently, because the poor girl looked truly exhausted.

She blinked, giving her head a little shake. "I'm sorry, what did you say?"

"Why are you wandering the halls?"

"Your grandmother is not feeling well," she said with a rueful smile. And then she abruptly added, "You're home late."

"I had business in Stamford," he said brusquely. He considered Grace one of his only true friends, but she was still every inch a lady, and he would never insult her by mentioning Celeste in her presence.

Besides, he was still rather annoyed with himself for his indecisiveness. Why the devil had he driven all the way to Stamford just to turn around?

Grace cleared her throat. "We had an . . . exciting evening," she said, adding almost reluctantly, "We were accosted by highwaymen."

"Good God," he exclaimed, looking at her more closely. "Are you all right? Is my grandmother well?"

"We are both unharmed," she assured him, "although our driver has a nasty bump on his head. I took the liberty of giving him three days to convalesce."

"Of course," he said, but inside he was berating himself. He should not have allowed them to travel alone. He should have realized they'd be returning late. And what of the Willoughbys? It was unlikely their carriage would have been accosted; they would have traveled in the opposite direction. But still, this did not sit well with him. "I must offer my apologies," he said. "I should have insisted that you take more than one outrider."

"Don't be silly," Grace responded. "It's not your fault. Who would have—" She shook her head. "We are unhurt. That is all that matters."

"What did they take?" he asked, because it seemed an obvious question.

"Not very much," Grace said lightly, sounding as if she was attempting to minimize the situation. "Nothing at all from me. I imagine it was obvious I am not a woman of means."

"Grandmother must be spitting mad."

"She is a bit overset," Grace admitted.

He almost laughed. Inappropriate and unkind, he knew, but he had always adored understatement. "She was wearing her emeralds, wasn't she?" He shook his head. "The old bat is ridiculously fond of those stones."

"She kept the emeralds, actually," Grace replied, and he knew that she must be exhausted, because she did not scold him for calling his grandmother an old bat. "She hid them under the seat cushions."

He was impressed despite himself. "She did?"

"I did," Grace corrected. "She thrust them at me before they breached the vehicle."

He smiled at her resourcefulness, and then, after a moment of uncharacteristically awkward silence, he said, "You did not mention why you're up and about so late. Surely you deserve a rest as well."

She hemmed and hawed, leaving him to wonder what on earth could have her feeling so embarrassed. Finally she admitted, "Your grandmother has a strange request."

"All of her requests are strange," he replied immediately.

"No, this one . . . well . . . " She let out an exasperated sigh. "I don't suppose you'd like to help me remove a painting from the gallery."

Not what he was expecting. "A painting," he echoed.

She nodded.

"From the gallery."

She nodded again.

He tried to imagine . . . then gave up. "I don't suppose she's asking for one of those modestly sized square ones."

She looked as if she *might* smile. "With the bowls of fruit?"

He nodded.

"No."

Good Lord, his grandmother had finally gone insane. This was a good thing, really. Perhaps he could have her committed to an asylum. He could not imagine anyone would protest.

"She wants the portrait of your uncle."

"My uncle? Which one?"

"John."

Thomas nodded, wondering why he'd even asked. He'd never known his uncle, of course; John Cavendish perished a year before he was born. But Belgrave Castle had long lived under his shadow. The dowager had always loved her middle son best, and everyone had known it, especially her other sons. "He was always her favorite," he murmured.

Grace looked at him quizzically. "But you never knew him."

"No, of course not," he said brusquely. "He died before I was born. But my father spoke of him."

Quite often. And never with fondness.

Still, he supposed he should help Grace wrestle the painting from the wall. The poor girl would be unable to manage it herself. He shook his head. "Isn't that portrait life-sized?"

"I'm afraid so."

Good Lord. The things his grandmother did . . . No. No. He wasn't going to do it.

He looked Grace squarely in the eye. "No," he said. "You will *not* get that for her this evening. If she wants the bloody painting in her room, she can ask a footman for it in the morning."

"I assure you, I want nothing more than to retire this very minute, but it is easier just to accommodate her."

"Absolutely not," Thomas replied. Good Lord, his grandmother was enough of a terror as it was. He turned and marched up the stairs, intending to give her the tongue-lashing she so sorely deserved, but halfway up he realized he was alone.

What *was* it with the women of Lincolnshire this evening?

"Grace!" he barked.

And then, when she did not materialize immediately at the foot of the stairs, he ran down and said it louder.

"Grace!"

"I'm right here," she retorted, hurrying around the corner. "Good gracious, you'll wake the entire house."

He ignored that. "Don't tell me you were going to get the painting by yourself."

"If I don't, she will ring for me all night, and then I will never get any sleep."

He narrowed his eyes. "Watch me."

She looked alarmed. "Watch you what?"

"Dismantle her bell cord," he said, heading upstairs with renewed purpose.

"Dismantle her . . . Thomas!"

He didn't bother to stop. He could hear her scurrying along behind him, almost able to keep up.

"Thomas, you can't," she huffed, out of breath from taking the stairs two at a time.

He stopped and turned. Grinned, even, because really, this was almost fun. "I own the house," he said. "I can do anything I want."

His feet ate up the carpet with long strides, barely pausing when he reached his grandmother's door, which was conveniently ajar for easy entry.

"What," he snapped, when he'd made his way to the side of her bed, "do you think you're doing?"

But his grandmother looked . . .

Wrong.

Her eyes lacked their usual hardness, and truth be told, she didn't look quite enough like a witch to resemble the Augusta Cavendish he knew and didn't quite love.

"Good heavens," he said despite himself, "are you all right?"

"Where is Miss Eversleigh?" his grandmother asked, her eyes darting frantically about the room.

"I'm right here," Grace said, skidding across the room to the other side of her bed.

"Did you get it? Where is the painting? I want to see my son."

"Ma'am, it's late," Grace tried to explain. She edged forward, then looked at the dowager intently as she said it again: "Ma'am."

"You may instruct a footman to procure it for you in the morning," Thomas said, wondering why he thought that something unspoken had just passed between the two women. He was fairly certain his grandmother did not take Grace into her confidence, and he knew that Grace did not return the gesture. He cleared his throat. "I will not have Miss Eversleigh undertaking such manual labor, and certainly not in the middle of the night."

"I need the painting, Thomas," the dowager said, but it was not her usual brittle snap. There was a catch in her voice, a weakness that was unnerving. And then she said, "Please."

He closed his eyes. His grandmother never said please.

"Tomorrow," he said, recomposing himself. "First thing if you wish it."

"But—"

"No," he interrupted. "I am sorry you were accosted this evening, and I shall certainly do whatever is necessary—*within reason*—to facilitate your comfort and health, but this does not include whimsical and ill-timed demands. Do you understand me?"

Her lips pursed, and he saw a flash of her usual, haughty self in her eyes. For some reason, he found this reassuring. It wasn't that he viewed her usual, haughty self with much fondness, but the world was a more balanced place when everyone behaved as expected.

She stared at him angrily.

He stared back. "Grace," he said sharply, without turning around, "go to bed."

There was a long beat of silence, and then he heard Grace depart.

"You have no right to order her about that way," his grandmother hissed.

"No, *you* have no right."

"She is my companion."

"*Not* your slave."

His grandmother's hands shook. "You don't understand. You could never understand."

"For which I am eternally grateful," he retorted. Good Lord, the day he understood her was the day he ceased to like himself altogether. He'd spent a lifetime trying to please this woman, or if not that, then half a life trying to please her and the next half trying to avoid her. She had never liked him. Thomas could recall his childhood well enough to know that much. It did not bother him now; he'd long since realized she did not like anyone.

But apparently she once had. If his father's resentful ramblings were any indication, Augusta Cavendish had adored her middle son, John. She had always bemoaned the fact that he had not been born the heir, and when Thomas's father had unexpectedly inherited, she had made it abundantly clear that he was a weak substitute. John would have been a better duke, and if not him, then Charles, who, as the eldest, had been groomed for the spot. When he had perished, Reginald, born third, had been left alone with a bitter mother and a wife he did not like or respect. He had always felt that he had been forced to marry beneath him because no one thought he'd inherit, and he saw no reason not to make this opinion clear and loud.

For all that Reginald Cavendish and his mother appeared to detest one another, they were in truth remarkably alike. Neither one of them liked *anyone*, and certainly not Thomas, ducal heir or not.

"It's a pity we can't choose our families," Thomas murmured.

His grandmother looked at him sharply. He had not spoken loudly enough for her to make out his words, but his tone would have been clear enough to interpret.

"Leave me alone," she said.

"What *happened* to you this evening?" Because this made no sense. Yes, perhaps she'd been accosted by highwaymen, and perhaps she'd even had a gun pointed at her chest. But Augusta Cavendish was no frail flower. She'd be spitting nails when they laid her in her grave, of that he had no doubt.

Her lips parted and a vengeful gleam sparked in her eyes, but in the end she held her tongue. Her back straightened and her jaw tightened, and finally she said, "Leave."

He shrugged. If she did not wish to allow him to play the dutiful grandson, then he considered himself absolved of the responsibility. "I heard they did not get your emeralds," he said, heading for the door.

"Of course not," she snapped.

He smiled. Mostly because she could not see it. "It was not well done of you," he said, turning to face her when he reached the door. "Foisting them upon Miss Eversleigh."

She scoffed at that, not dignifying his comment with a reply. He hadn't expected her to; Augusta Cavendish would never have valued her companion over her emeralds.

"Sleep well, dear grandmother," Thomas called out, stepping into the corridor. Then he popped his head back into the doorway, just far enough to deliver a parting shot. "Or if you can't manage that, be silent about it. I'd ask for invisibility, but you keep insisting you're not a witch."

"You are an unnatural grandson," she hissed.

Thomas shrugged, deciding to allow her the last word. She'd had a difficult night. And he was tired.

And besides that, he didn't really care.

Chapter 4

The most irritating part of it, Amelia thought as she sipped her tea, which had (of course) gone cold, was that she could have been reading a book.

Or riding her mare.

Or dipping her toes in a stream or learning to play chess or watching the footmen at home polish silver.

But instead she was here. In one of Belgrave Castle's twelve drawing rooms, sipping cold tea, wondering if it would be impolite to eat the last biscuit, and jumping every time she heard footsteps in the hall.

"Oh, my heavens! Grace!" Elizabeth was exclaiming. "No wonder you appear so distracted!"

"Hmmm?" Amelia straightened. Apparently she had missed something of interest whilst pondering how to avoid her fiancé. Who, it was worth noting, might or might not be in love with Grace.

And had kissed *her*, anyway.

Shabby behavior, indeed. Toward *both* of the ladies.

Amelia looked at Grace a bit more closely, pondering her dark hair and blue eyes, and realized that she was actually quite beautiful. This shouldn't have come as a surprise; she'd known Grace her entire life. Before Grace had become the dowager's companion, she'd been the daughter of a local squire.

Amelia supposed she still was, only now she was the daughter of a dead squire, which did not offer much in the way of livelihood or protection. But back when Grace's family had been living, they were all part of the same general country set, and if perhaps the parents had not been close, the children certainly were. She had probably seen Grace once every week; twice, she supposed, if one counted church.

But in truth, she hadn't ever really thought about Grace's appearance. It wasn't that she didn't care, or that she considered her beneath notice. It was just that . . . well . . . *why?* Grace had always been simply there. A regular and dependable part of her world. Elizabeth's closest friend, tragically orphaned and then taken in by the dowager duchess.

Amelia reconsidered. *Taken in* was perhaps a euphemism. Truly, Grace worked hard for her keep. She might not be performing menial labor, but time spent with the dowager was exhausting.

As Amelia knew firsthand.

"I am quite recovered," Grace said. "Just a bit tired, I'm afraid. I did not sleep well."

"What happened?" Amelia asked, deciding there was no point in pretending she'd been listening.

Elizabeth actually shoved her. "Grace and the dowager were accosted by highwaymen!"

"Really?"

Grace nodded. "Last night. On the way home from the assembly."

Now this *was* interesting. "Did they take anything?" Amelia asked, because really, it seemed a pertinent question.

"How can you be so dispassionate?" Elizabeth demanded. "They pointed a gun at her!" She turned to Grace. "Did they?"

"They did, actually."

Amelia pondered this. Not the gun, but rather, her lack of horror at the retelling. Perhaps she was a cold person.

"Were you terrified?" Elizabeth asked breathlessly. "I would have been. I would have swooned."

"I wouldn't have swooned," Amelia remarked.

"Well, of course you wouldn't," Elizabeth said irritably. "You didn't even gasp when Grace told you about it."

"It sounds rather exciting, actually." Amelia looked at Grace with great interest. "Was it?"

And Grace—good heavens, she blushed.

Amelia leaned forward, lips twitching. A blush could mean all sorts of things—all of them quite splendid. She felt a rush of excitement in her chest, a heady, almost weightless sort of feeling—the sort one got when told a particularly juicy piece of gossip. "Was he handsome, then?"

Elizabeth looked at her as if she were mad. "Who?"

"The highwayman, of course."

Grace stammered something and pretended to drink her tea.

"He *was*," Amelia said, feeling much better now. If Wyndham was in love with Grace . . . well, at least she did not return the emotion.

"He was wearing a *mask*," Grace retorted.

"But you could still tell that he was handsome," Amelia urged.

"No!"

"Then his accent was terribly romantic. French? Italian?" Amelia actually shuddered with delight, thinking of all the Byron she'd read recently. *"Spanish."*

"You've gone mad," Elizabeth said.

"He didn't *have* an accent," Grace said. "Well, not much of one. Scottish, perhaps? Irish? I couldn't tell, precisely."

Amelia sat back with a happy sigh. "A highwayman. How romantic."

"Amelia Willoughby!" her sister scolded. "Grace was just attacked at gunpoint, and you are calling it romantic?"

She would have responded with something very cutting and clever—because really, if one couldn't be cutting and clever with one's sister, who *could* one be cutting and clever with?—but at that moment she heard a noise in the hall.

"The dowager?" Elizabeth whispered to Grace with a grimace. It was so lovely when the dowager did *not* join them for tea.

"I don't think so," Grace replied. "She was still abed

when I came down. She was rather . . . ehrm . . . distraught."

"I should think so," Elizabeth remarked. Then she gasped. "Did they make away with her emeralds?"

Grace shook her head. "We hid them. Under the seat cushions."

"Oh, how clever!" Elizabeth said approvingly. "Amelia, wouldn't you agree . . . "

But Amelia wasn't listening. It had become apparent that the movements in the hall belonged to a more sure-footed individual than the dowager, and sure enough, Wyndham walked past the open doorway.

Conversation stopped. Elizabeth looked at Grace, and Grace looked at Amelia, and Amelia just kept looking at the now empty doorway. After a moment of held breath, Elizabeth turned to her sister and said, "I think he does not realize we are here."

"I don't care," Amelia declared, which wasn't *quite* the truth.

"I wonder where he went," Grace murmured.

And then, like a trio of idiots (in Amelia's opinion), they sat motionless, heads turned dumbly toward the doorway. A moment later they heard a grunt and a crash, and as one they rose (but still did not otherwise move) and watched.

"Bloody hell," they heard the duke snap.

Elizabeth's eyes widened. Amelia was rather warmed by the outburst. She approved of anything that indicated he was not in complete control of a situation.

"Careful with that," they heard him say.

A rather large painting moved past the doorway, two footmen struggling to keep it perpendicular to the ground. It was a singularly odd sight. The painting was a portrait—life-sized, which explained the difficulty in balancing it—and it was of a man, quite a handsome one, actually, standing with his foot on a large rock, looking very noble and proud.

Except for the fact that he was now tilted at a forty-five-degree angle, and—from Amelia's vantage point—appeared to be bobbing up and down as he floated past. Which cut away significantly at noble and proud.

"Who was that?" she asked, once the painting had disappeared from sight.

"The dowager's middle son," Grace replied distractedly. "He died twenty-nine years ago."

Amelia thought it odd that Grace knew so precisely the date of his death. "Why are they moving the portrait?"

"The dowager wants it upstairs," Grace murmured.

Amelia thought to ask why, but who knew why the dowager did anything? And besides, Wyndham chose that moment to walk past the doorway once again.

The three ladies watched in silence, and then, as if time were playing in reverse, he backed up a step and looked in. He was, as always, impeccably dressed, his shirt a crisp, snowy white, his waistcoat a marvelous brocade of deep blue. "Ladies," he said.

They all three bobbed immediate curtsies.

He nodded curtly. "Pardon." And was gone.

"Well," Elizabeth said, which was a good thing, because no one else seemed to have anything to fill the silence.

Amelia blinked, trying to figure out just what, precisely, she thought of this. She did not consider herself knowledgeable in the etiquette of kisses, or of the appropriate behavior after the event, but surely after what had happened the previous evening, she warranted more than a "pardon."

"Perhaps we should leave," Elizabeth said.

"No, you can't," Grace replied. "Not yet. The dowager wants to see Amelia."

Amelia groaned.

"I'm sorry," Grace said, and it was quite clear that she meant it. The dowager positively reveled in picking Amelia to pieces. If it wasn't her posture, then it was her expression, and if it wasn't her expression, then it was the new freckle on her nose.

And if it wasn't the new freckle, then it was the freckle she was *going* to get, because even if Amelia happened to be standing inside, entirely in the shadows, the dowager *knew* that her bonnet would not be affixed with the proper vigor when the time came to step into the sun.

Truly, the things the dowager knew about her were frightening, both in their scope and inaccuracy.

You will bear the next Duke of Wyndham! the dowager had snapped, more than once. *Imperfection is not an option!*

Amelia envisioned the rest of the afternoon and let

out a sigh. "I'm eating the last biscuit," she announced, sitting back down.

The two other ladies nodded sympathetically and resumed their seats as well. "Perhaps I should order more?" Grace asked.

Amelia nodded dejectedly.

And then Wyndham came back. Amelia let out a growl of displeasure, because now she had to sit up straight again, and of course her mouth was full of crumbs, and of course *of course*, he wasn't even addressing her, anyway, so she was agitating herself for naught.

Inconsiderate man.

"We nearly lost it on the stairs," the duke was saying to Grace. "The whole thing swung to the right and nearly impaled itself on the railing."

"Oh, my," Grace murmured.

"It would have been a stake through the heart," he said with a wry smile. "It would have been worth it just to see the look on her face."

Grace started to stand. "Your grandmother rose from bed, then?"

"Only to oversee the transfer," he told her. "You're safe for now."

Grace looked relieved. Amelia couldn't say that she blamed her.

Wyndham looked over to the plate where the biscuits had once sat, saw only crumbs, then turned back to Grace. "I cannot believe she had the temerity to demand that you fetch it for her last night. Or," he added, in a

voice that was not quite so sharp as it was dry, "that
you actually thought you could do it."

Grace turned to her guests and explained, "The
dowager requested that I bring her the painting last
night."

"But it was huge!" Elizabeth exclaimed.

Amelia said nothing. She was too busy being impressed by Grace's verbal restraint. They all knew the
dowager never *requested* anything.

"My grandmother always favored her middle son,"
the duke said grimly. And then, as if only just noticing
the woman he planned to marry, he glanced at Amelia
and said, "Lady Amelia."

"Your grace," she replied dutifully.

But she rather doubted he heard her. He was already
back to Grace, saying, "You will of course support me
if I lock her up?"

Amelia's eyes widened. She thought it was a question, but it *might* have been a directive. Which was far
more interesting.

"Thom—" Grace began, before clearing her throat
and correcting herself. "Your grace. You must grant her
extra patience this day. She is distraught."

Amelia swallowed the bitter, acidic taste that rose in
her throat. How had she not known that Grace used
Wyndham's Christian name? They were friendly, of
course. They lived in the same house—huge, to be
sure, and filled with a flotilla of servants, but Grace
dined with the dowager, which meant she often dined
with Wyndham, and after five years they must have had
countless conversations.

Amelia knew all that. She didn't care. She had never cared. She didn't even care that Grace had called him Thomas, and she, his fiancée, had never even *thought* of him as such.

But how could she not have known? Shouldn't she have known?

And why did it bother her so much that she *hadn't* known?

She watched his profile closely. He was still speaking with Grace, and his expression was one that he'd never—not even once—used with her. There was familiarity in his gaze, a warmth of shared experiences, and—

Oh, dear Lord. Had he kissed her? Had he kissed Grace?

Amelia clutched the edge of the chair for support. He couldn't have. *She* wouldn't have. Grace was not her friend so much as she was Elizabeth's, but even so, she would never have committed such a betrayal. It was simply not in her. Even if she had thought herself in love with him, even if she'd thought a dalliance could lead to marriage, she would not have been so ill-bred or disloyal as to—

"Amelia?"

Amelia blinked her sister's face into focus.

"Are you unwell?"

"I'm perfectly fine," she said sharply, because the last thing she wanted was everyone looking at her when she was certain she'd gone quite green.

And of course, everyone was.

But Elizabeth was not the sort to be put off. She laid

a hand on Amelia's forehead, murmuring, "You're not warm."

"Of course not," Amelia muttered, brushing her away. "I was just standing too long."

"You were sitting," Elizabeth pointed out.

Amelia stood. "I believe I need some air."

Elizabeth also rose to her feet. "I thought you wanted to sit."

"I'll sit outside," Amelia ground out, dearly wishing she had not outgrown her childhood penchant for smacking her sister on the shoulder. "Excuse me," she muttered, crossing the room even though it meant she had to brush right past Wyndham and Grace.

He had already risen, gentleman that he was, and now bowed his head ever so slightly as she passed.

And then—oh, God, could anything be more mortifying—out of the corner of her eye she saw Grace elbow him in the ribs.

There was a terrible moment of silence, during which he was surely glaring at Grace (Amelia had already made it to the door, and thankfully was not required to look at his face), and then, in his usual polite voice, Wyndham said, "Allow me to escort you."

Amelia paused in the doorway and slowly turned around. "Thank you for your concern," she said carefully, "but it is not necessary."

She saw on his face that he would have liked to accept the exit option she'd offered, but he must have felt guilty for ignoring her, because he let out a crisp,

"Of course it is," and the next thing she knew, her hand was on his arm and they were walking outside.

And she wanted to don her blandest smile and say—

Oh, how lucky *I am to be your bride.*

Or if not that then—

Will I be required to make conversation?

Or at the very least—

Your cravat is askew.

But of course she didn't.

Because he was the duke, and she was his betrothed, and if perhaps she'd managed a small show of spirit the night before . . .

That was before he'd kissed her.

Funny how that changed everything.

Amelia stole a glance at him. He was staring straight ahead, and the line of his jaw was impossibly proud and resolute.

He hadn't looked at Grace in that manner.

She swallowed, suppressing a sigh. She couldn't make a sound, because then he would turn, and then he'd look at her in that way of his—piercing, icy—really, her life would be so much simpler if his eyes were not quite so blue. And then he'd ask her what was wrong, but of course he would not care about the answer, and she'd *know* that from his tone, and that would just make her feel worse, and—

And what? What did she care, really?

He paused, a slight break in his stride, and she glanced up at him again. He was looking over his shoulder, back at the castle.

Back at Grace.

Amelia suddenly felt rather sick.

This time she was not able to suppress her sigh. Apparently she cared rather a lot.

Blast it all.

It was, Thomas realized almost dispassionately, a spectacular day. The sky was equal parts blue and white, and the grass just long enough to ruffle gently in the breeze. There were trees ahead, a peculiarly wooded area, right in the middle of farmland, with gentle hills sloping down toward the coast. The sea was more than two miles away, but on days like this, when the wind came in from the east, the air held the faint tang of salt. There was nothing but nature ahead, left as God had made it, or at least as the Saxons had cleared it hundreds of years ago.

It was marvelous, and marvelously wild. If one kept one's back to the castle, one might be able to forget the existence of civilization. There was almost the sense that if you kept walking, you could just go on and on . . . away. Disappear.

He had pondered this on occasion. It was tempting.

But behind him lay his birthright. It was huge and imposing, and from the outside, not particularly friendly.

Thomas thought of his grandmother. Belgrave wasn't always particularly friendly on the inside, either.

But it was his, and he loved it, even with the massive weight of responsibility that came with it. Belgrave Castle was in his bones. It was in his soul. And no matter how much he was occasionally tempted, he could never walk away.

There were other, more immediate obligations, however, the most pressing of which was walking at his side.

He sighed inside, the only indication of weariness an ever so slight roll of his eyes. He probably should have danced attendance on Lady Amelia when he'd seen her in the drawing room. Hell, he probably should have spoken to her before addressing Grace. In fact, he *knew* he should have done, but the scene with the painting had been so farcical, he had to tell someone about it, and it wasn't as if Lady Amelia would have understood.

Still, he had kissed her last night, and even if he had a perfect right to do so, he supposed that required a bit of postencounter finesse. "I trust your journey home last evening went without incident," he said, deciding that was as good a conversational introduction as any.

Her eyes remained focused on the trees ahead. "We were not accosted by highwaymen," she confirmed.

He glanced over at her, attempting to gauge her tone. There had been a hint of irony in her voice, but her face was magnificently placid.

She caught him looking at her and murmured, "I thank you for your concern."

He could not help wondering if she thought she was mocking him. "Lovely weather this morning," he said, because it seemed like the right thing to say to needle her. He wasn't sure why. And he wasn't sure why he wanted to.

"It's very pleasant," she agreed.

"And you are feeling improved?"

"Since last night?" she asked, blinking with surprise.

He looked down at her pinking cheeks with some amusement. "I'd thought since five minutes ago, but last night will do just as well."

It was good to know he still knew how to kiss a blush onto a woman's cheeks.

"I am much better now," she said crisply, batting at her hair, which, unconfined by a bonnet, was now blowing about in the breeze. It kept getting caught in the corner of her mouth. He would have found that vastly annoying. How did women tolerate it?

"I was feeling overly closed-in in the drawing room," she added.

"Ah yes," he murmured. "The drawing room is a bit confined."

It could seat forty.

"The company was stifling," she said pointedly.

He smiled to himself. "I had no idea you were on such uncomfortable terms with your sister."

She'd been directing her barbs at the trees down the hill, but at this she snapped her head in his direction. "I wasn't talking about my sister."

"I was aware," he murmured.

Her skin flushed even deeper, and he wondered which was the cause—anger or embarrassment. Both, probably. "Why are you here?" she demanded.

He paused to consider this. "I live here."

"With me." This, between her teeth.

"Unless I am mistaken, you are to be my wife."

She stopped walking, turned, and looked him straight in the eye. "You don't like me."

She didn't sound particularly saddened by this, more exasperated than anything. Which he found curious. "That's not true," he replied. Because it wasn't. There was a huge difference between dislike and disregard.

"You don't," she persisted.

"Why would you think so?"

"How could I not?"

He offered her a sultry gaze. "I believe I liked you quite well last night."

She said nothing, but her body was so tense, and her face such a picture of concentration, that he could almost hear her counting to ten before grinding out, "I am a duty to you."

"True," he agreed, "but possibly a pleasant one."

Her face moved with charming intensity. He had no idea what she was thinking; any man who said he could read females was a fool or a liar. But he found it rather entertaining to watch her think, to see her expressions shift and sway as she tried to figure out how best to deal with him.

"Do you ever think about me?" she finally asked.

It was such a typically female question; he felt as if he were defending mankind everywhere when he promptly answered, "I'm thinking about you right now."

"You *know* what I mean."

He thought about lying. It was, most likely, the kind thing to do. But he'd recently discovered that this creature he was meant to marry was far more intelligent than she'd originally let on, and he didn't think she would be appeased by platitudes. And so he told the truth.

"No."

She blinked. And then again. And then several more times. Clearly, this was not what she had been expecting. "No?" she finally echoed.

"You should consider it a compliment," he instructed. "If I thought less of you, I'd lie."

"If you thought more of me, I'd not have to ask you this question right now."

He felt his patience begin to drip away. He was here, wasn't he, escorting her across the fields, when the truth was, all he really wanted to do was . . .

Something, he thought crossly. He wasn't sure what, but the truth was, he had at least a dozen matters that required his attention, and if he didn't particularly want to *do* them, he dearly wanted to have them done.

Did she think herself his only responsibility? Did she think he had time to sit about, composing poems to a woman he hadn't even chosen for a wife? She'd been *assigned* to him, for God's sake. In the bloody cradle.

He turned to her, his eyes piercing hers. "Very well, Lady Amelia. What are your expectations of me?"

She seemed flummoxed by the question, stammering some sort of nonsense he doubted even she understood. Good God, he didn't have time for this. He'd got no sleep the night before, his grandmother was even more of an aggravation than usual, and now his affianced bride, who had heretofore never uttered a peep beyond the usual claptrap about the weather, was suddenly acting as if he had obligations toward her.

Beyond marrying her, of course. Which he fully intended to do. But good Lord, not this afternoon.

He rubbed his brow with his thumb and middle finger. His head had started to ache.

"Are you all right?" Lady Amelia inquired.

"I'm fine," he snapped.

"At least as well as *I* was in the drawing room," he heard her mutter.

And really, that was too much. He lifted his head, pinned her with a stare. "Shall I kiss you again?"

She said nothing. But her eyes grew round.

He let his gaze fall upon her lips and murmured, "It seemed to make the both of us far more agreeable."

Still she said nothing. He decided to take that as a yes.

Chapter 5

$\mathcal{N}$o!" Amelia exclaimed, jumping back a step.

And if she hadn't been so discombobulated by his sudden swerve into amorous territory, she would have greatly enjoyed *his* discombobulation when he stumbled forward, his lips finding nothing but air.

"Really?" he drawled, once he'd regained his footing.

"You don't even want to kiss me," she said, backing up another step. He was starting to look dangerous.

"Indeed," he murmured, eyes glittering. "Just as I don't like you."

Her heart dropped about a foot. "You don't?" she echoed.

"According to you," he reminded her.

She felt her skin burn with embarrassment—the sort only possible when one's own words were being tossed in one's face. "I don't want you to kiss me," she stammered.

"Don't you?" he asked, and she wasn't sure how he managed it, but they weren't quite so far apart any longer.

"No," she said, fighting to maintain her equilibrium. "I don't, because . . . because . . . " She thought about this—thought frantically about it, because there was no way her thoughts could be anything approaching calm and rational in such a position.

And then it was clear.

"No," she said again. "I don't. Because you don't."

He froze, but just for a moment. "You think I don't wish to kiss you?"

"I know you don't," she replied, in what had to be the bravest moment of her life. Because in that moment he was *everything* ducal.

Fierce. Proud. Possibly furious. And, with the wind ruffling his dark hair until it was just ever so slightly mussed, so handsome it almost hurt to look at him.

And the truth was, she very much did wish to kiss him. Just not if he didn't want to kiss her.

"I believe you think too much," he finally said.

She could think of no possible reply. But she did add to the space between them.

Which he eliminated immediately. "I very much wish to kiss you," he said, moving forward. "In fact, it might very well be the *only* thing I wish to do with you right now."

"You don't," she said quickly, inching away. "You only think you do."

He laughed then, which would have been insulting if she weren't so focused on keeping her footing—*and* her pride.

"It's because you think you can control me that way," she said, glancing down to make sure she wasn't about to step into a mole hole as she scooted back another foot. "You think if you seduce me, I shall turn into a spineless, mushy blob of a woman, unable to do anything but sigh your name."

He looked as if he wanted to laugh again, although this time she thought—*maybe*—it would be with her, not at her.

"Is that what you think?" he asked, smiling.

"It's what I think you think."

The left corner of his mouth quirked up. He looked charming. Boyish. Completely unlike himself—or at least unlike the man she ever got to see.

"I think you're right," he said.

Amelia was so flummoxed she actually felt her jaw drop. "You do?"

"I do. You're far more intelligent than you let on," he said.

Was that a compliment?

"But," he added, "that doesn't change the fundamental essence of the moment."

Which was . . . ?

He shrugged. "I'm still going to kiss you."

Her heart began to pound, and her feet—traitorous little appendages that they were—grew *roots*.

"The thing is," he said softly, reaching out and taking her hand, "that while you are correct—I do rather enjoy turning you into a—what was that charming phrase of yours?—a spineless blob of a woman, whose only purpose in life is to agree with my every word, I find myself rather perplexed by a certain rather self-evident truth."

Her lips parted.

"I want to kiss you."

He tugged at her hand, pulled her toward him.

"Very much."

She wanted to ask him why. No, she didn't, because she was quite certain the answer would be something that would only melt whatever portion of her resolve still remained. But she wanted to . . . Oh, good Lord, she didn't know what she wanted to do. Something. Anything. Anything that might remind them both that she was still in possession of a brain.

"Call it luck," he said softly. "Or serendipity. But for whatever reason, I wish to kiss you . . . it's very enjoyable." He brought her hand to his lips. "Wouldn't you agree?"

She nodded. However much she wanted to, she could not bring herself to lie.

His eyes seemed to darken, from azure to dusk. "I'm so glad we are in accord," he murmured. He touched her chin, tipping her face up toward his. His mouth found hers, softly at first, teasing her lips open, waiting for her sigh before he swooped in, capturing her breath, her will, her very ability to form thoughts, except that . . .

This was different.

Truly, that was the only rational, fully-formed idea she could manage. She was lost in a sea of breathless sensation, driven by a need she barely understood, but all the while, she could feel this one thing inside—

This was different.

Whatever his purposes, whatever his intent, his kiss was not the same as the time before.

And she could not resist him.

He hadn't meant to kiss her. Not when he'd found himself strong-armed into accompanying her on a stroll, not when they'd walked down the hill, out of sight of the house, and not even, really, when he'd mocked her with: *Shall I kiss you again?*

But then she'd made her mushy-blobby speech, and he couldn't do anything but agree with her, and she looked so unexpectedly fetching, fighting her hair, which had completely escaped its coiffure, all the while staring him down—or, if not precisely doing that, at least standing her ground and defending her opinions in a way no one did with him. Except maybe Grace, and even then, only when no one else was present.

It was in that moment that he noticed her skin, pale and luminescent, with the most delightful sprinkle of freckles; and her eyes, not quite green, but not brown, either, lit with a fierce, if suppressed, intelligence.

And her lips. He very much noticed her lips. Full, and soft, and trembling so slightly that one would only notice if one stared.

Which he did. He couldn't look away.

How was it he had never noticed her before? She'd always been there, a part of his life almost as long as he could remember.

And then—damn the reasons why, he wanted to kiss her. Not to control her, not to subdue her (although he wouldn't mind either of those as an added boon), but just to kiss her.

To know her.

To feel her in his arms, and absorb whatever it was inside of her that made her . . . *her*.

And maybe, just maybe, to learn who that was.

But five minutes later, if he'd learned anything, he couldn't tell, because once he started to kiss her— really kiss her, in every way a man dreamed about kissing a woman—his brain had ceased to function in any recognizable manner.

He couldn't imagine why he suddenly wanted her with an intensity that made his head spin. Maybe it was because she was his, and he knew it, and maybe all men had a primitive, possessive streak. Or maybe it was because he liked it when he rendered her speechless, even if the endeavor left him in a similarly stunned state.

Whatever the case, the moment his lips parted hers, and his tongue slipped inside to taste her, the world around them had spun and faded and dropped away, and all that was left was *her*.

His hands found her shoulders, then her back, and then her bottom. He squeezed and pressed, groaning as he felt her mold against him. It was insane. They were in a field. In the full sun. And he wanted to take her right there. Right then. Lift her skirts and tumble her until they'd worn the grass right off the ground.

And then he wanted to do it again.

He kissed her with all the mad energy that was coursing through his blood, and his hands moved instinctively to her clothing, searching for buttons, clasps, anything that would open her to him, allow him to feel her skin, her heat. It was when he'd finally got two of them open at her back that he regained at least a portion of his sensibility. He wasn't sure exactly what had brought reason back to the fore—it might have been her moan, husky and accommodating and completely inappropriate from an innocent virgin. But it was probably his reaction to the sound—which was swift and hot and involved rather detailed images of her, unclothed and doing things she probably didn't even know were possible.

He pushed her away, at once reluctant and determined. He sucked in his breath, then shuddered an exhalation, not that it seemed to do anything to calm the rapid tattoo of his heart. The words *I'm sorry* hung on his tongue, and honestly, he meant to say them, because that was what a gentleman did, but when he looked up and saw her, lips parted and wet, eyes wide and dazed and somehow greener than before, his mouth formed words with absolutely no direction from his brain, and he said, "That was . . . surprising."

She blinked.

"Pleasantly so," he added, somewhat relieved that he sounded more composed than he actually felt.

"I've never been kissed," she said.

He smiled, somewhat amused. "I kissed you last night."

"Not like that," she whispered, almost as if she were saying it to herself.

His body, which had begun to calm, started to fire up again.

"Well," she said, still looking rather stunned herself, "I suppose you *have* to marry me now."

At any other moment, from any other woman . . . hell, after any other kiss, he would have descended into instant irritation. But something about Amelia's tone, and *everything* about her face, which still carried a rather fetchingly dubious expression, brought about the exact opposite reaction, and he laughed.

"What's so funny?" she demanded. But didn't demand, really, because she was still too befuddled to manage anything shrill.

"I have no idea," he said quite honestly. "Here, turn around, I'll do you up."

Her hand flew to the back of her neck, and from her gasp he wondered if she'd even realized he had undone two of her buttons. She tried to refasten them herself, and he rather enjoyed watching the attempt, but after about ten seconds of frantic fumbling, he took pity on her and gently brushed her fingers aside.

"Allow me," he murmured.

As if she had any other choice.

His hands worked slowly, even though every rational corner of his brain knew that a quick frock closure was in order. But he was mesmerized by that small patch of skin, peachy smooth and his alone. Faint blond tendrils slid down her nape, and when his breath touched her, her skin seemed to shiver.

He leaned down. He couldn't help himself. He kissed her.

And she moaned again.

"We had better return," he said roughly, stepping back. Then he realized he'd never done the last button of her frock. He swore under his breath, because it couldn't possibly be a good idea to touch her again, but he couldn't very well send her back to the house like that, so back to the buttons he went, moving with considerably more diligence this time.

"There you are," he muttered.

She turned, eyeing him warily. It made him feel like a despoiler of innocents.

And oddly, he didn't mind. He held out his arm. "Shall I escort you back?"

She nodded, and he had the strangest, most intense need in that moment—

To know what she was thinking.

Funny, that. He'd never cared to know what anyone had thought before.

But he didn't ask. Because he didn't do such things. And really, what was the need? They'd marry eventually, so it didn't matter what either of them thought, did it?

Amelia hadn't thought it was possible for a blush of embarrassment to stain one's cheeks for a full hour, but clearly it was, because when the dowager intercepted her in the hall, at *least* sixty minutes after she had rejoined Grace and Elizabeth in the drawing room, the dowager took one look at her face and her own face went nearly purple with fury.

Now she was stuck, standing like a tree in the hall, forced to remain motionless as the dowager snapped away at her, her voice rising to an astonishing crescendo on, "Damn *damn* freckles!"

Amelia flinched. The dowager had berated her for her freckles before (not that they even numbered in the double digits), but this was the first time her anger had turned profane.

"I don't have any new freckles," she ground out, wondering how Wyndham had managed to escape this scene. He'd slipped away the moment he returned her, pink-cheeked, to the drawing room, a sitting duck for the dowager, who had always held the sun in about as much affection as did a vampire bat.

Which did hold a certain ironic justice, as she held the *dowager* in about as much affection as she did a vampire bat.

The dowager drew back at her comment. "What did you just say?"

As Amelia had never talked back to her before, she could not be surprised at her reaction. But she seemed to be turning over a new leaf these days, one of assertiveness and cheek, so she swallowed and said, "I don't have any new freckles. I looked in the washroom mirror and counted."

It was a lie, and a very satisfying one at that.

The dowager's mouth pinched like a fish. She glared at Amelia for a good ten seconds, which was nine seconds longer than was required to make Amelia squirm, and then barked, "Miss Eversleigh!"

Grace practically leapt through the drawing room doorway and into the hall.

The dowager seemed not to notice her arrival and continued with her tirade. "Does no one care about our name? Our blood? Good God above, am I the only person in this damnable world who understands the importance of . . . the meaning of . . . "

Amelia stared at the dowager in horror. For a moment it looked as if she might cry. Which could not be possible. The woman was biologically incapable of tears. She was sure of it.

Grace stepped forward, stunning them all when she placed her arm around the dowager's shoulders. "Ma'am," she said soothingly, "it has been a difficult day."

"It has not been difficult," the dowager snapped, shaking her off. "It has been anything *but* difficult."

"Ma'am," Grace said again, and again Amelia marveled at the gentle calmness of her voice.

"Leave me alone!" the dowager roared. "I have a *dynasty* to worry about! You are nothing! Nothing!"

Grace lurched back. Amelia saw her throat work, and she could not tell if she was near tears or absolute fury.

"Grace?" she said carefully, and she wasn't even sure *what* she was asking, just that she thought she should say something.

Grace responded with a quick little shake of her head that clearly meant *don't ask*, leaving Amelia to wonder just what, exactly, had happened the night before. Because no one was acting normally. Not Grace, not the dowager, and certainly not Wyndham.

Apart from his disappearance from the scene. That, at least, was precisely as expected.

"We will accompany Lady Amelia and her sister back to Burges Park," the dowager ordered. "Miss Eversleigh, have our carriage readied at once. We will ride with our guests and then return in our own conveyance."

Grace's lips parted with surprise, but she was accustomed to the dowager and her furious whims, and so she nodded and hurried toward the front of the castle.

"Elizabeth!" Amelia said desperately, spotting her sister in the doorway. The traitorous wretch had already turned on the ball of her foot and was attempting to slink away, leaving her to deal with the dowager by herself.

Amelia reached out and grabbed her elbow, reeling her in with a teeth-grinding, "Sister, dear."

"My tea," Elizabeth said feebly, motioning toward the drawing room.

"Is cold," Amelia said firmly.

Elizabeth attempted a weak smile in the dowager's direction, but the expression did not make it much beyond grimace.

"Sarah," the dowager said.

Elizabeth didn't bother to correct her.

"Or Jane," the dowager snapped. "Which is it?"

"Elizabeth," Elizabeth said.

The dowager's eyes narrowed, as if she didn't quite believe her, and her nostrils flared most unattractively as she said, "I see you accompanied your sister again."

"She accompanied me," Elizabeth said, in what Amelia was quite certain was the most controversial sentence she'd ever uttered in the dowager's presence.

"What is that supposed to mean?"

"Er, I was returning the books my mother borrowed," Elizabeth stammered.

"Bah! Your mother doesn't read, and we all know it. It's a silly and transparent excuse to send *her*"—at this she motioned to Amelia—"into our midst."

Amelia's lips parted with surprise, because she'd always thought that the dowager *wanted* her in her midst. Not that the dowager liked her, just that she wanted her to hurry up and marry her grandson so she might start growing little Wyndhams in her belly.

"It's an acceptable excuse," the dowager grumbled, "but it hardly seems to be working. Where is my grandson?"

"I do not know, your grace," Amelia answered. Which was the absolute truth. He'd not given her any indication of his plans when he abandoned her earlier. He'd apparently kissed her so senseless he hadn't thought any explanations were necessary.

"Stupid chit," the dowager muttered. "I don't have time for this. Does *no one* understand their duty? I've heirs dying off right and left, and *you*"—at this she shoved Amelia in the shoulder—"can't even lift your skirts to—"

"Your grace!" Amelia exclaimed.

The dowager's mouth clamped shut, and for a moment Amelia thought she might have realized she'd gone too far. All she did, however, was narrow her eyes to vicious little slits and stalk off.

"Amelia?" Elizabeth said, moving to her side.

Amelia blinked. Several times. Quickly. "I want to go home."

Elizabeth nodded comfortingly.

Together the sisters walked toward the front door. Grace was giving instructions to a footman, so they walked outside and waited for her in the drive. The afternoon had grown a bit chilly, but Amelia would not have cared if the heavens had opened up and drenched them both. She just wanted to be out of that wretched house. "I'm not coming next time," she said to Elizabeth, hugging her arms to her chest. If Wyndham wished to finally court her, he could come to see her.

"I'm not coming, either," Elizabeth said, glancing dubiously back at the house. Grace emerged at that moment, so she waited for her to step into the drive, then linked her arm in hers and asked, "Was it my imagination or was the dowager worse than usual?"

"Much worse," Amelia agreed.

Grace sighed, and her face moved a little, as if she were thinking the better of the first set of words that had come to mind. Finally, she just said, "It's . . . complicated."

There didn't seem to be anything to say in response to that, so Amelia watched curiously as Grace pretended to adjust the straps of her bonnet, and then—

Grace froze.

They all froze. And then Amelia and Elizabeth followed Grace's stare. There was a man at the end of the drive, much too far away to see his face, or really anything other than the dark hue of his hair and the fact that he sat atop a horse as if he'd been born to the saddle.

The moment hung suspended in time, silent and still, and then, seemingly for no reason at all, he rode away.

Amelia's lips came together to ask Grace who he was, but before she could speak, the dowager stepped outside and barked, "Into the carriage!" And as Amelia did not wish to enter into any sort of dialogue with her, she decided to follow orders and keep her mouth shut.

A few moments later they were all settled into the Crowland carriage, Grace and Elizabeth facing back, Amelia stuck facing front next to the dowager. She kept her face forward, focusing on a little spot behind Grace's ear. If she could just hold this pose for the next half an hour, she might escape without having to lay eyes on the dowager.

"Who was that man?" Elizabeth asked.

No response.

Amelia shifted her gaze to Grace's face. This was most interesting. She was pretending that she had not heard Elizabeth's query. It was easy to see through the ruse if one was facing her; the right corner of her mouth had tightened with concern.

"Grace?" Elizabeth said again. "Who was it?"

"No one," Grace said quickly. "Are we ready to depart?"

"Do you know him, then?" Elizabeth asked, and Amelia wanted to muzzle her. *Of course* Grace knew him. It had been clear as day.

"I do not," Grace said sharply.

"What are you talking about?" the dowager asked, all irritation.

"There was a man at the end of the drive," Elizabeth explained. Amelia wanted desperately to kick her, but there was just no way; she was seated across from the dowager and completely unreachable.

"Who was it?" the dowager demanded.

"I do not know," Grace answered. "I could not see his face."

Which wasn't a lie. Not the second part, at least. He'd stood much too far away for any of them to have seen his face. But Amelia would have bet her dowry that Grace had known exactly who he was.

"Who was it?" the dowager thundered, her voice rising over the sound of the wheels, beginning their rumble down the drive.

"I don't know," Grace repeated, but they could all hear the cracks that were forming in her voice.

The dowager turned to Amelia, her eyes as biting as her voice. "Did you see him?"

Amelia's eyes caught Grace's. Something passed between them.

Amelia swallowed. "I saw no one, ma'am."

The dowager dismissed her with a snort, turning the full weight of her fury on Grace. "Was it he?"

Amelia sucked in her breath. Who were they talking about?

Grace shook her head. "I don't know," she stammered. "I couldn't say."

"Stop the carriage," the dowager yelled, lurching forward and shoving Grace aside so she could bang on the wall separating the cabin and the driver. "Stop, I tell you!"

The carriage came to a sudden halt, and Amelia, who had been sitting face-front beside the dowager, tumbled forward, landing at Grace's feet. She tried to get up, but the dowager had reached across the carriage and clamped her hand around Grace's chin.

"I will give you one more chance, Miss Eversleigh," she hissed. "Was it he?"

Amelia stopped breathing.

Grace did not move, and then, very slightly, she nodded.

And the dowager went mad.

Amelia had just regained her seat when she had to duck to avoid being decapitated by her walking stick. "Turn the carriage around!" the dowager was yelling. They slowed, then turned sharply when the dowager screeched, "Go! Go!"

In less than a minute they were back at the front of Belgrave Castle, and Amelia was staring in horror as the dowager shoved Grace out of the carriage. She and Elizabeth both rose to stare out the doorway as the dowager hopped down after her.

"Was Grace limping?" Elizabeth asked.

"I—" She'd been about to say, *I don't know,* but the dowager had cut her off, slamming the carriage door shut without a word.

"What just happened?" Elizabeth asked as the carriage lurched forward toward home.

"I have no idea," Amelia whispered. She turned and watched the castle receding into the distance. "None at all."

Chapter 6

$\mathcal{L}$ater that day, Thomas was sitting in his study, re-
flecting upon the rather enticing curve of his fiancée's
backside (as he pretended to inspect some contracts his
secretary had drawn up). It was a most pleasant pas-
time, and he might well have continued in this manner
through to supper if not for the tremendous commotion
that erupted in the hall.

"Don't you want to know my name?" an unfamiliar
male voice called out.

Thomas paused, setting down his pen but not otherwise making any motion to rise. He didn't really
care to investigate, and when he heard nothing more
in the next few moments, he decided to return to his
contracts. He'd just dipped his point in ink when his
grandmother's voice rent the air as only her voice
could.

"Will you leave my companion alone!"

At that, Thomas stood. Possible harm to his grandmother could be easily ignored, but not to Grace. He strode into the corridor and glanced out toward the front. Good Lord. What was his grandmother up to now? She was standing by the drawing room door, a few paces away from Grace, who looked as miserable and mortified as he had ever seen her. Next to Grace was a man Thomas had never seen before.

Whose hands his grandmother appeared to have had bound behind his back.

Thomas groaned. The old bat was a menace.

He moved forward, intending to free the man with an apology and a bribe, but as he approached the threesome, he heard the bloody cur whisper to Grace, "I might kiss your mouth."

"What the devil?" Thomas demanded. He closed the distance between them. "Is this man bothering you, Grace?"

She shook her head quickly, but he saw something else on her face. Something very close to panic. "No, no," she said, "he's not. But—"

Thomas turned on the stranger. He did not like the look in Grace's eyes. "Who are you?"

"Who are *you*?" was the other man's reply. That and a rather disrespectful smirk.

"I am Wyndham," Thomas shot back, prepared to put an end to this nonsense. "And you are in my home."

The man's expression changed. Or rather it flickered. For just a moment, and then it was back to insolence. He was tall, almost as tall as Thomas, and of a similar age. Thomas disliked him instantly.

"Ah," the other man said, suddenly all charm. "Well, in that case, I am Jack Audley. Formerly of His Majesty's esteemed army, more recently of the dusty road."

Thomas opened his mouth to tell him just what he thought of that answer, but his grandmother beat him to the punch. "Who are these Audleys?" she demanded, striding angrily to his side. "You are no Audley. It is there in your face. In your nose and chin and in every bloody feature save your eyes, which are quite the wrong color."

Thomas turned to her with impatient confusion. What could she possibly be blithering on about this time?

"The wrong color?" the other man responded. "Really?" He turned to Grace, his expression all innocence and cheek. "I was always told the ladies *like* green eyes. Was I misinformed?"

"You are a Cavendish!" the dowager roared. "You are a Cavendish, and I demand to know why I was not informed of your existence."

A Cavendish? Thomas stared at the stranger, and then at his grandmother, and then back to the stranger. "What the *devil* is going on?"

No one had an answer, so he turned to the only person he deemed trustworthy. "Grace?"

She did not meet his eyes. "Your grace," she said with quiet desperation, "perhaps a word in private?"

"And spoil it for the rest of us?" Mr. Audley said. He let out a self-righteous huff. "After all I've been through . . . "

Thomas looked at his grandmother.

"He is your cousin," she said sharply.

He paused. He could not have heard that correctly. He looked to Grace, but *she* added, "He is the highwayman."

While Thomas was attempting to digest *that*, the insolent sod turned so that they might all make note of his bound hands and said, "Not here of my own volition, I assure you."

"Your grandmother thought she recognized him last night," Grace said.

"I *knew* I recognized him," the dowager snapped. She flicked her hand toward the highwayman. "Just look at him."

The highwayman looked at Thomas and said, as if he were as baffled as the rest of them, "I was wearing a mask."

Thomas brought his left hand to his forehead, his thumb and fingers rubbing and pinching hard at the headache that had just begun to pound. Good God. And then he thought—*the portrait*.

Bloody hell. So that was what that had been about. At half three in the godforsaken morning, Grace had been up and about, trying to yank the portrait of his dead uncle off the wall and—

"Cecil!" he yelled.

A footman arrived with remarkable speed.

"The portrait," Thomas snapped. "Of my uncle."

The footman's Adam's apple bobbed with dismay. "The one we just brought up to—"

"Yes. In the drawing room." And when Cecil did not move fast enough, Thomas practically barked, "Now!"

He felt a hand on his arm. "Thomas," Grace said quietly, obviously trying to settle his nerves. "Please, allow me to explain."

"Did you know about this?" he demanded, shaking her off.

"Yes," she said, "but—"

He couldn't believe it. Grace. The one person he had come to trust for complete honesty. "Last night," he clarified, and he realized that he bloody well *treasured* last night. His life was sorely lacking in moments of pure, unadulterated friendship. The moment on the stairs, bizarre as it was, had been one of them. And that, he thought, had to explain the gut-punched feeling he got when he looked at her guilty face. "Did you know last night?"

"I did, but Thomas—"

"Enough," he spat. "Into the drawing room. All of you."

Grace tried to get his attention again, but he ignored her. Mr. Audley—his bloody cousin!—had his lips puckered together, as if he might whistle a happy tune at any moment. And his grandmother . . . well, the devil only knew what she was thinking. She looked dyspeptic, but then again, she always looked dyspeptic. But she was watching Audley with an intensity that was positively frightening. Audley, for his part, seemed not to notice her maniacal stare. He was too busy ogling Grace.

Who looked miserable. As well she should.

Thomas swore viciously under his breath and slammed the door to the drawing room shut once they were all out of the hall. Audley held up his hands and cocked his head to the side. "D'you think you might . . . ?"

"For the love of Christ," Thomas muttered, grabbing a letter opener off a nearby writing table. He grasped one of Audley's hands and with one angry swipe sliced through the bindings.

"Thomas," Grace said, situating herself in front of him. Her eyes were urgent as she said, "I really think you ought to let me speak with you for a moment before—"

"Before what?" he snapped. "Before I am informed of another long-lost cousin whose head may or may not be wanted by the Crown?"

"Not by the Crown, I think," Audley said mildly, "but surely a few magistrates. And a vicar or two." He turned to the dowager. "Highway robbery is not generally considered the most secure of all possible occupations."

"Thomas." Grace glanced nervously over at the dowager, who was glowering at her. "Your grace," she corrected, "there is something you need to know."

"Indeed," he bit off. "The identities of my true friends and confidantes, for one thing."

Grace flinched as if struck, but Thomas brushed aside the momentary pang of guilt that struck his chest. She'd had ample time to fill him in the night before. There was no reason he should have come into this situation completely unprepared.

"I suggest," Audley said, his voice light but steady, "that you speak to Miss Eversleigh with greater respect."

Thomas froze. Who the hell did this man think he was? "I *beg* your pardon."

Audley's head tilted very slightly to the side, and he seemed to lick the inside of his teeth before saying, "Not used to being spoken to like a man, are we?"

Something foreign seemed to invade Thomas's body. It was furious and black, with rough edges and hot teeth, and before he knew it, he was leaping through the air, going for Audley's throat. They went down with a crash, rolling across the carpet into an end table. With great satisfaction, Thomas found himself straddling his beloved new cousin, one hand pressed against his throat as the other squeezed itself into a deadly weapon.

"Stop!" Grace shrieked, but Thomas felt nothing as she grabbed at his arm. She seemed to fall away as he lifted his fist and slammed it into Audley's jaw. But Audley was a formidable opponent. He'd had years to learn how to fight dirty, Thomas later realized, and with a vicious twist of his torso, he slammed his head into Thomas's chin, stunning him for just enough time to reverse their positions.

"Don't . . . you . . . ever . . . strike . . . me . . . again!" Audley ground out, slamming his own fist into Thomas's cheek as punctuation.

Thomas freed an elbow, jabbed it hard into Audley's stomach, and was rewarded with a low grunt.

"Stop it! Both of you!" Grace managed to wedge herself between them, which was probably the only thing that would have stopped the fight. Thomas just barely had time to halt the progress of his fist before it clipped her in the face.

"You should be ashamed of yourself," she said, and Thomas would have agreed with her, except he was still breathing too hard to speak. And then it became apparent that she was speaking to *him*. It was galling, and he was filled with a not very admirable urge to embarrass her, just as she had embarrassed him.

"You might want to remove yourself from my, er . . ." He looked down at his midsection, upon which she was now seated.

"Oh!" Grace yelped, jumping up. She did not let go of Audley's arm, however, and she yanked him along with her, peeling the two men apart. Audley, for his part, seemed more than happy to go with her.

"Tend to my wounds?" he asked, gazing upon her with all the pitiable mournfulness of an ill-treated puppy.

"You have no wounds," she snapped, then looked over at Thomas, who had risen to his feet as well. "And neither do you."

Thomas rubbed his jaw, thinking that their faces would both prove her wrong by nightfall.

And then his grandmother—oh now *there* was a person who ought be giving lessons in kindness and civility—decided it was time to enter the conversation. Unsurprisingly, her first statement was a hard shove to his shoulder.

"Apologize at once!" she snapped. "He is a guest in our house."

"*My* house."

Her face tightened at that. It was the one piece of leverage he held over her. She was there, as they all knew, at his pleasure and discretion.

"He is your first cousin," she said. "One would think, given the lack of close relations in our family, that you would be eager to welcome him into the fold."

One would, Thomas thought, looking warily over at Audley. Except that he had disliked him on sight, disliked that smirky smile, that carefully studied insolence. He knew this sort. This Audley knew nothing of duty, nothing of responsibility, and he had the *gall* to waltz in here and criticize?

And furthermore, who the hell was to say that Audley actually *was* his cousin? Thomas's fingers clawed then straightened as he attempted to calm himself down. "Would someone," he said, his voice clipped and furious, "do me the service of explaining just how this man has come to be in my drawing room?"

The first reaction was silence, as everyone waited for someone else to jump into the breach. Then Audley shrugged, motioned with his head toward the dowager, and said, "She kidnapped me."

Thomas turned slowly to his grandmother. "You kidnapped him," he echoed, not because it was hard to believe but rather because it *wasn't*.

"Indeed," she said sharply. "And I would do it again."

Thomas looked to Grace. "It's true," she said. And then—bloody hell—she turned to Audley and said, "I'm sorry."

"Accepted, of course," he said, with enough charm and grace to pass muster in the most discerning of ballrooms.

Thomas's disgust must have shown on his face, because when Grace looked at him, she added, "She *kidnapped* him!"

Thomas just rolled his eyes. He did not care to discuss it.

"And forced me to take part," Grace muttered.

"I recognized him last night," the dowager announced.

"In the dark?" Thomas asked dubiously.

"Under his mask," she answered with pride. "He is the very image of his father. His voice, his laugh, every bit of it."

Everything made sense now, of course. The portrait, her distraction the night before. Thomas let out a breath and closed his eyes, somehow summoning the energy to treat her with gentle compassion. "Grandmother," he said, which ought to have been recognized as the olive branch it was, given that he usually called her *you*, "I understand that you still mourn your son—"

"Your uncle," she cut in.

"My uncle," he corrected, although it was difficult to think of him as such, given that they had never met. "But it has been thirty years since his death."

"Twenty-nine," she corrected sharply.

Thomas looked to Grace for he wasn't sure what. Support? Sympathy? Her lips stretched into an apologetic line, but she remained silent.

He turned back to his grandmother. "It has been a long time," he said. "Memories fade."

"Not mine," she said haughtily, "and certainly not the ones I have of John. *Your* father I have been more than pleased to forget entirely—"

"In that we are agreed," Thomas interrupted tightly, because the only thing more farcical than the present situation was imagining his father witnessing it.

"Cecil!" he bellowed again, flexing his fingers lest he give in to the urge to strangle someone. Where the hell was the bloody painting? He'd sent the footman up ages ago. It should have been a simple endeavor. Surely his grandmother had not had time to affix the damned thing to her bedchamber wall yet.

"Your grace!" he heard from the hall, and sure enough there was the painting for the second time that afternoon, bobbing along as two footmen attempted to keep it balanced as they rounded the corner.

"Set it down anywhere," Thomas instructed.

The footmen found a clear spot and set the painting down on the floor, leaning it gently against the wall. And for the second time that day Thomas found himself staring into the long-dead face of his uncle John.

Except this time was completely different. How many times had he walked by the portrait, never once bothering to look closely? And why should he? He'd never known the man, never had cause to see anything familiar in his expression.

But now . . .

Grace was the first to find words to express it. *"Oh my God."*

Thomas stared in shock at Mr. Audley. It was as if he were one with the painting.

"I see no one is disagreeing with me now," his grandmother announced smugly.

"Who *are* you?" Thomas whispered, staring at the man who could only be his first cousin.

"My name," he stammered, unable to tear his eyes off the portrait. "My given name . . . My full name is John Augustus Cavendish-Audley."

"Who were your parents?" Thomas whispered. But he didn't reply, and Thomas heard his own voice grow shrill as he demanded, "Who was your father?"

Audley's head snapped around. "Who the bloody hell do you think he was?"

Thomas felt the world dropping away. Every last moment, every memory, every breath of air that made him think he actually knew who he was—they all slid away, leaving him alone, stark, and completely without bearings.

"Your parents," he said, and his voice shook like the wind. "Were they married?"

"What is your implication?" Audley snarled.

"Please," Grace pleaded, jumping between them yet again. "He doesn't know." She looked at Thomas, and he knew what she was trying to tell him. Audley didn't know. He had no idea what it meant if his birth was indeed legitimate.

Grace looked at him with apology. Because she was also saying that they had to tell him. They could not keep it a secret, no matter what the consequences. She said, "Someone needs to explain to Mr. Audley—"

"Cavendish," the dowager snapped.

"Mr. Cavendish-Audley," Grace amended, ever the diplomat. "Someone needs to tell him that . . . that . . . " She looked frantically from person to person, and then her gaze finally settled upon Audley's stunned face. "Your father—the man in the painting, that is—assuming he *is* your father—he was his grace's father's . . . *elder* brother."

No one said anything.

Grace cleared her throat. "So, if . . . if your parents were indeed lawfully married—"

"They were," Audley bit off.

"Yes, of course. I mean, not of course, but—"

"What she means," Thomas cut in sharply, because by God, he could not stand another moment of this, "is that if you are indeed the legitimate offspring of John Cavendish, then *you* are the Duke of Wyndham."

And then he waited. For what, he wasn't sure, but he was through with this. He'd said his part. Someone else could chime in and offer their bloody opinion.

"No," Audley finally said, sitting down in the closest chair. "No."

"You will remain here," the dowager announced, "until this matter can be settled to my satisfaction."

"No," Audley repeated, with considerably more conviction. "I will not."

"Oh, yes, you will," she responded. "If you do not, I will turn you in to the authorities as the thief you are."

"You wouldn't do that," Grace blurted out. She turned to the man in question. "She would never do that. Not if she believes that you are her grandson."

"Shut up!" the dowager growled. "I don't know what you think you are doing, Miss Eversleigh, but you are not family, and you have no place in this room."

Thomas stepped forward to intercede, but before he could utter a word, Audley stood, his back ramrod straight, his eyes hard.

And for the first time, Thomas no longer believed he'd been lying about his military service. For Audley was every inch an officer as he ordered, "Do not speak to her in that manner ever again."

The dowager recoiled, stunned that he would speak to her in that manner, and over someone she considered beneath notice. "I am your grandmother," she bit off.

Audley did not remove his eyes from her face. "That remains to be determined."

"What?" Thomas burst out, before he had the chance to temper his reaction.

Audley looked at him with cool assessment.

"Are you now trying to tell me," Thomas said disbelievingly, "that you *don't* think you are the son of John Cavendish?"

The other man shrugged, suddenly looking more like the rogue he'd been playing earlier. "Frankly, I'm not so certain I wish to gain entry into this charming little club of yours."

"You don't have a choice," the dowager said.

Audley glanced at her sideways. "So loving. So thoughtful. Truly, a grandmother for the ages."

Grace let out the choked sound that Thomas would have made—in any other circumstances. No, he would have laughed aloud, truly. But not now. Not with a potential usurper standing in his godforsaken drawing room.

"Your grace," Grace said hesitantly, but he just didn't want to hear it right now. He didn't want to hear anything—no one's opinions, no one's suggestions, nothing.

Good God, they were all looking at him, waiting for him to make a decision, as if he were in charge. Oh, now, that was rich. He didn't even know who the bloody hell he was any longer. No one, possibly. No one at all. Certainly not the head of the family.

"Wyndham—" his grandmother began.

"Shut *up*," he snapped. He grit his teeth, trying not to show weakness. What the *hell* was he supposed to do now? He turned to Audley—*Jack*, he supposed he ought start thinking of him, since he couldn't quite manage to think of him as Cavendish, or God help him, Wyndham. "You should remain," he said, hating the weary sound in his voice. "We will need—" Good Lord, he could hardly believe he was saying this. "We will need to get this sorted out."

Audley did not answer immediately, and when he did, he sounded every bit as exhausted as Thomas felt. "Could someone please explain . . . " He paused, pressing his fingers into his temples. Thomas knew that motion well. His own head was pounding like the devil.

"Could someone explain the family tree?" Audley finally asked.

"I had three sons," the dowager said crisply. "Charles was the eldest, John the middle, and Reginald the last. Your father left for Ireland just after Reginald married"—her face took on a visible expression of distaste, and Thomas almost rolled his eyes as she jerked her head in his direction—"*his* mother."

"She was a cit," Thomas said, because hell, it wasn't a secret. "Her father owned factories. Piles and piles of them." Ah, the irony. "We own them now."

The dowager did not acknowledge him, instead keeping her attention firmly on Audley. "We were notified of your father's death in July of 1790. One year after that, my husband and my eldest son died of a fever. I did not contract the ailment. My youngest son was no longer living at Belgrave, so he, too, was spared. Charles had not yet married, and we believed John to have died without issue. Thus Reginald became duke." There was a brief pause, followed by: "It was not expected."

And then everyone turned and looked at him. Wonderful. Thomas said nothing, refusing to give any indication that she deserved a reply.

"I will remain," Audley finally said, and although he sounded resigned, as if he hadn't been offered a choice, Thomas was not fooled. The man was a thief, for God's sake. A thief who had been given a chance to legally snatch one of the highest titles in the land. Not to mention the riches that accompanied it.

Riches that were unfathomable. Even, at times, to him.

"Most judicious of you," the dowager said, clapping her hands together. "Now then, we—"

"But first," Audley cut in, "I must return to the inn to collect my belongings." He glanced around the drawing room, as if mocking the opulence. "Meager though they are."

"Nonsense," the dowager said briskly. "Your things will be replaced." She looked down her nose at his traveling costume. "With items of far greater quality, I might add."

"I wasn't asking your permission," Audley responded coolly.

"Nonethe—"

"Furthermore," he cut in, "I must make explanations to my associates."

Thomas started to intercede. He could not have Audley spreading rumors across the county. Within a week it would be all over Britain. It wouldn't matter if the claims were proved baseless. No one would ever judge him in the same way again. There would always be whispers.

He might not really be the duke.

There was another claim, hadn't you heard? His own grandmother supported it.

It would be a bloody nightmare.

"Nothing approaching the truth," Audley added dryly, with a look in his direction. It made Thomas uncomfortable. He did not like that he could be read so easily. And by this man, most especially.

"Don't disappear," the dowager directed. "I assure you, you will regret it."

"There's no worry of that," Thomas said, echoing what they all had to know. "Who would disappear with the promise of a dukedom?"

Audley seemed not amused. Thomas didn't much care.

"I will accompany you," Thomas told him. He needed to take this man's measure. He needed to see how he conducted himself, how he behaved with no female audience to woo.

Audley gave him a mocking smile, and his left eyebrow rose, just like—good *God,* it was frightening—the dowager's. "Need I worry for my safety?" he murmured.

Thomas forced himself not to respond. The afternoon hardly needed another fistfight. But the insult was acute. His entire life he had put Wyndham first. The title, the legacy, the lands. Nothing had ever been about him, about Thomas Cavendish, a gentleman born in the English county of Lincolnshire; who loved music but abhorred the opera; who preferred to ride astride rather than in a carriage, even when the weather was inclement; who loved strawberries, especially with clotted cream; who had taken a first at Cambridge and could recite most of the sonnets of Shakespeare but never did, because he preferred to linger over each word in his own mind. It never seemed to matter that he found satisfaction in manual labor, or that he had no patience for inefficiency. And no one cared that he had never acquired a taste for port, or that he found the current habit of snuff asinine at best.

No, when the time came to make a decision—any decision—none of this had ever mattered. He was Wyndham. It was that simple.

And apparently, that complicated. Because his loyalty to his name and his legacy was unchecked. He would do what was right, what was proper. He always did. It was laughable, really, too ironic to contemplate. He did the right thing because he was the Duke of Wyndham. And it seemed the right thing might very well mean handing over his very name to a stranger.

If he wasn't the duke . . . Did that make him free? Could he then do whatever he wished, rob coaches and despoil virgins and whatever it was men with no encumbrances chose to do?

But after all he had done, for someone to suggest that he would put his own personal gain above his duty to his family name—

It did not cut to the bone. It burned.

And then Audley turned to Grace, offering her that annoyingly smarmy smile, and said, "I am a threat to his very identity. Surely any reasonable man would question his safety." It was all Thomas could do to keep his hands—fisted though they were—at his sides.

"No, you're wrong," Grace said to Audley, and Thomas found himself oddly comforted by the fervor in her voice. "You misjudge him. The duke—" She stopped for a moment, choking on the word, but then squared her shoulders and continued. "He is as honorable a man as I have ever met. You would never come to harm in his company."

"I assure you," Thomas said smoothly, regarding his new cousin with a cool eye, "whatever violent urges I possess, I shall not act upon them."

Grace turned her temper upon him at that. "That is a terrible thing to say." And then, more quietly, so that only he could hear. "And after I defended you."

"But honest," Audley acknowledged with a nod.

The two men locked eyes, and a silent truce was met. They would travel to the inn together. They would not ask questions, they would not offer opinions . . . Hell, they would not even speak unless absolutely necessary.

Which suited Thomas perfectly.

Chapter 7

"*Y*our eye's gone black."

That was the first thing Audley said to him on the journey, nearly an hour after they'd departed.

Thomas turned and looked at him. "Your cheek is purple."

They were almost to the posting inn where Audley had his belongings stashed, and so they had slowed their gait down to a walk. Audley was riding one of the horses from the Belgrave stables; he was, Thomas could not help but note, an extremely accomplished rider.

Audley touched his cheek, and not with any delicacy. He patted it briskly, the three central fingers of his right hand. "It's nothing," he said, apparently assessing the injury. "Certainly not as bad as your eye."

Thomas gave him a haughty look. Because, really, how could he know? The cheek was purple, quite lividly so.

Audley looked at him with remarkable blandness, then said, "I have been shot in the arm and stabbed in the leg. And you?"

Thomas said nothing. But he felt his teeth clenching together, and he was painfully aware of the sound of his breath.

"The cheek is nothing," Audley said again, and he looked forward anew, his eyes focusing on the bend in the road, just up ahead.

They were nearly to the posting inn. Thomas knew the area well. Hell, he owned half of it.

Or thought he owned it. Who knew any longer? Maybe he wasn't the Duke of Wyndham. What would it mean if he was merely another random Cavendish cousin? There were certainly enough of them. Maybe not as first relations, but the country was positively awash with seconds and thirds.

It was an interesting question. Interesting, of course, being the only word he could use that did not make him want to explode in mad laughter. If he wasn't the Duke of Wyndham, who the hell was he? Did he own anything? Have a stick or stone or rubbly little patch of land to call his own?

Was he even still betrothed to Amelia?

Good God. He looked over his shoulder at Audley, who, damn him, looked cool and unperturbed as he stared at the horizon.

Would *he* get her? Lands, title, every last penny in his accounts—tally ho, mateys! Let's toss in the fiancée while we're at it.

And judging from Grace's reaction to the annoying

sod, Amelia would be head over heels for him at first sight.

He snorted in exasperation. If the day descended any further, he'd reach the seventh level of hell before nightfall. "I'm getting a pint," he announced.

"Of ale?" Audley asked in surprise, as if he could not imagine the Duke of Wyndham drinking anything so plebeian.

"While you do whatever it is you wish to do," Thomas said. He glanced at him out of the corner of his eye. "I assume you don't need me to help you fold up your unmentionables."

Audley turned, his eyebrows arched. "Not unless you have a preference for other men's undergarments. Far be it for me to put a halt to your jollies."

Thomas met his stare with cool purpose. "Don't make me hit you again."

"You'd lose."

"*You'd* die."

"Not at your hand," Audley muttered.

"What did you say?"

"You're still the duke," Audley said with a shrug.

Thomas gripped his reins with far greater vigor than was necessary. And even though he knew exactly what Audley was saying, he found himself gripped—by a peevish little need to make him spell it out. And so, his tone sharp and clipped—and yes, quite ducal—he said, "By this you mean . . . "

Audley turned. He looked lazy, and self-possessed, and completely at ease with himself, which *infuri-*

ated Thomas because Audley was—or looked to be—everything that he himself normally was.

But not now. His heart was pounding, and his hands felt itchy, and more than anything the world seemed somewhat dizzy. It wasn't *him*. *He* did not feel off-balance. Everything else did. He was almost afraid to close his eyes, because when he opened them the sky would be green and the horses would be speaking French, and every time he tried to take a step, the ground would not be quite where he expected it.

And then Audley said, "You are the Duke of Wynd-ham. The law is always on your side."

Thomas *really* wanted to hit him again. Especially since it would prove Audley right. No one would dare cross him here in the village. He could beat Audley to a bloody pulp, and his remains would be swept neatly aside.

All hail the Duke of Wyndham. Just think of all the perks of the title he'd never got around to taking advantage of.

They reached the posting inn, and he tossed the reins to the stable boy who came running out to greet them. Bobby, his name was. Thomas had known him for years. His parents were tenants—honest, hardworking folk, who insisted upon bringing a basket of shortbread to Belgrave every year at Christmas, even though they knew that the Cavendishes could not possibly be in need of food.

"Your grace," Bobby said, beaming up at him, even as he panted from his run.

"You'll take good care of them, Bobby?" Thomas nodded toward Audley's mount as the boy took those reins as well.

"The best, sir."

"Which is why I would never trust them to someone else." Thomas tossed him a coin. "We'll be an . . . hour?" He looked to Audley.

"If that," Audley confirmed. He turned down toward Bobby then, looked the lad straight in the eye, which Thomas found surprising. "You weren't here yesterday," he said.

"No, sir," Bobby replied. "I only works five days each week."

Thomas saw to it that the innkeeper got a little bonus each month for giving the younger boys an extra day off. Not that anyone save the innkeeper knew about it.

"Have you met Lucy?"

Lucy? Thomas listened with interest.

"The black gelding?" Bobby's eyes lit up.

"You have a gelding named Lucy?" Thomas asked.

"That's the one," Audley said to Bobby. And then to Thomas, "It's a long story."

"He's a beauty," Bobby said, his eyes round with awe. Thomas could not help but be amused. Bobby had been mad for horses since before he could walk. Thomas had always thought he'd end up hiring him to run the Belgrave stables some day.

"I'm rather fond of him myself," Audley said. "Saved my life once or twice."

Bobby's eyes went round as saucers. "Really?"

"Really. Napoleon doesn't stand a chance against a fine British horse like that." Audley glanced over toward the stables. "He's well?"

"Watered and brushed. I did it myself."

While Audley made arrangements to have his ridiculously named gelding readied for the ride home, Thomas headed over to the taproom. He supposed he disliked Audley slightly less than before—one had to respect a man who had so much respect for a horse—but still, a pint of ale could not possibly be out of place on a day like this.

He knew the innkeeper well. Harry Gladdish had grown up at Belgrave, the son of the assistant to the stable master. Thomas's father had judged him to be an acceptable companion—he was so far below Thomas in rank that there could be no arguing who was in charge. "Better a stable hand than a cit," Thomas's father had often said.

Usually in front of Thomas's mother, who was the daughter of a cit.

Harry and Thomas did, however, argue about who was in charge, and quite frequently, too. As a result, they'd become fast friends. The years had sent them their separate ways—Thomas's father let Harry share in Thomas's lessons at Belgrave, but he wasn't about to sponsor his education any further than that. Thomas had gone off to Eton and Cambridge, and then to the glittering excesses of London. Harry had stayed in Lincolnshire, eventually taking over the inn his father had bought when his wife had come into an unexpected inheritance. And while they were perhaps a bit more aware of the differences in their rank than they had been as children, the easygoing friendship of their youth had proven remarkably enduring.

"Harry," Thomas said, sliding onto a stool near the bar.

"Your grace," Harry said, with that wicked smile he always used when using an honorific.

Thomas started to scowl at him for his cheek, then almost laughed. If he only knew.

"Pretty eye, there," Harry said, quite conversationally. "Always did like the royal purple."

Thomas thought of ten different retorts, but in the end lacked the energy to bother with any of them.

"A pint?" Harry asked.

"Of your best."

Harry pulled the pint, then set it down on the bar. "You look like hell," he said baldly.

"Warmed over?"

"Not even that," Harry said, shaking his head. "Your grandmother?"

Harry knew his grandmother well.

"Among other things," Thomas said vaguely.

"Your fiancée?"

Thomas blinked. He hadn't given Amelia much thought that afternoon, which was remarkable, considering that he'd nearly tupped her in a meadow just six hours earlier.

"You have one," Harry reminded him. "About this high . . . " He made an indication in the air.

She was taller than that, Thomas thought absently.

"Blond," Harry continued, "not too buxom, but—"

"Enough," Thomas snapped.

Harry grinned. "It is your fiancée, then."

Thomas took a swig of his ale and decided to let him believe it. "It's complicated," he finally said.

Harry immediately leaned against the bar with a sympathetic nod. Truly, he was born to the job. "It always is."

As Harry had married his sweetheart at the age of nineteen and now had six little urchins tearing through the small house he had behind the inn, Thomas wasn't completely convinced that he was qualified to offer judgments on matters of the heart.

"Had a bloke in here just the other day . . . " Harry began.

Then again, he'd surely heard every sob story and sad tale from here to York and back.

Thomas drank his ale as Harry nattered on about nothing in particular. Thomas wasn't really listening, but it did occur to him, as he sucked down the last dregs, that never in his life had he been more grateful for mindless chatter.

And then in walked Mr. Audley.

Thomas stared at his tankard, wondering if he ought to ask for another. Downing it in under a minute sounded rather appealing just then.

"Good evening to you, sir!" Harry called out. "How's your head?"

Thomas looked up. Harry knew him?

"Much better," Audley replied.

"Gave him my morning mixture," Harry told Thomas. He looked back up to Audley. "It always works. Just ask the duke here."

"Does the duke often require a balm for overindulgence?" Audley inquired politely.

Thomas looked at him sharply.

Harry did not answer. He'd seen the look that passed between them. "You two know each other?"

"More or less," Thomas said.

"Mostly less," Audley added.

Harry looked at Thomas. Their eyes met for barely a second, but there were a hundred questions in the exchange, along with one astoundingly comforting reassurance.

If he needed him, Harry would be there.

"We need to go," Thomas said, pushing his stool back to stand. He turned to Harry and gave him a nod.

"You're together?" Harry asked with surprise.

"He's an old friend," Thomas said. More of a grunt, really.

Harry did not ask from where. Harry always knew which questions not to ask.

He turned to Audley. "You didn't mention you knew the duke."

Audley shrugged. "You didn't ask."

Harry appeared to consider this, then turned back to Thomas. "Safe journeys, friend."

Thomas tipped his head in response, then headed out the door, leaving Audley to follow in his wake.

"You're friends with the innkeeper," Audley stated once they were outdoors.

Thomas turned to him with a broad, false smile. "I'm a friendly fellow."

And that was the last thing either of them said until they were just minutes from Belgrave, when Audley said, "We'll need a story."

Thomas looked at him askance.

"I assume you don't wish to set it about that I am your cousin—your father's *elder* brother's son, to be precise—until you have verification."

"Indeed," Thomas said. His voice was clipped, but that was mostly because he was angry at himself for not having brought the same thing up earlier.

The look Audley gave him was blindingly annoying. It started with a smile but quickly turned to a smirk. "Shall we be old friends, then?"

"From university?"

"Eh, no. Do you box?"

"No."

"Fence?"

Like a master. "I'm passable," he said with a shrug.

"Then that's our story. We studied together. Years ago."

Thomas kept his eyes straight ahead. Belgrave was looming ever closer. "Let me know if you wish to practice," he said.

"You've equipment?"

"Everything you could possibly need."

Audley glanced at Belgrave, which now hung over them like a stone ogre, blotting out the last dusky rays of the sun. "And everything one doesn't need, too, I imagine."

Thomas didn't comment, just slid off his mount and handed the reins to a waiting footman. He strode inside, eager to put his back to the man behind him. It wasn't that he wished to cut him, exactly. It was more that he wished to forget him.

Just think how lovely his life had been, merely twelve hours earlier.

No, make that eight. Eight, and he'd have had a bit of fun with Amelia as well.

Yes, that was the optimal cut-off point between his old life and new. Post-Amelia, pre-Audley.

Perfection.

But ducal powers, far-reaching though they were, did not extend to the turning back of time, and so, refusing to be anything but the sophisticated, utterly self-contained man he used to be, he gave the butler a quick set of orders about what to do with Mr. Audley, and then entered the drawing room, where his grandmother was waiting with Grace.

"Wyndham," his grandmother said briskly.

He gave her a curt nod. "I had Mr. Audley's belongings sent up to the blue silk bedroom."

"Excellent choice," his grandmother replied. "But I must repeat. Do not refer to him as Mr. Audley in my presence. I don't know these Audleys, and I don't care to know them."

"I don't know that they would care to know you, either." This, from Mr. Audley, who had entered the room on swift but silent feet.

Thomas looked to his grandmother. She merely lifted a brow, as if to point out her own magnificence.

"Mary Audley is my late mother's sister," Audley stated. "She and her husband, William Audley, took me in at my birth. They raised me as their own and, *at my request*, gave me their name. I don't care to relinquish it."

Thomas could not help it. He was enjoying this.

Audley then turned to Grace and bowed. "You may refer to me as Mr. Audley if you wish, Miss Eversleigh."

Grace bobbed an idiotic little curtsy then looked over at Thomas. For what? Asking permission?

"She can't sack you for using his legal name," Thomas said impatiently. Good God, this was getting tedious. "And if she does, I shall retire you with a lifelong bequest and have her sent off to some far-flung property."

"It's tempting," Audley murmured. "How far can she be flung?"

Thomas almost smiled. As irritating as Audley was, he did have his moments. "I am considering adding to our holdings," Thomas murmured. "The Outer Hebrides are lovely this time of year."

"You're despicable," his grandmother hissed.

"Why do I keep her on?" Thomas wondered aloud. And then, because it had been a bloody long day, and he'd lost whatever comfort he'd gleaned from his ale, he walked over to a cabinet and poured himself a drink.

And then Grace spoke up, as she frequently did whe she thought she was required to defend the dowa "She is your grandmother."

"Ah yes, blood." Thomas sighed. He was beginning to feel punchy. And he wasn't even the least bit soused. "I'm told it's thicker than water. Pity." He looked over at Audley. "You'll soon learn."

Audley just shrugged. Or maybe he didn't. Maybe Thomas just imagined it. He needed to get out of here, away from these three people, away from anything that screamed Wyndham or Cavendish or Belgrave or any one of the other fifteen honorifics attached to his name.

He turned, looking squarely at his grandmother. "And now my work here is done. I have returned the prodigal son to your loving bosom, and all is right with the world. Not *my* world," he could not resist adding, "but someone's world, I'm sure."

"Not mine," Audley said with a slow, careless smile. "In case you were interested."

Thomas just looked at him. "I wasn't."

Audley smiled blandly, and Grace, God bless her, looked ready to jump between them again, should they attack each other anew.

He dipped his head toward her, in an expression of wry salute, then tossed back his liquor in one shockingly large swallow. "I am going out."

"Where?" demanded the dowager.

Thomas paused in the doorway. "I have not yet decided."

Truly, it didn't matter. Anything was fine. Just not here.

Chapter 8

"Isn't that Wyndham over there?"

Amelia blinked, shading her eyes with her hand (a fat lot of good her bonnet seemed to be doing her this morning) as she peered across the street. "It does look like him, doesn't it?"

Her younger sister Milly, who had accompanied her on the outing to Stamford, leaned into her for a better view. "I think it *is* Wyndham. Won't Mother be pleased."

Amelia glanced nervously over her shoulder. Her mother, who was inside a nearby shop, had resembled nothing so much as a woodpecker all morning. *Peck peck peck*, do this, Amelia, *peck peck peck*, don't do that. Wear your bonnet, you're getting freckles, don't sit so inelegantly, the duke will never get around to marrying you.

Peck peck peck peck peck peck peck.

Amelia had never been able to make the connection between her posture whilst in the privacy of her own breakfast room and her fiancé's inability to choose a date for the wedding, but then again, she'd never been able to understand how her mother could know exactly which of her five daughters had nicked a bit of her marzipan, or accidentally let the dogs in, or (Amelia winced; this one had been her fault) knocked over the chamber pot.

Onto her mother's favorite dressing gown.

Blinking her eyes into focus, Amelia looked back across the street at the man Milly had pointed out.

It *couldn't* be Wyndham. It was true, the man in question did look remarkably like her fiancé, but he was clearly . . . how did one say it . . . ?

Disheveled.

Except disheveled was putting it a bit kindly.

"Is he sotted?" Milly asked.

"It's not Wyndham," Amelia said firmly. Because Wyndham was never so unsteady.

"I really think—"

"It's *not*." But she wasn't so sure.

Milly held her tongue for all of five seconds. "We should tell Mother."

"We should *not* tell Mother," Amelia hissed, whipping around to face her.

"Ow! Amy, you're hurting me!"

Amelia reluctantly loosened her grip on her sister's upper arm. "Listen to me, Milly. You will not say a word to Mother. Not . . . a . . . word. Do you understand me?"

Milly's eyes grew very round. "Then you *do* think it's Wyndham."

Amelia swallowed, unsure of what to do. It certainly looked like the duke, and if it was, surely she had a duty to aid him. Or hide him. She had a feeling his preference would be for the latter.

"Amelia?" Milly whispered.

Amelia tried to ignore her. She had to *think*.

"What are you going to do?"

"Be quiet," Amelia whispered furiously. She did not have much time to figure out how to proceed. Her mother would emerge from the dress shop at any second, and then—

Good Lord, she didn't even want to imagine the scene.

Just then, the man across the street turned and looked at her. He blinked a few times, as if trying to place her in his memory. Stumbled, righted himself, stumbled again, and finally leaned up against a stone wall, yawning as he rubbed his eye with the heel of his hand.

"Milly," Amelia said slowly. She was still watching Wyndham—for surely it was he—until at the last moment she pulled her gaze away to face her sister. "Can you lie?"

Milly's eyes positively sparkled. "Like a rug."

"Tell Mother I saw Grace Eversleigh."

"Elizabeth's friend?"

"She's my friend, too."

"Well, she's more Elizabeth's—"

"It doesn't matter whose friend she is," Amelia

snapped. "Just tell her I saw Grace, and Grace invited me back to Belgrave."

Milly blinked a few times; rather owlishly, Amelia thought. Then Milly said, "At this time in the morning?"

"Milly!"

"I'm just trying to make sure we have a believable story."

"Fine, yes. This time in the morning." It was a bit early for a visit, but Amelia could see no way around it. "You won't have to explain anything. Mother will just cluck about and say something about it being curious, and that will be the end of it."

"And you're going to just leave me here on the street?"

"You'll be fine."

"I know I'll be fine," Milly shot back, "but Mother will question it."

Blast it, she hated when Milly was right. They had gone out for a sweet and were meant to return together. Milly was seventeen and perfectly able to walk three storefronts on her own, but their mother always said that proper young ladies did not walk anywhere alone.

Lady Crowland had not been amused when Amelia had asked her if that included the water closet. Apparently, proper young ladies did not say "water closet," either.

Amelia looked quickly over her shoulder. The sun was hitting the window of the dress shop, and it was difficult to see inside through the resulting glare.

"I think she's still in the back," Milly said. "She said she planned to try on three different dresses."

Which meant she'd almost certainly try on eight, but still, they could not count on it.

Amelia thought quickly, then said to Milly, "Tell her that Grace had to leave straightaway, so I didn't have time to come in and inform her of the change of plans myself. Tell her Grace had no choice. The dowager needed her."

"The dowager," Milly echoed, nodding. They all knew the dowager.

"Mother won't mind," Amelia assured her. "She'll be delighted, I'm sure. She's always trying to send me over to Belgrave. Now go." She gave her sister a little push, then thought the better of it and yanked her back. "No, don't go. Not yet."

Milly looked at her with patent aggravation.

"Give me a moment to get him out of view."

"To get your*self* out of view," Milly said pertly.

Amelia jammed down the urge to shake her sister senseless, and instead gave her a hard stare. "Can you do this?"

Milly looked miffed that she'd even asked. "Of course."

"Good." Amelia gave her a brisk nod. "Thank you." She took a step, then added, "Don't watch."

"Oh, *now* you ask too much," Milly warned her.

Amelia decided she couldn't push the matter. If their positions were reversed, she would *never* look away. "Fine. Just don't say a word."

"Not even to Elizabeth?"

"*No* one."

Milly nodded, and Amelia knew she could trust her. Elizabeth might not know how to keep her mouth shut, but Milly (with the proper motivation) was a vault. And as Amelia was the only person who knew precisely how Lord Crowland's entire collection of imported cigars had gotten soaked by an overturned teapot (her mother had detested the cigars and thus declared herself uninterested in finding the culprit) . . .

Well, let it be said that Milly had ample motivation to hold her tongue.

With one final glance in her sister's direction, Amelia dashed across the street, taking care to avoid the puddles that had accumulated during the previous night's rainfall. She approached Wyndham—still somewhat hoping that it wasn't actually he—and, with a tentative tilt of her head, said, "Er, your grace?"

He looked up. Blinked. Cocked his head to the side, then winced, as if the motion had been unwise. "My bride," he said simply.

And nearly knocked her over with his breath.

Amelia recovered quickly, then grabbed his arm and held tight. "What are you doing here?" she whispered. She looked about frantically. The streets were not terribly busy, but anyone could happen along. "And good heavens, what happened to your eye?"

It was amazingly purple underneath, from the bridge of his nose straight out to his temple. She had never seen anything like it. It was far worse than the time she had accidentally hit Elizabeth with a cricket bat.

He touched the bruised skin, shrugged, scrunched his nose as he apparently considered her question. Then he looked back at her and tilted his head to the side. "You *are* my bride, aren't you?"

"Not yet," Amelia muttered.

He regarded her with a strange, intense concentration. "I *think* you still are."

"Wyndham," she said, trying to cut him off.

"Thomas," he corrected.

She almost laughed. Now would be the time he granted her use of his given name? "Thomas," she repeated, mostly just to get him to stop interrupting. "What are you doing here?" And then, when he did not answer her: "Like this?"

He stared at her uncomprehendingly.

"You're drunk," she whispered furiously.

"No," he said, thinking about it. "I was drunk last night. Now I'm indisposed."

"Why?"

"Do I need a reason?"

"You—"

"'Course, I *have* a reason. Don't really care to share it with you, but I do have a reason."

"I need to get you home," she decided.

"Home." He nodded, tilting his head and looking terribly philosophical. "Now *there's* an interesting word."

While he was talking nonsense, Amelia looked up and down the street, searching for something—anything—that might indicate how he'd gotten there the night before. "Your grace—"

"Thomas," he corrected, with a rather wiggly sort of grin.

She held up a hand, her fingers spread wide, more in an attempt to control her own aggravation than to scold him. "How did you get here?" she asked, very slowly. "Where is your carriage?"

He pondered this. "I don't rightly know."

"Good God," she muttered.

"Is He?" he mused. "*Is* He good? Really?"

She let out a groan. "You *are* drunk."

He looked at her, and looked at her, and looked at her even more, and then just when she'd opened her mouth to tell him that they needed to find his carriage immediately, he said, "I might be a little bit drunk." He cleared his throat. "Still."

"Wyndham," she said, adopting her sternest voice. "Surely you—"

"Thomas."

"Thomas." She clenched her teeth. "Surely you remember how you *got* here."

Again, that moronic silence, followed by, "I rode."

Wonderful. That was *just* what they needed.

"In a carriage!" he said brightly, then laughed at his own joke.

She stared at him in disbelief. Who *was* this man?

"Where is the carriage?" she ground out.

"Oh, just over there," he said, waving vaguely behind him.

She turned. "Over there" appeared to be a random street corner. Or it could have been the street that ran around the corner. Or, given his current state, he might have been referring to the whole of Lincolnshire, straight back to the Wash and on to the North Sea.

"Could you be more precise?" she asked, followed by a rather slow and deliberately enunciated: "Can you lead me there?"

He leaned in, looking very jolly as he said, "I *could* . . ."

"You *will*."

"You sound like my grandmother."

She grabbed his chin, forcing him to hold still until they were eye-to-eye. "*Never* say that again."

He blinked a few times, then said, "I *like* you bossy."

She let go of him as if burned.

"Pity," he said, stroking his chin where she'd touched him. He pushed off the stone wall and stood straight, wobbling for only a second before finding his balance. "Shall we be off?"

Amelia nodded, intending to follow until he turned to her with a weak smile and said, "I don't suppose you'd take my arm?"

"Oh, for heaven's sake," she muttered. She slipped her arm in his, and together they walked off the high street and onto a side alley. He was setting the direction, but she was providing the balance, and their progress was slow. More than once he nearly stumbled, and she could see that he was watching his steps closely, every now and then taking a deliberate pause before trying to navigate the cobbles. Finally, after crossing two streets and turning another corner, they reached a middling-sized, mostly empty, square.

"I thought it was here," Wyndham said, craning his neck.

"There," Amelia said, jabbing her finger out in a most unladylike point. "In the far corner. Is that yours?"

He squinted. "So it is."

She took a long, fortifying breath and led him across the square to the waiting carriage. "Do you think," she murmured, turning toward his ear, "that you can act as if you are not sotted?"

He smiled down at her, his expression rather superior for someone who needed help remaining upright. "Jack Coachman!" he called out, his voice crisp and authoritative.

Amelia was impressed despite herself. "Jack Coachman?" she murmured. Weren't they all *John* Coachman?

"I've renamed all my coachmen Jack," Wyndham said, somewhat offhandedly. "Thinking of doing the same with the scullery maids."

She just managed to resist the impulse to check his forehead for fever.

The coachman, who had been dozing atop the driver's seat, snapped to attention and jumped down.

"To Belgrave," Wyndham said grandly, holding out his arm to help Amelia up into the carriage. He was doing a fine impression of someone who hadn't drunk three bottles of gin, but she wasn't certain she wished to lean on him for assistance.

"There's no way around it, Amelia," he said, his voice warm, and his smile just a little bit devilish. For a moment, he sounded almost like himself, always in control, always with the upper hand in a conversation.

She set her hand in his, and did he—did she, feel—

A squeeze. A tiny little thing, nothing seductive, nothing wicked. But it felt searingly intimate, speaking of shared memories and future encounters.

And then it was gone. Just like that. She was sitting in the carriage, and he was next to her, sprawled out like the somewhat inebriated gentleman she knew him to be. She looked at the opposite seat pointedly. They might be engaged, but he was certainly not supposed to take the position next to her. Not when they were alone in a closed carriage.

"Don't ask me to ride backwards," he said with a shake of his head. "Not after—"

"Say no more." She moved quickly to the rear-facing position.

"You didn't have to go." His face formed an expression entirely out of character. Almost like a wounded puppy, but with a hint of rogue shining through.

"It was self-preservation." She eyed him suspiciously. She'd seen that skin pallor before. Her youngest sister had an extremely sensitive stomach. Wyndham looked rather like Lydia did right before she cast up her accounts. "How much did you have to drink?"

He shrugged, having obviously decided there was no point in trying to cajole her further. "Not nearly as much as I deserved."

"Is this something you . . . do often?" she asked, very carefully.

He did not answer right away. Then: "No."

She nodded slowly. "I didn't think so."

"Exceptional circumstances," he said, then closed his eyes. "Historic."

She watched him for a few seconds, allowing herself the luxury of examining his face without worrying what he would think. He looked tired. Exhausted, really, but more than that. He looked . . . burdened.

"I'm not asleep," he said, even though he did not open his eyes.

"That's commendable."

"Are you always this sarcastic?"

She did not answer right away. Then: "Yes."

He opened one eye. "Really?"

"No."

"But sometimes?"

She felt herself smiling. "Sometimes. A little more than sometimes, when I'm with my sisters."

"Good." He closed his eyes again. "I can't bear a female without a sense of humor."

She thought about that for a moment, trying to figure out why it did not sit well with her. Finally she asked, "Do you find humor and sarcasm to be interchangeable?"

He did not answer, which led her to regret the question. She should have known better than to introduce a complicated concept to a man who reeked of liquor. She turned and looked out the window. They had left Stamford behind and were now traveling north on the Lincoln road. It was, she realized, almost certainly the same road Grace had been traveling the night she and the dowager were waylaid by highwaymen. It had probably been farther out of town, however; if she were to rob a coach, she would certainly choose a more out-of-the-way locale. Plus, she thought, craning her neck for a better view through the window, she did not see any good hiding spots. Wouldn't a highwayman need a place to lie in wait?

"No."

She started, then looked at Wyndham in horror. Had she been thinking aloud?

"I don't find humor and sarcasm interchangeable," he said. His eyes, interestingly, were still closed.

"You're only just answering my question now?"

He shrugged a little. "I had to think about it."

"Oh." She returned her attention to the window, preparing to resume her daydreams.

"It was a complicated query," he continued.

She turned back. His eyes were open and focused on her face. He appeared a bit more lucid than he had just a few minutes earlier. Which did not lend him the air of an Oxford professor, but he did look capable of carrying on a basic conversation.

"It really depends," he said, "on the subject of the sarcasm. And the tone."

"Of course," she said, although she was still not sure he had all his wits about him.

"Most people of my acquaintance intend their sarcasm as insult, so no, I do not find it interchangeable with humor." He looked at her with a certain level of question in his eyes, and she realized he desired her opinion on the matter. Which was astounding. Had he ever requested her opinion before? On anything?

"I agree," she said.

He smiled. Just a little, as if anything more vigorous might make him queasy. "I thought you would." He paused, just for a heartbeat. "Thank you, by the way."

It was almost embarrassing how lovely it felt to hear those words. "You're welcome."

His smile stayed small, but turned a little wry. "It has been some time since someone has saved me."

"I imagine it has been some time since you needed saving." She sat back, feeling oddly content. She believed him when he said he did not make a habit of drunken revelry, and she was glad for that. She had little experience with tipsy males, but what she had seen—usually at balls at which her parents had allowed her to stay later than usual—had not impressed her.

Still, she could not help but be glad that she had seen him this way. He was always in charge, always supremely composed and confident. It wasn't just that he was the Duke of Wyndham, second in rank to but a handful of men in Britain. It was simply *him*, the way he was—his authoritative manner, his cool intelligence. He stood at the back of the room, surveying the crowds, and people *wanted* to let him take charge. They wanted him to make their decisions, to tell them what to do.

John Donne had got it wrong. Some men *were* islands,

entire of themselves. The Duke of Wyndham was. He always had been, even to her earliest memories.

Except now, just this once, he had needed her.

He had needed her.

It was thrilling.

And the best part of it was that he hadn't even realized it. He hadn't had to ask for it. She had seen him in need, judged the situation, and acted.

She had made the decisions. She had taken control.

And he had liked it. He said he liked her bossy. It was almost enough to make her want to hug herself.

"What has you smiling?" he asked. "You look quite contented."

"Something you would never understand," she said, without a trace of bitterness. She did not begrudge him his self-possession. She envied it.

"That's unfair of you," he said with gentle accusation.

"I mean it as a compliment," she replied, knowing he'd be unable to understand *that* as well.

One of his brows rose. "I shall have to trust you on it, then."

"Oh, I would never lie about a compliment," she said. "I don't give them out willy-nilly. I think they should mean something, don't you?"

"Even if the subject does not understand the meaning?"

She smiled. "Even then."

He smiled back, a little wry thing involving just one corner of his mouth. But it was full of humor and maybe even a touch of affection, and for the first time in her life, Amelia Willoughby began to think that marriage to the Duke of Wyndham might be about something more than duty, something greater than rank.

It might turn out to be a most pleasant endeavor, indeed.

Chapter 9

$\mathcal{I}$t was probably a good thing that he'd still had rather too much liquor in his veins when Amelia came across him, Thomas reflected, because he hadn't had the good sense to be mortified. And now—when the only remnant of his night of drunken excess was a pounding in his left temple (and a throb in the right)— he reckoned she'd already seen the worst and hadn't gone off screaming. In fact, she seemed quite content to ride along in the carriage with him, gently scolding and rolling her eyes at him.

The thought would have made him smile, if the sudden bump in the road hadn't sent his brain jostling against his skull—if indeed that were possible. He was not a scholar of anatomy, but this scenario seemed far more likely than what it felt like, which was an anvil flying through the window and impaling itself in his left temple.

As to why his right temple was pounding in a similar manner, he could only assume it was out of sympathy.

He let out an unattractive groan and pinched hard at the bridge of his nose, as if the pain of *that* might be enough to blot out the rest of it.

Amelia didn't say anything, and in fact didn't even look as if she thought she ought to be saying something—further reinforcing his newly arrived belief that she was a most excellent female. She was just sitting there, her face remarkably placid, given that he must look like death itself, ready to spew noxious substances all over her.

Not to mention his eye. It had looked rather vicious the night before. Thomas couldn't imagine what sort of hue it had turned overnight.

He drew in a deep breath and opened his eyes, glancing at Amelia's face around his hand, which was still doing its completely ineffective magic on his nose.

"Your head?" she asked politely.

She'd been waiting for him to acknowledge her, he realized. "Pounds like the devil."

"Is there something you can take for that? Laudanum, perhaps?"

"God, no." He almost passed out at the thought. "It'd do me in completely."

"Tea? Coffee?"

"No, what I need is—"

A Gladdish Baddish.

Why hadn't he thought of it earlier?

It was a ridiculous name, but as it was only needed when one had behaved in a ridiculous manner, he supposed it was fitting. Harry Gladdish had perfected it the summer they were eighteen.

Thomas's father had elected to spend the season in London, leaving him to his own devices at Belgrave. He and Harry had run wild. Nothing too debauched, although at the time they fancied themselves the worst sorts of profligates. After having seen how other young men chose to ruin themselves in London, Thomas now looked back at that summer with some amusement. By comparison, he and Harry had been innocent lambs. But even so, they had drunk far too much and far too often, and the Gladdish Baddish, administered in the morning (with a pinched nose and a shudder), saved them more than once.

Or at the very least, rendered them able to walk straight enough to make it back to their beds, where they could sleep off the last of their miseries.

He looked at Amelia. "Can you spare another half an hour?"

She motioned around her. "Apparently I can spare the entire day."

It was a bit embarrassing, that. "Ah, yes"—he cleared his throat, trying to hold himself very steady as he did so—"sorry for that. I hope you were not forced to abandon important plans."

"Just the milliner and the cobbler." She pretended to pout, but anyone could see it was really a smile. "I shall be poorly hatted and shod for the winter, I'm afraid."

He held up a finger. "Just one moment." Then he reached across the carriage and gave the wall two pounds with his fist. Immediately, they rolled to a halt.

Normally, he would have hopped down to redirect the driver, but surely this time he could be forgiven for trying to limit his movements. The last thing any of them wanted was for him to lose his stomach in a closed carriage.

Once the new arrangements had been made, and the driver had got them back on their way, he resettled himself in his seat, feeling decidedly more chipper just at the thought of the Baddish that awaited him. Harry would wonder why he'd been drinking *and* why he'd been drinking somewhere else, but he would never ask. At least not this afternoon.

"Where are we going?" Amelia asked.

"The Happy Hare." It was a bit out of their way, but not drastically so.

"The posting inn?"

Indeed. "I shall be cured."

"At the Happy Hare?" She sounded dubious.

"Trust me."

"Said by a man reeking of gin," she said, shaking her head.

He looked over at her, lifting one of his brows into the famously regal Wyndham arch. "I wasn't drinking gin." Good Lord, he had more breeding than *that*.

She looked as if she might smile. "So sorry. What were you drinking, then?"

He was quite certain this wasn't the sort of conversation one ought to conduct with one's fiancée, but nothing about this meeting was the sort of thing one ought to do or see or say with one's fiancée. "Ale," he told her. "Have you ever tried it?"

"Of course not."

"Tsk tsk. Such outrage."

"That wasn't outrage," she shot back, outraged *now*. "It was simple fact. Who would have ever served me ale?"

She did have a point. "Very well," he said, everything gracious. "But it wasn't gin."

She rolled her eyes, and he almost laughed. They were like an old married couple. Not that he'd had much cause to witness old married couples doing anything but insulting (his father) and accepting it (his mother), but Grace had told him that her parents had been wondrously devoted to each other, and from what he'd seen of Lord and Lady Crowland—Amelia's parents—they seemed to get on reasonably well, too. Or at the very least, neither seemed consumed with desire to see the other one dead.

"Do your parents like each other?" he asked quite suddenly.

She blinked several times in rapid succession, obviously surprised by the change of topic. "My parents?"

"Do they get on?"

"Yes, I suppose." She paused, and her brow wrinkled adorably as she considered it. "They don't *do* very much together—their interests really don't mesh—but I do think they hold each other in some affection. I haven't given it much thought, to be honest."

It was not exactly a description of a grand passion, but still, it was so entirely different from his own experience that Thomas could not help but be intrigued.

She must have noticed the interest on his face, because she continued, "I suppose they must get on. If they didn't, I probably *would* have given it much thought, wouldn't you think?"

He thought about the endless hours he'd wasted thinking about his own parents. He nodded. For all her innocence and guileless speech, she could be extraordinarily astute.

"My mother can nag a bit," she said. "Well, more than a bit. But my father seems not to mind. He knows it is only because she feels it her duty to see all of her daughters settled. Which is of course his wish as well. He just doesn't wish to be involved in the details of it."

Thomas found himself nodding approvingly. Daughters had to be an incredible amount of work.

"He humors her for a few minutes," Amelia continued, "because he knows how much she likes an audience, but then he most often just shakes his head and walks away. I think he is happiest when out of doors, mucking about with his hounds."

"Hounds?"

"He has twenty-five of them."

"Gad."

She grimaced. "We keep trying to convince him it's got a bit excessive, but he insists that any man with five daughters deserves five times as many hounds."

He tried to suppress the image in his mind. "Please tell me none are included in your dowry."

"You should verify," she said, her eyes sparkling with mischief. "*I've* never seen the betrothal papers."

His eyes held hers for a long, steady moment, then he said, "That means no." But she held her blank expression for long enough to make him add, "I hope."

She laughed. "He could not bear to part with them. Me, I think he will be happy to get off his hands, but his dogs . . . Never." And then: "Did your parents get on well?"

He felt himself go grim, and his head began to pound anew. "No."

She watched his face for a moment, and he was not sure he wanted to know what she saw there, because she looked almost pitying when she said, "I'm sorry."

"Don't be," he said briskly. "It is done, and they are dead, and there is nothing to be done about it now."

"But—" She stopped, her eyes a little sad. "Never mind."

He didn't mean to tell her anything. He had never discussed his parents with anyone, not even Harry, and he'd been witness to it all. But Amelia was sitting there so silently, with an expression of such understanding on her face—even though . . . well, she couldn't possibly understand, not with her gloriously boring and traditional family. But there was something in her eyes, something warm and willing, and it felt as if she *knew* him already, as if she'd known him forever and was merely waiting for him to know her.

"My father hated my mother." The words fell from his lips before he even realized he was saying them.

Her eyes widened, but she did not speak.

"He hated everything she stood for. She was a cit, you know."

She nodded. Of course she knew. Everyone knew. No one seemed to care much anymore, but everyone knew that the most recent duchess had been born without even a connection to a title.

The title. Now that was rich. His father had spent his entire life worshipping at the altar of his own aristocracy, and now it seemed he'd never really been the duke at all. Not if Mr. Audley's parents had had the sense to marry.

"Wyndham?" she said softly.

His head jerked toward her. He must have drifted off in his own thoughts. "Thomas," he reminded her.

A faint blush spread across her cheeks. Not of embarrassment, he realized, but of delight. The thought warmed him, deep in his belly and then deeper still, to some little corner of his heart that had lain dormant for years.

"Thomas," she said softly.

It was enough to make him want to say more. "He married her before he gained the title," he explained. "Back when he was the third son."

"One of his brothers drowned, did he not?"

Ah yes, the beloved John, who might or might not have sired a legitimate son of his own.

"The second son, was it not?" Amelia asked quietly.

Thomas nodded, because there was nothing else he could do. He was not about to tell her what had transpired the day before. Good God, it was madness. Less than twenty-four hours earlier he'd been happily kissing her in the garden, thinking it was finally time to make her his duchess, and now he didn't even know who he was.

"John," he forced himself to say. "He was my grandmother's favorite. His ship went down in the Irish Sea. And then a year later a fever took the old duke and the heir—both within a week—and suddenly my father had inherited."

"It must have been a surprise," she murmured.

"Indeed. No one thought he'd be the duke. He had three choices: the military, the clergy, or marriage to an heiress." Thomas let out a harsh chuckle. "I cannot imagine anyone was surprised that he chose as he did. And as for my mother—now here's the funny part. *Her* family was disappointed as well. More so."

She drew back, faint surprise coloring her face. "Even marrying into the house of Wyndham?"

"They were wildly rich," Thomas explained. "Her father owned factories all across the North. She was his only child. They thought for certain they could buy her a title. At the time, my father had none. With little hope of inheriting."

"What happened?"

He shrugged. "I have no idea. My mother was pretty enough. And she was certainly wealthy enough. But she did not take. And so they had to settle for my father."

"Who thought he was settling for her," Amelia guessed.

Thomas nodded grimly. "He disliked her from the moment he married her, but when his two older brothers died and he became duke, he *loathed* her. And he never bothered to hide it. Not in front of me, not in front of anyone."

"Did she return the sentiment?"

"I don't know," Thomas replied, and he realized that it was odd, but he had never asked himself the same question. "She never retaliated, if that is what you are wondering." He saw his mother in his mind's eye— her perpetually stricken face, the constant exhaustion behind her pale blue eyes. "She just . . . accepted it. Listened to his insults, said nothing in return, and walked away. No. No," he said, remembering it correctly. "That's not how it happened. She never walked away. She always waited for him to leave. She would never have presumed to quit a room before he did. She would never have dared."

"What did she do?" Amelia asked softly.

"She liked the garden," Thomas recalled. "And when it rained, she spent a great deal of time looking out the window. She didn't really have many friends. I don't think . . . "

He'd been about to say that he could not recall her ever smiling, but then a memory fluttered through his head. He'd been seven, perhaps eight. He'd gathered a small posy of flowers for her. His father was enraged; the blooms had been part of an elaborately planned garden and were not for picking. But his mother had smiled. Right there in front of his father, her face lit up and she smiled.

Strange how he had not thought about that for so many years.

"She rarely smiled," he said softly. "Almost never."

She'd died when he was twenty, just a week before her husband. They'd been taken by the same lung fever. It had been a terrible, violent way to go, their bodies wracked by coughs, their eyes glazed with exhaustion and pain. The doctor, never one to speak delicately, said they were drowning in their own fluids. Thomas had always thought it bitterly ironic that his parents, who spent their lives avoiding each other, had died, essentially, together.

And his father had one last thing to blame her for. His final words, in fact, were, "She did this."

"It is why we are here now," he said suddenly, offering Amelia a dry smile. "Together."

"I beg your pardon?"

He shrugged, as if none of it mattered. "Your mother was supposed to marry Charles Cavendish, did you know that?"

She nodded.

"He died four months before the wedding," he said softly and without emotion, almost as if recounting a bit of news from the newspaper. "My father always felt that your mother should have been *his* wife."

Amelia started with surprise. "Your father loved my mother?"

Thomas chuckled bitterly. "My father loved no one. But your mother's family was as old and noble as his own."

"Older," Amelia said with a smile, "but not as noble."

"If my father had known he was to be duke, he would

never have married my mother." He looked at her with an unreadable expression. "He would have married yours."

Amelia's lips parted, and she started to say something utterly deep and incisive, like, "Oh," but he continued with:

"At any rate, it was why he was so quick to arrange my betrothal to you."

"It would have been Elizabeth," Amelia said softly, "except that my father wished his eldest to marry the son of his closest friend. He died, though, so Elizabeth had to go to London to look for a match."

"My father was determined to join the families in the next generation." Thomas laughed then, but there was an uncomfortable, exasperated note to it. "To rectify the unfortunate mongrelization caused by my mother's entrance into the bloodlines."

"Oh, don't be silly," Amelia said, even though she had a feeling he was not being silly at all. Still, she ached for the boy he must have been, growing up in such an unhappy household.

"Oh, no," he assured her, "he said it quite often. I must marry a noble bride, and I must make certain my sons did the same. It was going to take generations to get the bloodlines back to where they should be." He grinned at her then, but it was an utterly awful expression. "You, my dear, were meant to be our savior, even at the ripe old age of six months."

Amelia looked away from him, trying to take this all in. No wonder he had been so uneager to set a date for the marriage. Who would *want* to marry her, when it was put in such terms?

"Don't look so somber," he said, and when she turned back to face him, he reached out and touched her cheek. "It isn't *your* fault."

"It isn't yours, either," she said, trying to resist the urge to turn and nuzzle his hand.

"No," he murmured. "It isn't."

And then he leaned forward, and she leaned forward . . . because she couldn't *not* lean forward, and even then, as the carriage rocked gently beneath them, he brushed his lips against hers.

She tingled. She sighed. And she would have gladly melted into another kiss, except that they hit an exceptionally vicious rut in the road, which sent both of them back to their respective seats.

Amelia let out a frustrated snort. Next time she'd figure out how to adjust her balance so she'd land on his seat. It would be so lovely, and even if she happened to find herself in a scandalous position, she'd be (almost) completely blameless.

Except that Thomas looked dreadful. Quite beyond green. The poor man was puce.

"Are you all right?" she asked, very carefully scooting across the carriage so she was not sitting directly across from him.

He said something, but she must have misheard, because it *sounded* like, "I need a radish."

"I beg your pardon?"

"I'd kiss you again," he said, sounding very droll and

perhaps a bit queasy at the same time, "except that I'm quite certain you would not appreciate it."

While she was trying to formulate a reply to that, he added, "The next kiss—"

(Brief moment of silence, followed by a grunt, both brought on by another rut.)

He cleared his throat. "The next kiss, you will appreciate. *That*, Amelia, is a vow."

She was quite sure he was right, because the statement alone made her shiver.

Hugging her arms to her chest, she peered out the window. She'd noticed they were slowing down, and indeed, the carriage had wound into the small courtyard in front of the posting inn. The Happy Hare dated from Tudor times, and its black and white exterior was well-kept and inviting, each window adorned with a flower box, blooming all shades of red and gold. From the jettied upper story hung a rectangular sign featuring a toothsome rabbit, standing upright in his Elizabethan doublet and ruff.

Amelia found it all rather charming and intended to comment, but Thomas was already making for the door.

"Shouldn't you wait for the carriage to come to a complete stop?" she asked mildly.

His hand went still upon the door handle, and he did not say a word until they had halted completely. "I'll be but a moment," he said, barely looking at her.

"I believe I will accompany you," she replied.

He froze, then his head turned slowly toward her. "Wouldn't you prefer to remain in the comfort of the carriage?"

If he had been trying to douse her curiosity, he was going about it the wrong way.

"I would like to stretch my legs," she said, affixing her favorite bland smile onto her face. She'd used it with him a hundred times at least, but not since they had got to know each other a bit. She was no longer sure how well it would work.

He stared at her for a long moment, clearly baffled by her placid demeanor.

Like a charm, she decided. She blinked a couple of times—nothing too coy or obvious, just a couple of flutters in a row, as if she were patiently waiting for him to respond.

"Very well," he said, sounding resigned in a way she did not think she'd ever heard in his voice before. He always got everything he wanted. Why *would* he ever feel resigned?

He stepped down with far less bounce than his usual hop, then held up a hand to assist her. She took it gracefully and stepped down herself, pausing to smooth her skirts and take stock of the inn.

She'd never been to the Happy Hare. She'd passed it dozens of times, of course. It was on a main road, and she'd spent her entire life, save for two seasons in London, in this particular corner of Lincolnshire. But she'd never gone in. It was a posting inn, and thus primarily for travelers passing through the district. And besides that, her mother would *never* have stepped foot into such an establishment. As it was, there were only three inns that she would deign to visit on the way to London, which did make travels somewhat restricted.

"Do you come here often?" Amelia asked, taking his arm when he offered it to her. It was surprisingly thrilling, this, to be on the arm of her betrothed, and not because it was a requirement he felt he must fulfill. It was almost as if they were a young married couple, off on an outing, just the two of them.

"I consider the innkeeper a friend," he replied.

She turned to him. "Really?" Until this very day, he had been the Duke to her, raised high on a pedestal, too rarefied to converse with mere mortals.

"Is it so difficult to imagine that I might have a friend who is of inferior rank?" he asked.

"Of course not," she replied, since she could not tell him the truth—that it was difficult to imagine him with a friend of any stripe. Not, of course, because *he* was lacking. Quite the contrary. He was so splendid in every way that one could not imagine walking up to him and uttering anything benign or banal. And wasn't that how friendships were usually formed? With an ordinary moment, a shared umbrella, or perhaps two seats next to each other at a bad musicale?

She had seen the way people treated him. Either they fawned and preened and begged his favors, or they stood to the side, too intimidated to attempt a conversation.

She'd never really thought about it before, but it must be rather lonely to be him.

They entered the inn, and although Amelia kept her face politely forward, her eyes were darting this way and that, trying to take it all in. She wasn't sure what her mother had found so repellent; everything looked respectable enough to her. It smelled heavenly, too, of meat pies and cinnamon and something else she couldn't quite identify—something tangy and sweet.

They walked into what had to be the taproom, and were immediately greeted by the innkeeper, who called out, "Wyndham! Two days in a row! To what do I owe your gilded presence?"

"Stuff it, Gladdish," Thomas muttered, leading Amelia to the bar. Feeling very risqué, she sat atop a stool.

"You've been drinking," the innkeeper said, grinning. "But not here with me. I'm crushed."

"I need a Baddish," Thomas said.

Which didn't really make any more sense than a radish, Amelia thought.

"I need an introduction," the innkeeper returned.

Amelia grinned. She'd never heard anyone speak to him in this manner. Grace came close . . . sometimes. But it wasn't like this. She would never have been so audacious.

"Harry Gladdish," Thomas said, sounding supremely irritated that he was being made to dance to someone else's tune, "may I present the Lady Amelia Willoughby, daughter of the Earl of Crowland."

"And your affianced bride," Mr. Gladdish murmured.

"I am most delighted to make your acquaintance," Amelia said, holding out her hand.

He kissed it, which made her grin. "I've been waiting to meet you, Lady Amelia."

She felt her face light up. "You have?"

"Since . . . Well, da—dash it all, Wyndham, how long have we known that you were engaged?"

Thomas crossed his arms, his expression bored. "*I* have known since I was seven."

Mr. Gladdish turned to her with a devilish smile. "Then I have known since I was seven as well. We are of an age, you see."

"You have known each other a long time, then?" Amelia asked.

"Forever," Mr. Gladdish confirmed.

"Since we were three," Thomas corrected. He rubbed his temple. "The Baddish, if you will."

"My father was assistant to the stable master at Belgrave," Mr. Gladdish said, ignoring Thomas completely. "He taught us to ride together. I was better."

"He was not."

Mr. Gladdish leaned forward. "At everything."

"Recall that you are married," Thomas bit off.

"You're married?" Amelia said. "How delightful! We shall have to have you and your wife over to Belgrave once we are wed." She caught her breath, feeling almost light-headed. She'd never anticipated their life as a married couple with such certainty. Even now she could not quite believe she'd been so bold as to say it.

"Why, we would be delighted," Mr. Gladdish said,

giving Thomas a bit of a look. Amelia wondered if he'd never invited him over.

"The Baddish, Harry," Thomas almost growled. "Now."

"He's drunk, you know," Mr. Gladdish told her.

"Not anymore," she replied. "But he was. Quite." She turned to Thomas and grinned. "I like your friend."

"Harry," Thomas said, "if you do not place a Baddish upon this counter within the next thirty seconds, as God is my witness, I shall have this place razed to the ground."

"Such an abuse of power," Mr. Gladdish said, shaking his head as he went to work. "I pray that you will be a good influence on him, Lady Amelia."

"I can only do my best," Amelia said, using her most prim and pious voice.

"Truly," Mr. Gladdish said, placing a hand on his heart, "it is all any of us can do."

"You sound just like the vicar," Amelia told him.

"Really? What a compliment. I have been cultivating my vicarish tone. It aggravates Wyndham, and is thus something to aspire to."

Thomas's arm shot across the bar and he grabbed his friend's collar with strength remarkable in one so impaired. "Harry . . . "

"Thomas, Thomas, Thomas," Mr. Gladdish said, and Amelia nearly laughed aloud at the sight of her betrothed being scolded by an innkeeper. It was marvelous.

"No one likes a surly drunk," Mr. Gladdish continued. "Here you are. For the sake of the rest of us." He plunked a short glass on the counter. Amelia leaned forward to inspect the contents. It was yellowish, and rather slimy-looking, with a dark brown swirl and a few flecks of red.

It smelled like death.

"Good heavens," she said, looking up at Thomas. "You're not going to drink that, are you?"

He grabbed the glass, brought it to his lips, and downed it in one gulp. Amelia actually flinched.

"Ew," she let out, unable to suppress her groan. She felt sick to her stomach just watching him.

Thomas shuddered, and his chin seemed to tense and shake, as if he were steeling himself for something very unpleasant. And then, with a gasp, he let out a breath.

Amelia backed away from the fumes. That kiss he had promised . . .

He had better not be planning on it today.

"Tastes just as good as you remembered, eh?" Mr. Gladdish said.

Thomas met his gaze dead even. "Better."

Mr. Gladdish laughed at that, and then Thomas laughed, and Amelia just looked at them with a complete lack of comprehension. Not for the first time, she wished she'd had brothers. Surely she could have used a bit of practice with the males of the species before trying to understand these two.

"You'll be cured before long," Mr. Gladdish said.

Thomas gave a nod. "That's why I'm here."

"You've had one of these before?" Amelia asked, trying not to wrinkle her nose.

Mr. Gladdish cut Thomas off before he could reply.

"He'd have my head if I told you just how many of these he's tossed back."

"Harry . . . " Thomas said warningly.

"We were young and foolish," Harry said, holding up his hands as if that were explanation enough. "Truly, I haven't served him one of these in years."

Amelia was glad to hear it; as amusing as it had been to finally see Thomas at less than his best, she did not relish the thought of marriage to a habitual drunkard. Still, it did make her wonder—just what had happened that made him want to go out and overindulge?

"Served one of these to your friend the other day," Mr. Gladdish said offhandedly.

"My friend," Thomas repeated.

Amelia hadn't been paying much attention, but the tone of his voice when he replied was enough to make her look sharply in his direction. He sounded bored . . . and dangerous, if the combination was possible.

"You know the one," Mr. Gladdish said. "You were in here with him just yesterday, wasn't it?"

"Is someone visiting?" Amelia asked. "Who is it?"

"No one," Thomas said, barely looking at her. "Just an acquaintance from London. Someone I used to fence with."

"He *is* handy with a sword," Mr. Gladdish put in, motioning to Thomas. "He trounced me every time, pains me though it does to admit it."

"You were invited to share his fencing lessons?" Amelia said. "How lovely."

"I shared all his lessons," Mr. Gladdish said with a

smile. It was a real smile, too; nothing teasing or silly.

"It was my father's only generous gesture," Thomas confirmed. "Not generous enough, of course. Harry's education was stopped when I left for Eton."

"Wyndham couldn't be rid of me *that* easily, though," Harry said. He leaned toward Amelia and said, "Everyone should have someone in his life who knows his every secret."

Her eyes widened. "Do you?"

"Know his every secret? Absolutely."

Amelia turned to Thomas. He did not contradict. She turned back to Harry with delight. "Then you *do*!"

"You didn't believe me the first time?"

"It seemed only polite to verify," she demurred.

"Well, yes, you do have to marry the old chap, whereas I must only bear his company once a week or so." Mr. Gladdish turned to Thomas and took the empty Baddish glass off the counter. "Do you need another one?"

"One was quite enough, thank you."

"Your color is returning already," Amelia said with some amazement. "You're not so green."

"Yellow, I thought," Mr. Gladdish put in. "Except for the purple under the eye. Very regal-like."

"Harry." Thomas looked quite close to the edge of his patience.

Harry leaned closer to Amelia. "Those ducal types never get black eyes. Always purple. Goes better with the robes."

"There are robes?"

Harry waved a hand. "There are always robes."

Thomas took hold of Amelia's arm. "We're leaving, Harry."

Harry grinned. "So soon?"

Amelia waved with her free hand, even as Thomas tugged her away from the bar. "It was lovely meeting you, Mr. Gladdish!"

"You are welcome any time, Lady Amelia."

"Why, thank you, I—"

But Thomas had already yanked her from the room.

"He's very sweet," Amelia said as she skipped along beside him, trying to keep up with his lengthier stride.

"Sweet," Thomas repeated, shaking his head. "He'd like that." He steered her around a puddle, although not so deftly that she didn't have to take a little hop to save her boots.

The coachman was already holding the door open when they approached. Amelia let Thomas help her up, but she'd not even taken her seat before she heard him say, "To Burges Park."

"No!" she exclaimed, popping her head back out. "We can't."

Good heavens, that would be a disaster.

Chapter 10

Thomas stared at her for longer than was strictly necessary, then motioned to the coachman to leave them to their privacy. As Amelia was already half hanging outside the carriage, he was not required to lean forward in order to ask, "Why not?"

"To preserve your dignity," she said, as if that made perfect sense. "I told Milly—"

"Milly?"

"My sister." Her eyes widened in that way women affected when they were frustrated that their companion (usually male) could not immediately discern the nature of their thoughts. "You do recall that I have one."

"I recall that you have several," he said dryly.

Her expression turned positively peevish. "Not that it could have been helped, but Milly was with me this morning when I saw you—"

Thomas swore under his breath. "Your sister saw me."

"Just one of them," she assured him. "And luckily for you, it was the one who can actually keep a secret."

There *should* have been something amusing in that, but he wasn't seeing it. "Go on," he ordered.

She did. With great animation. "I had to give my mother *some* reason for abandoning Milly on the Stamford high street, so I told Milly to tell her that I'd come across Grace, who was running errands for your grandmother. Then she was to say that Grace invited me back to Belgrave, but that if I wished to go, I had to depart immediately, because the dowager had ordered Grace to return right away."

Thomas blinked, trying to follow.

"Because I had to have a reason why I did not have time enough to go into the dress shop and inform Mama of the change of plans myself."

She stared at him as if he ought to have a response. He did not.

"Because," she added, noticeably impatient now, "if I spoke to my mother directly, she would have insisted upon coming outside, and pretty though you are, I must confess to being at a loss as to how I might disguise you as Grace Eversleigh."

He waited until he was certain she was finished, then murmured, "Sarcasm, Amelia?"

"When the conversation calls for it," she returned, after a beat of highly irritated silence. She looked at him, her brows arched almost defiantly.

He looked at her, hiding his amusement. If arrogance was the game, she would never win.

And indeed, after but five seconds of their staring

competition, she took a breath, and it was as if she'd never halted her recounting. "So you see why I cannot return to Burges just yet. There is no way I could have gone to Belgrave, visited with whomever it was I'm supposed to have been visiting with, and then gone home again."

"Me," he said.

She looked at him dumbly. Or rather, as if she thought *he* were dumb. "I beg your pardon."

"You shall have to have been visiting with me," he further clarified.

Now her expression turned incredulous. "Mother will be beyond delighted, but no one else will believe it."

Thomas was not quite certain why that stung, but it did, and it turned his own voice to ice. "Would you care to explain that comment?"

She let out a laugh, and then, when he did not say anything, jerked to attention and said, "Oh, you're serious."

"Did I give you some indication that I was not?"

Her lips pressed together and for a moment she almost looked humble. "Of course not, your grace."

He did not bother to remind her to call him Thomas.

"But surely you must see my point," she continued, just when he thought she was through. "Do I ever visit with you at Belgrave?"

"You visit all the time."

"And see you for the prescribed ten minutes, fifteen if you are feeling generous."

He stared at her in disbelief. "You were far more amenable when you thought I was drunk."

"You *were* drunk."

"Regardless." He bowed his head for a moment, pinching the bridge of his nose. Blast it all, what was he going to do about *this*?

"Is your head bothering you?" she asked.

He looked up.

"You do that"—she imitated his gesture—"when your head is bothering you.

He'd been doing it so much during the past twenty-four hours, it was a wonder the spot wasn't as bruised as his eye. "Any number of things are bothering me," he said curtly, but she looked so stricken he was compelled to add, "I do not refer to you."

Her lips parted but she did not comment.

He did not speak, either, and a full minute passed before she said, her voice careful, and indeed almost rueful, "I think we shall have to go. To Belgrave," she clarified, when his gaze caught hers.

"I am sure you were thinking as I was," she continued, "that we could simply take the carriage out to the country and while away an hour or two before returning me home."

He was, actually. It would be hell on her reputation, were they discovered, but somehow that seemed the least of his concerns.

"But you don't know my mother," she added. "Not as I do. She will send someone to Belgrave. Or perhaps come herself, under some guise or another. Probably something about borrowing more books from your grandmother. If she arrives, and I am not there, it will be a disaster."

He almost laughed. The only reason he did not was that it would be the height of insult, and there were certain gentlemanly traits he could not abandon, even when the world was falling down around him.

But really, after the events of yesterday—his new cousin, the possible loss of his title, his home, probably even the clothes on his back—the ramifications of an illicit country picnic seemed trivial. What could possibly happen? Someone would see them and they would be forced to marry? They were already betrothed.

Or were they? He no longer knew.

"I know that it would only hasten a ceremony that has been preordained for decades, but"—here her voice became tremulous, and it pierced his heart with guilt—"you don't want that. Not yet. You've made that clear."

"That's not true," he said quickly. And it wasn't. But it had been. And they both knew it. Looking at her now, her blond hair shining in the morning light, her eyes, not so hazel today, this time almost green—he no longer knew why he'd put this off for so long.

"*I* don't want it," she said, her voice almost low enough to be a whisper. "Not like that. Not some hastily patched-up thing. Already no one thinks you really want to marry me."

He wanted to contradict her, to tell her she was being foolish, and silly, and imagining things that were simply not true. But he could not. He had not treated her badly, but nor had he treated her well.

He found himself looking at her, at her face, and it was

as if he'd never truly seen her before. She was lovely. In every way. And she could have been his wife by now.

But the world was a very different place than it had been this time yesterday, and he no longer knew if he had any right to her. And good Lord, the last thing he wished to do was take her to Belgrave. Wouldn't that be fun? He could introduce her to Highwayman Jack! He could imagine the conversation already.

Amelia, do meet my cousin.

Your cousin?

Indeed. He might be the duke.

Then who are you?

Excellent question.

Not to mention the other excellent questions she was sure to come up with, most notably—what, exactly, was the state of their betrothal?

Good God. The mind boggled, and *his* mind, on the mend but still worse for the wear after a night of drink, preferred to remain boggle-free.

It would be so easy to insist that they not go to Belgrave. He was used to making the decisions, and she was used to having to abide by them. His overriding of her wishes would not seem at all out of character.

But he couldn't do it. Not today.

Maybe her mother would not seek her out. Maybe no one would ever know that she'd not been where she said she'd be.

But Amelia would know. She would know that she had looked him in the eye and told him why she needed to go to Belgrave, and she would know that he had been too callous to consider her feelings.

And he would know that he'd hurt her.

"Very well," he said brusquely. "We shall head to Belgrave." It wasn't exactly a cottage. Surely they could avoid Mr. Audley. He was probably still abed, anyway. He didn't seem the sort to enjoy the morningtide.

Thomas directed the driver to take him home and then climbed into the carriage beside Amelia. "I don't imagine you are eager for my grandmother's company," he said.

"Not overmuch, no."

"She favors the rooms at the front of the castle." And if Mr. Audley was indeed awake, that was where he would also be, probably counting the silver or estimating the worth of the collection of Canalettos in the north vestibule.

Thomas turned to Amelia. "We shall enter at the back."

She nodded, and it was done.

When they reached Belgrave, the driver made straight for the stables, presumably, Amelia thought, on the duke's orders. Indeed, they reached their destination without ever coming within sight of the castle's front windows. If the dowager was where Wyndham had said she would be—and indeed, in all her visits to the castle, Amelia had only ever seen the dowager in three separate rooms, all at the front—then they would be able to carry out the rest of the morning in relative peace.

"I don't believe I've ever been 'round to this side of Belgrave," Amelia commented as they entered through a set of French doors. She almost felt like a thief, sneaking about as she was. Belgrave was so still and quiet over here at the back. It made one aware of every noise, every footfall.

"I'm rarely in this section," Thomas commented.

"I can't imagine why not." She looked about her. They had entered a long, wide hall, off which stood a row of rooms. The one before her was some sort of study, with a wall of books, all leather-bound and smelling like knowledge. "It's lovely. So quiet and peaceful. These rooms must receive the morning sun."

"Are you one of those industrious sorts, always rising at dawn, Lady Amelia?"

He sounded so formal. Perhaps it was because they were back at Belgrave, where everything was formal. She wondered if it was difficult to speak guilelessly here, with so much splendor staring down upon one. Burges Park was also quite grand—there was no pretending otherwise—but it held a certain warmth that was lacking at Belgrave.

Or perhaps it was just that she knew Burges. She'd grown up there, laughed there, chased her sisters and teased her mother. Burges was a home, Belgrave more of a museum.

How brave Grace must be, to wake up here every morning.

"Lady Amelia," came Thomas's reminding voice.

"Yes," she said abruptly, recalling that she was meant to answer his question. "Yes, I am. I cannot sleep when it is light out. Summers are particularly difficult."

"And winters are easy?" He sounded amused.

"Not at all. They're even worse. I sleep far too much. I suppose I should be living at the equator, with a perfect division of day and night, every day of the year."

He looked at her curiously. "Do you enjoy the study of geography?"

"I do." Amelia wandered into the study, idly running her fingers along the books. She liked the way the spine of each volume bowed slightly out, allowing her fingers to bump along as she made her way into the room. "Or I should say I *would*. I am not very accomplished. It was not considered an important subject by our governess. Nor by our parents, I suppose."

"Really?"

He sounded interested. This surprised her. For all their recent rapprochement, he was still . . . well . . . *him*, and she was not used to his taking an interest in her thoughts and desires.

"Dancing," she replied, because surely that would answer his unspoken question. "Drawing, pianoforte, maths enough so that we can add up the cost of a fancy dress ensemble."

He smiled at that. "Are they costly?"

She tossed a coquettish look over her shoulder. "Oh, dreadfully so. I shall bleed you dry if we host more than two masquerades per year."

He regarded her for a moment, his expression almost wry, and then he motioned to a bank of shelves on the far side of the room. "The atlases are over there, should you wish to indulge your interests."

She smiled at him, a bit surprised at his gesture. And then, feeling unaccountably pleased, she crossed the room. "I thought you did not come to this section of the house very often."

He quirked a dry half smile, which somehow sat at odds with his blackened eye. "Often enough to know where to find an atlas."

She nodded, pulling a tall, thin tome at random from the shelf. She looked down at the gold lettering on the cover. MAPS OF THE WORLD. The spine creaked as she cracked it open. The date on the title page was 1796. She wondered when the book had last been opened.

"Grace is fond of atlases," she said, the thought popping into her head, seemingly from nowhere.

"Is she?"

She heard his steps drawing near. "Yes. I seem to recall her saying so at some point. Or perhaps it was Elizabeth who told me. They have always been very good friends." Amelia turned another page, her fingers careful. The book was not particularly delicate, but something about it inspired reverence and care. Looking down, she saw a large, rectangular map, crossing the length of both pages, with the caption: *Mercator projection of our world, the Year of our Lord, 1791.*

Amelia touched the map, her fingers trailing softly across Asia and then down, to the southernmost tip of Africa. "Look how big it is," she murmured, mostly to herself.

"The world?" he said, and she heard the smile in his voice.

"Yes," she murmured.

Thomas stood next to her, and one of his fingers found Britain on the map. "Look how small *we* are," he said.

"It does seem odd, doesn't it?" she remarked, trying not to notice that he was standing so close that she could feel the heat emanating from his body. "I am always amazed at how far it is to London, and yet here"—she motioned to the map—"it's nothing."

"Not nothing." He measured the distance with his smallest finger. "Half a fingernail, at least."

She smiled. At the book, not at him, which was a much less unsettling endeavor. "The world, measured in fingernails. It would be an interesting study."

He chuckled. "There is someone at some university attempting it right now, I assure you."

She looked over at him, which was probably a mistake, because it left her feeling somewhat breathless. Nonetheless, she was able to say (and in a remarkably reasonable voice), "Are professors so very eccentric, then?"

"The ones with long fingernails are."

She laughed, and he did, too, and then she realized that neither of them was looking at the map.

His eyes, she thought, with a strange kind of detachment, as if she were regarding a piece of art. She liked his eyes. She liked looking at them.

How was it that she had never realized that the right one had a stripe in it? She'd thought the irises were blue—not pale, or clear, or even azure, but a dark, smoky shade with the barest hint of gray. But now she could see quite clearly that there was a brown stripe in one of them. It ran from the pupil down to where one would find the four on a clock.

It made her wonder how she'd never seen it before. Maybe it was just that she'd never looked closely enough. Or maybe he'd never allowed her close enough, for long enough, to do so.

And then, in a voice as contemplative and muted as hers surely would have been, had she had the nerve to speak, he murmured, "Your eyes look almost brown just now."

Amelia felt herself jolted back into reality. And she said, "You have a stripe."

And promptly wanted to flee the room. What a pea-brained thing to say.

He touched the bruised skin of his cheekbone. "A stripe?"

"No, *in* your eye," she clarified, because it wasn't as if she could take the comment back. She might as well make her meaning clear. She motioned awkwardly in the air with her right hand, darting forward as if to point it out, but then jerking back since she could not touch him, and certainly not in his eye.

"Oh. Oh, that. Yes, it's odd, isn't it?" He made a strange sort of face. Well, no, not really. It would not have been strange on anyone else, but on *him* it was. It was a little bit modest, almost a little bit sheepish, and so thoroughly and wonderfully human that her heart skipped a beat.

"No one else has ever noticed it," he added. "It's probably for the best, really. It's a foolish little imperfection."

Was he fishing for compliments? She pressed her lips together, avoiding a smile. "I like it," she told him. "I like anything that makes you less than perfect."

Something in his expression warmed. "Is that so?"

She nodded, then looked away. Funny how it was easier to be frank and brave when he was angry (or, she supposed, tipsy) than when he was smiling at her.

"You will find many things to like about me, then," he said, his voice too close to her ear for her comfort, "once you get to know me better."

She pretended to study the map. "Are you telling me you are not perfect?"

"I would never presume to say *that*," he teased.

She swallowed. He was leaning far too close. He probably didn't even notice the nearness; his voice sounded completely unaffected, his breathing controlled and even to her ears.

"Why did you say my eyes were brown?" she asked, still keeping her eyes on the atlas.

"I didn't. I said they looked brown."

She felt a completely unbecoming swell of vanity rise within her. She'd always been proud of her hazel eyes. They were her best feature. Certainly her most unique. All of her sisters shared the same blond hair and skin tone, but she was the only one with such interesting eyes.

"They looked green this morning," he continued. "Although I suppose that could have been the drink. Another pint of ale and there would have been butterflies coming out of your ears."

She turned at that, utterly indignant. "It was not the drink. My eyes are hazel. Far more green than brown," she added in a mutter.

He smiled rather stealthily. "Why, Amelia, have I discovered your vanity?"

He had, not that he was going to get her to admit it. "They're hazel," she said again, a little primly. "It's a family trait."

Someone's family, at least.

"Actually," he said quite softly, "I was rather marveling on their changeability."

"Oh." She swallowed, discomfited by his gentle compliment. And at the same time rather pleased. "Thank you." She turned back to the map, which sat, safe and comforting, on the table before her. "Look how big Greenland is," she said, mostly because the big blob at the top was the first thing she saw.

"It's not really that big," he said. "The map distorts area."

"It does?"

"You did not know that?"

His tone was not insulting. It was not even condescending, but nonetheless, she felt foolish. It seemed like the sort of thing she ought to have known. And certainly it was the sort of thing she'd *like* to have known.

"It comes from having to spread a spherical object onto a flat plane," he explained. "Try to envision wrapping this map around a sphere. You'd have a great deal of extra paper at the poles. Or conversely, try to imagine taking the surface of a sphere and laying it out flat. You would not get a rectangle."

She nodded, cocking her head to the side as she considered this. "So the tops and bottoms are stretched. Or rather, the north and the south."

"Exactly. Do you see how Greenland looks nearly equal in size to Africa? It's actually less than one tenth the area."

She looked up at him. "Nothing is as it seems, is it?"

He was silent for just long enough to make her wonder if they were still talking about maps. And then he said, his face devoid of emotion, "No."

She shook her head, turning back to the map. "Strange."

And she *thought* she heard him say, "You have no idea." She glanced at him curiously, intending to ask what he meant, but he'd already returned his attention to the map.

"These projections do have their advantages," he said, sounding somewhat brisk, as if it were his turn to wish to change the subject. "It is true that they do not preserve actual area, but the local angles remain true, which is why they are so useful in navigation."

She was not sure that she fully understood what he was saying, but she enjoyed listening to him discuss something so academic. And she *adored* that he had not brushed it aside as a topic that would surely be of no interest to a lady. She looked over at him and smiled. "You certainly seem to know a great deal about this."

He shrugged modestly. "It is an interest of mine."

She sucked in her lips, a habit of hers that her mother detested. But she could not seem to help it. It was something she always did when she was deciding what to say. Or whether to say it.

"There is a name for this subject, is there not?" she asked. One of her feet was tapping nervously in her shoe. She wanted to know the name, because she wanted to try to look it up in her father's encyclopedia at home, but she hated revealing her ignorance. It brought to mind all those times she'd been forced to smile politely when her mother described her as smart (but not too smart).

"You mean mapmaking?"

She nodded.

"It is called cartography. From the Greek *chartis*, for map, and *graphein*, to write."

"I should have known that," she muttered. "Not the Greek, I suppose, but at least the word. Did my parents think we would never have use for a map?"

"I imagine they thought you would have others to read them for you," Thomas said gently.

She looked over at him in dismay. "You agree, then? That I have been educated appropriately?"

It was a terrible question to ask him. She'd put him in a dreadful spot, but she couldn't help it.

"I think," he said, his voice soft and deliberate, "that if you showed a desire for more knowledge, you should have been given the opportunity to acquire it."

And that was the moment. She didn't realize it right

away, and in fact she wouldn't realize it—or rather, she wouldn't *let* herself realize it—for several weeks to come. But that was the moment she fell in love with him.

Chapter 11

An hour later, after pulling fourteen atlases from the shelves and explaining to Amelia the difference between Mercator, sinusoidal, and conical map projections, Thomas deposited her in one of the front drawing rooms and notified the butler that she was there to see Miss Eversleigh.

Grace would have to be informed of the morning's activities, there was no getting around that. If a lie could not be made as close as possible to the truth, then Thomas was of the opinion that the truth ought to be made as close as possible to the lie. Everyone was far less likely to get confused that way. This meant, however, that Amelia needed to visit with Grace, and more important, that Grace understood that she was to have been shopping in Stamford that morning and invited Amelia back to Belgrave.

He, however, needed to speak with Grace first, without Amelia's knowledge, and so he positioned himself in the doorway of another drawing room, closer to the stairs, where he might intercept her before she reached her destination.

After five minutes he heard footsteps coming softly down the stairs. Definitely a feminine footfall. He moved closer to the doorway, confirmed that it was indeed Grace, and, when the time came, reached out and yanked her inside.

"Thomas!" she exclaimed after her initial yelp of shock. Her eyes widened as she took in his disheveled appearance. "What happened to you?"

He put his finger to his lips and shut the door behind them. "Were you expecting someone else?" he asked, since her surprise had seemed more to the *who* than the actual event.

"No, of course not," she said quickly. But her skin colored all the same. She looked about the room, probably to discern if they were alone. "What is wrong?"

"I needed to speak with you before you see Lady Amelia."

"Oh, then you know she is here?"

"I brought her," he confirmed.

Grace silenced, her face showing her surprise. She glanced over at the mantel clock, which revealed the time to be still before noon.

"It is a long story," he said preemptively. "But suffice it to say, Amelia will inform you that you were in Stamford this morning, and you invited her back to Belgrave."

"Thomas, any number of people know quite well that I was not in Stamford this morning."

"Yes, but her mother is not among that number."

"Er, Thomas . . ." Grace began, sounding very much as if she was not certain how to proceed. "I feel I must tell you, given the number of delays thus far, I would imagine that Lady Crowland would be delighted to know—"

"Oh for God's sake, it is nothing like that," he muttered, half expecting her to cry out, *"Despoiler of innocents!"*

He ground his teeth together, not at all enjoying the singular experience of having to explain his actions to another human being. "She assisted me home when I was . . . impaired."

"That was most charitable of her," Grace said primly.

Thomas glared at her. She looked as if she were about to laugh.

Grace cleared her throat. "Have you, er, considered tidying up?"

"No," he bit off, all sarcasm now, "I rather enjoy looking like a slovenly fool."

She winced—audibly—at that.

"Now listen," he continued, eager to bypass her embarrassment, "Amelia will repeat what I have told you, but it is imperative that you not tell her about Mr. Audley." He nearly growled the last; it was difficult to utter his name without an accompanying wave of revulsion.

"I would never do that," Grace replied. "It is not my place."

"Good." He'd known he could trust her.

"But she will want to know why you were, er . . ."

"You don't know why," he said firmly. "Just tell her that. Why would she suspect that you would know more?"

"She knows that I consider you a friend," Grace said. "And furthermore, I live here. Servants always know everything. She knows that, too."

"You're not a servant," he muttered.

"I am and you know it," she replied, her lips twitching with amusement. "The only difference is that I am allowed to wear finer clothing and occasionally converse with the guests. But I assure you, I am privy to all of the household gossip."

Good Lord, what went on in this house? Had any of his actions been private? Ever? Thomas turned his head and swore, and then, after taking a long, fortifying breath, looked back at her and said, "For me, Grace, will you please just tell her you don't know?"

Soon Amelia would know everything, but he just didn't want it to be today. He was too tired to make explanations, too worn-out from his own shock to deal with hers, and beyond that . . .

For the first time in his life he was *glad* she was his fiancée. Surely no one would begrudge him the desire to hold onto that for a few more days.

"Of course," Grace said, not quite looking at him. And then, because she had been brought up to look people in the eye, she met his gaze and added, "You have my word."

He nodded. "Amelia will be expecting you," he said gruffly.

"Yes. Yes, of course." She hurried to the door, then stopped and turned around. "Will you be all right?"

What a question.

"No, don't answer that," she mumbled, and dashed from the room.

Amelia waited patiently in the silver drawing room, trying not to tap her toes while she waited for Grace. Then she realized that she was drumming her fingers, which was an even worse habit (according to her mother), so she forced herself to stop *that*.

Her toes immediately started tapping again.

She let out a long breath and decided she didn't care. There was no one here to see her, anyway, and despite what her mother insisted, toe tapping was *not* a bad habit when done in private. As opposed to chewing one's fingernails (which she would *never* do), which left one stubby and unkempt, all 'round the clock.

She'd tried to explain the difference to Milly, who could sit still as stone for six hours straight but hadn't seen the whites of her nails for years. Milly had declared herself quite unable to detect the distinction. For purely selfish reasons, of course.

Amelia examined her own nails, which she noticed looked not quite as clean as usual. Probably from hauling Wyndham across Stamford. Heaven only knew what sort of dirt he'd been rolling about in. She supposed he was upstairs now, cleaning up. She'd never seen him look so untidy. She rather thought he'd never *been* so untidy. And, in fact—

Was that him? Striding past the doorway? She jumped up. "Thomas? Is that—"

The gentleman stopped, turned, and then Amelia realized that it was someone else. He was of a similar height and coloring, but she had never seen him before, of that she was quite certain. He was tall, although not awkwardly so, and his hair was perhaps a shade or two darker than Thomas's. And his cheek was bruised.

How interesting.

"I'm so sorry," she said hastily. But she was curious, and so she stepped toward the door. If she moved in his direction, he could not continue on his way without being unforgivably rude.

"Sorry to disappoint," the gentleman said, smiling at her in a most flirtatious fashion. Amelia felt rather pleased despite herself. She wondered if he knew who she was. Probably not. Who would dare flirt with the Duke of Wyndham's fiancée in his own house?

"No," she said quickly, "of course not. It was my mistake. I was just sitting back there." She motioned behind her. "You looked rather like the duke as you walked by."

Indeed, the two gentlemen even shared the same stride. How odd. Amelia had not realized that she could recognize Thomas's walk, but the moment she'd seen this man, she immediately realized that they moved in the same way.

He swept into a gracious bow. "Captain Jack Audley, at your service, ma'am."

She bobbed a polite curtsy. "Lady Amelia Willoughby."

"Wyndham's fiancée."

"You know him, then? Oh, well, of course you do. You are a guest here." Then she recalled their conversation back at the Happy Hare. "Oh, you must be his fencing partner."

Captain Audley stepped forward. "He told you about me?"

"Not much," she admitted, trying not to look at the bruise on his cheek. It could not be a coincidence that both he and Thomas showed signs of an altercation.

"Ah, this," Captain Audley murmured. He looked somewhat embarrassed as he touched his fingers to his cheek. "It looks much worse than it actually is."

She was trying to figure out the best way to ask him about it when he added, in a most conversational tone, "Tell me, Lady Amelia, what color is it today?"

"Your cheek?" she asked, surprised by his forthrightness.

"Indeed. Bruises tend to look worse as they age, have you noticed? Yesterday it was quite purple, almost regally so, with a hint of blue in it. I haven't checked in the mirror lately." He turned his head, offering her a better view. "Is it still as attractive?"

Amelia stared at him in awe, unsure of what to say. She had never met anyone quite so glib. It had to be a talent.

"Er, no," she finally replied, since it made absolutely no sense to lie when he was within ten feet of a mirror. "I would not call it attractive."

He laughed. "No mincing words for you, eh?"

"I'm afraid those blue undertones of which you were so proud have gone a bit green." She smiled, rather pleased with her analysis.

He leaned in, smiling wickedly. "To match my eyes?"

"No," she said, finding herself quite immune to his charms, although she did recognize them to be legion, indeed. The man probably had women falling at his feet at every turn. "Not with the purple overlaying it," she explained. "It looks quite horrible."

"Purple mixed with green makes . . . ?"

"Quite a mess."

He laughed again. "You are charming, Lady Amelia. But I am sure your fiancé tells you that on every possible occasion."

She was not quite certain how to reply to that. Certainly not every possible occasion. But today had been different. Better.

"Do you await him here?" the captain asked.

"No, I just—" She caught herself before she said that she'd just seen Thomas. She had never been good at telling tales. "I am here to see Miss Eversleigh."

Something intriguing flickered in his eyes, so she asked, "Have you met Miss Eversleigh?"

"Indeed I have. She is most lovely."

"Yes," Amelia said. Everyone thought so, didn't they? She pressed her tongue against the roof of her mouth just long enough to hide the fact that she wanted to frown, and added, "She is universally admired."

"Are you and Miss Eversleigh acquaintances?" the captain asked.

"Yes. I mean, no. More than that, I should say. I have known Grace since childhood. She is most friendly with my elder sister."

"And surely with you, as well."

"Of course." Amelia dipped her chin in acknowledgment. To do anything else would imply that Grace was less than gracious, which would be a falsehood. It was not Grace's fault that Thomas held her in such high esteem. And this gentleman, too, if his interest was any indication. "But more so with my sister. They are of an age, you see."

"Ah, the plight of the younger sibling," he murmured sympathetically.

Amelia looked at him with interest. "You share the experience?"

"Not at all," he said with a grin. "I was the one ignoring the hangers-on. I was the eldest of the brood. A fortuitous position, I think. I should have been most unhappy not to have been in charge."

Amelia understood that well. She'd often thought she was a different person with Elizabeth than she was with Milly. "I am the second of five," she said, "so I can appreciate your sentiments as well."

"Five!" He looked impressed. "All girls?"

Amelia's lips parted with surprise. "How did you know?"

"I have no idea," he replied, "except that it is such a

charming image. It would have been a shame to have sullied it with a male."

Good heavens, he was a rogue. "Is your tongue always this silver, Captain Audley?"

And, indeed, the smile he gave her was positively lethal. "Except," he said, "when it's gold."

"Amelia!"

They both turned. Grace had entered the room. "And Mr. Audley," she said, with some surprise.

"Oh, I'm sorry," Amelia said, somewhat confused. "I thought it was *Captain* Audley."

"It is," he said with a very slight shrug. "Depending upon my mood." He turned to Grace and bowed. "It is indeed a privilege to see you again so soon, Miss Eversleigh."

Grace curtsied in return. "I did not realize you were here."

"There is no reason why you should have done," Mr. Audley said politely. "I was heading outside for a restorative walk when Lady Amelia intercepted me."

"I thought he was Wyndham," Amelia told Grace. "Isn't that the oddest thing?"

"Indeed," Grace replied.

Amelia thought Grace's voice sounded a bit irregular, but it was probably just a bit of dust in her throat. It seemed impolite to mention it, however, and so she said, "Of course I was not paying much attention, which I am sure explains it. I only caught sight of him out of the corner of my eye as he strode past the open doorway."

Captain, er, *Mister* Audley turned to Grace. "It makes so much sense when put that way, does it not?"

"So much sense," Grace echoed. She glanced over her shoulder.

"Are you waiting for someone, Miss Eversleigh?" he inquired.

"No, I was just thinking that his grace might like to join us. Er, since his fiancée is here, of course."

Amelia swallowed awkwardly, grateful that neither one of them was looking at her. Grace did not know that she had spent the entire morning with Thomas. Or that she was supposed to have been shopping in Stamford. And she never would, Amelia thought, with the beginnings of irritation, if Mr. Audley did not go on his way. Hadn't he said he wanted to take a walk?

"Is he returned, then?" Mr. Audley asked. "I was not aware."

"That is what I have been told," Grace said. "I have not seen him myself."

"Alas," Mr. Audley said, "he has been absent for some time."

Amelia tried to catch Grace's attention but was unable to do so. Thomas would not like it to be well-known that he had been so impaired the night before—and this morning as well, for that matter.

"I think I should get him," Grace said.

"But you only just got here," Mr. Audley said.

"Nonetheless—"

"We shall ring for him," Mr. Audley said firmly, and he crossed the room to the bellpull. "There," he said, giving it a good yank. "It is done."

Amelia looked at Grace, whose face now held a vague expression of alarm, and then back to Mr. Audley, who was placidity personified. Neither spoke, nor did either seem to recall that she was in the room with them.

It did make one wonder just what, exactly, was going on.

Amelia looked back to Grace, since she knew her better, but Grace was already hurrying across the room to the sofa. "I believe I will sit down," she mumbled.

"I will join you," Amelia said, recognizing an opportunity to have a private word. She took a seat directly next to Grace, even though there was quite a length of cushion. All she needed was for Mr. Audley to excuse himself, or look the other way, or do anything other than follow the two of them about the room with those catlike green eyes of his.

"What a fetching tableau the two of you make," he said. "And me, without my oils."

"Do you paint, Mr. Audley?" Amelia asked. She had been brought up to make polite conversation whenever the situation called for it, and even, quite frequently, when it did not. Some habits were hard to break.

"Alas, no," he said. "But I have been thinking I might take some lessons. It is a noble pursuit for a gentleman, wouldn't you say?"

"Oh, indeed," she replied, although privately she thought that he would have been better served had he begun his studies at a younger age. Amelia looked at Grace, since it seemed only natural that she would add to the conversation. When she did not, Amelia gave her a polite nudge.

"Mr. Audley is a great appreciator of art," Grace blurted out.

Mr. Audley smiled enigmatically.

And Amelia was once again left to fill the breach. "You must be enjoying your stay at Belgrave Castle, then," she said to him.

"I look forward to touring the collections," he replied. "Miss Eversleigh has consented to show them to me."

"That was very kind of you, Grace." Amelia said, working to keep her surprise off her face. Not that there was anything wrong with Mr. Audley, except perhaps for his inability to leave the room when she wished him to. But as Grace was the dowager's companion, it seemed odd that she would have been asked to show Thomas's friend the collections.

Grace grunted something that was probably meant to be a response.

"We plan to avoid cupids," Mr. Audley said.

"Cupids?" Amelia echoed. Good heavens, he did move from topic to topic.

He shrugged. "I have discovered that I am not fond of them."

How could anyone not be fond of cupids?

"I can see that you disagree, Lady Amelia," Mr. Audley said. But Amelia noticed that he glanced at Grace before he spoke.

"What is there not to like about cupids?" Amelia asked him. She had not intended to engage him in such a ridiculous conversation, but really, he'd brought it up.

He perched himself on the arm of the opposite sofa. "You don't find them rather dangerous?" he asked, clearly out to make mischief.

"Chubby little babies?"

"Carrying deadly weapons," he reminded her.

"They are not *real* arrows."

Mr. Audley turned to Grace. Again. "What do you think, Miss Eversleigh?"

"I don't often think about cupids," she replied.

"And yet we have already discussed them twice, you and I."

"Because you brought them *up*."

Amelia drew back in surprise. She'd never heard Grace so short of temper.

"My dressing room is positively awash in them," Mr. Audley said.

Amelia turned to Grace. "You were in his dressing room?"

"Not *with* him," Grace practically snapped. "But I have certainly seen it before."

No one spoke, and then Grace finally muttered, "Pardon."

"Mr. Audley," Amelia said, deciding it was well past time to take the situation in hand. She was turning over a new leaf today, she'd decided. She had managed Thomas and she could manage these two if she had to.

"Lady Amelia," he said with a gracious tilt of his chin.

"Would it be rude if Miss Eversleigh and I took a turn about the room?"

"Of course not," he said immediately, even though it *was* rude, given that they were only a threesome, and he'd be left with nothing to do.

"Thank you for your understanding," Amelia said, linking her arm through Grace's and pulling them both to their feet. "I do feel the need to stretch my legs, and I fear that your stride would be far too brisk for a lady."

Good gad, she could not believe she was uttering such tripe, but it seemed to do the trick. Mr. Audley said nothing more, and she steered Grace over to a spot by the windows.

"I need to speak with you," she whispered, modulating their pace into something even and graceful.

Grace nodded.

"This morning," Amelia continued, glancing surreptitiously at Mr. Audley to see if he was watching them (he was), "Wyndham was in need of assistance, and I came to his aid, but I had to tell my mother that it was you I had seen, and that you had invited me back to Belgrave."

Grace nodded again, her eyes straight ahead, and then at the door, but never on her.

"I doubt it will come to it, but should you see my mother, I beg of you not to contradict."

"Of course not," Grace said quickly. "You have my word."

Amelia nodded, somewhat surprised at how easy that had been. She had not expected Grace to decline, but all the same, she thought she'd have to offer something more of an explanation. Grace hadn't even asked *why*

Wyndham had been in need of assistance. Surely that warranted some curiosity. When had either of them known him to need anything?

They fell silent as they promenaded past Mr. Audley, who looked rather amused at the spectacle they presented.

"Miss Eversleigh," he murmured. "Lady Amelia."

"Mr. Audley," Amelia returned. Grace said the same.

They continued around the room, Amelia picking up the conversation once they were again out of his earshot. "I do hope I do not overstep," she whispered. Grace was very silent, and Amelia was well aware that she was asking a great deal in asking her to lie.

They heard footsteps in the hall, and Grace's entire body jerked toward the door. But it was just a footman, walking by with a large trunk, probably empty, given that he had it perched easily on his shoulder.

"Sorry," Grace said. "Did you say something?"

Amelia started to repeat her comment, but instead just said, "No." She'd never seen Grace so distracted.

They continued around the room, taking, as they had the first time, the longest possible perimeter. As they drew close to the door, they heard more footsteps.

"Excuse me," Grace said, pulling away. She hurried to the open doorway, looked out, and then returned. "It wasn't the duke," she said.

Amelia glanced through the open doorway. Two more footmen were moving through the hall, one with a trunk and another with a hatbox.

"Is someone going somewhere?" Amelia asked.

"No," Grace replied. "Well, I suppose someone might be, but I do not know about it."

Her voice sounded so abrupt and unsettled that Amelia finally asked, "Grace, are you all right?"

Her head turned, but not far enough for Amelia to see into her eyes. "Oh, no . . . I mean, yes, I'm quite fine."

Amelia glanced back toward Mr. Audley. He waved. She turned back to Grace, whose face had flushed to a deep pink.

Which was reason enough to look back at Mr. Audley. He was looking at Grace. It was true that the two ladies were arm in arm, but it was more than obvious which was the recipient of his sultry gaze.

Grace knew it, too. Her breath caught, and indeed, her whole body stiffened. Amelia felt it tensing through her arm.

And then she was struck with the most marvelous thought.

"Grace," she whispered, keeping her voice extra low, "are you in love with Mr. Audley?"

"No!"

Grace's cheeks, which had begun to return to their normal tone, went right back to crimson. Her refusal had come out quite loudly, and Mr. Audley was regarding them with amused curiosity. Grace smiled weakly, nodded, and said, "Mr. Audley," even though he couldn't possibly hear her from where he sat.

"I've only just met him," Grace whispered furiously. "Yesterday. No, the day before. I can't recall."

"You've been meeting many intriguing gentlemen lately, have you not?"

Grace turned to her sharply. "Whatever can you mean?"

"Mr. Audley . . . " Amelia teased. "The Italian highwayman."

"Amelia!"

"Oh, that's right, you said he was Scottish. Or Irish. You weren't certain." Amelia caught sight of Mr. Audley just then, and it occurred to her that his accent was very slightly foreign as well. "Where is Mr. Audley from? He has a bit of a lilt as well."

"I do not know," Grace said, rather impatiently, in Amelia's opinion.

"Mr. Audley," Amelia called out.

He immediately tilted his head in question.

"Grace and I were wondering where you are from. Your accent is unfamiliar to me."

"Ireland, Lady Amelia, a bit north of Dublin."

"Ireland! My goodness, you are far afield."

He merely smiled.

The two ladies found themselves back at their original seating area, and so Amelia disconnected her arm from Grace's and sat down. "How are you enjoying Lincolnshire, Mr. Audley?"

"I find it most surprising."

"Surprising?" Amelia glanced at Grace to see if she, too, found that answer curious, but Grace was now standing near the door, nervously looking out.

"My visit here has not been what I expected."

"Really? What did you expect? I assure you, we are quite civilized in this corner of England."

"Very much so," he agreed. "More so than is my preference, as a matter of fact."

"Why, Mr. Audley, whatever can that mean?"

He smiled enigmatically but did not say more, which Amelia found quite out of character. Then it occurred to her that she'd known him but fifteen minutes; how odd that she would find anything out of character.

"Oh," she heard Grace say, and then: "Excuse me."

Grace hurried from the room.

Amelia and Mr. Audley looked at each other, and then in unison both turned to the doorway.

Chapter 12

$\mathcal{A}$side from Harry Gladdish, the man who knew Thomas best was his valet, Grimsby, who had been with the duke since the day he left for university. Unlike most valets, Grimsby was of an exceedingly strong constitution. (Not that one would know this to look at him; he was quite slender, with pale skin that always worried the housekeeper, who kept trying to get him to eat more beef.)

When Thomas returned from a hell-for-leather gallop in the rain, his clothes soaked and muddied, Grimsby merely inquired after the horse.

When Thomas spent a day in the field, doing manual labor alongside his tenants, returning with any number of layers of grime on his skin, in his hair, and under his nails, Grimsby asked him if he preferred his bathwater warm, hot, or steaming.

But when Thomas staggered into his bedchamber,

presumably still reeking of alcohol (he'd long since stopped noticing the odor), his cravat completely missing, and his eye a most remarkable shade of purple, Grimsby dropped his shoe brush.

It was possibly the only outward show of alarm he had ever displayed.

"Your eye," Grimsby said.

Oh, right. He hadn't seen Grimsby since his tussle with his lovely new cousin. Thomas gave him a flip sort of smile. "Perhaps we can choose a waistcoat to match."

"I don't believe we have one, your grace."

"Is that so?" Thomas crossed to the basin. As usual, Grimsby had made sure it was filled with water. Lukewarm by this point, but he was in no position to complain. He splashed a bit on his face, rubbed himself with a hand towel, then repeated the entire process after a quick glance in the mirror revealed that he'd barely scratched the surface of his disrepair.

"We shall have to remedy that, Grimsby," Thomas said, giving his forehead a good scrub. He looked back at his valet with a sarcastic grin. "Do you think you can memorize the hue for the next time we are in London?"

"Might I suggest, your grace, that you consider not subjecting your face to such abuse again?" Grimsby handed him another towel, even though Thomas had not requested one. "This would eliminate our need to consider the color when choosing your wardrobe for the upcoming year." He held out a bar of soap. "You could still purchase a new waistcoat of the color, if you wish. I imagine the shade would be most handsome when displayed upon fabric, as opposed to one's skin."

"Elegantly said," Thomas murmured. "It almost didn't sound like a scolding."

Grimsby smiled modestly. "I do try, your grace." He held forth another towel. Good gad, Thomas thought, he must be more of a mess than he'd thought.

"Shall I ring for a bath, your grace?"

The question was purely rhetorical, as Grimsby had already done so before the *your* in *your grace*. Thomas stripped off his clothing, which Grimsby then picked up with tongs, and donned his dressing robe. He flopped onto his bed, and was seriously considering postponing the bath in favor of a good nap when a knock sounded at the door.

"That was quick," Grimsby commented, crossing the room.

"His grace has a visitor," came the unexpected voice of Penrith, Belgrave's longtime butler.

Thomas did not bother to open his eyes. There could be no one worth rising for at this moment.

"The duke is not receiving at this time," Grimsby said. Thomas resolved to raise his wages with all possible haste.

"It is his fiancée," the butler said.

Thomas sat up like a shot. What the devil? Amelia was supposed to be here for Grace. It had all been planned. The two women would chitter chatter for an hour, and then he would make his usual appearance, and no one would suspect that Amelia had actually been at Belgrave all morning.

What could possibly have gone awry?

"Your grace," Grimsby said when Thomas swung his legs over the side of the bed to get down, "you cannot possibly think of receiving Lady Amelia in such a state."

"I do plan to dress, Grimsby," Thomas said rather dryly.

"Yes, of course, but . . . "

Grimsby appeared unable to complete his sentence aloud, but his nose flared a bit, then wrinkled, which Thomas took to mean—*Sir, you stink.*

Nothing to be done about it, though. He couldn't leave Amelia on her own if all had not gone according to plan. And indeed, Grimsby was able to work a small miracle in the space of ten minutes. By the time Thomas left his room, he looked wholly like himself again. (Himself in need of a shave, but this could not be helped.) But his hair was no longer sticking up like an exotic bird, and even though his eye still looked like death underneath, he no longer appeared quite so bloodshot and exhausted.

A bit of tooth powder and he was ready to go. Grimsby, on the other hand, gave every indication that he needed a good lie-down.

Thomas made his way downstairs, intending to head straight to the drawing room, but as he entered the hall, he saw Grace, standing about six feet from its entrance, gesticulating madly and holding one finger to her lips.

"Grace," he said as he approached, "what is the meaning of this? Penrith told me that Amelia was here to see me?"

He did not pause, assuming that she would fall in step beside him. But just as he passed, she grabbed his arm and yanked him to a stop. "Thomas, wait!"

He turned, lifting one of his brows in question.

"It's Mr. Audley," she said, pulling him back even farther from the door. "He is in the drawing room."

Thomas glanced toward the drawing room and then back at Grace, wondering why he'd been told that Amelia was there.

"With Amelia," Grace practically hissed.

He cursed, unable to stop himself, despite the presence of a lady. "Why?"

"I don't know," Grace said, her voice quite snappish. "He was in there when I arrived. Amelia said she saw him walking by the doorway and thought he was you."

Oh now, that was rich. Blessed with a family resemblance, they were. How quaint.

"What did he say?" Thomas finally asked.

"I don't know. I wasn't there. And then I couldn't very well interrogate her in his presence."

"No, of course not." He pinched the bridge of his nose, thinking. This was a disaster.

"I'm quite sure he did not reveal his . . . identity to her."

Thomas gave her a dry look.

"It is not my fault, Thomas," Grace said angrily.

"I did not say that it was." He let out his own irritated snort and then pressed on toward the drawing room. Mr. Audley was a cancer in their midst. In all the years Grace had worked here, they had never exchanged angry words. And God only knew what the man was saying to Amelia.

From the moment Grace rushed from the room, neither Amelia nor Mr. Audley had uttered a word. It was as if they had reached an unspoken agreement; silence would prevail while they both tried to make out what was being said in the hall.

But unless Mr. Audley's hearing was superior to hers, Amelia accepted that they had both been stymied. She could not make out a thing. Grace must have intercepted Thomas at the far end of the hall.

Grace did seem exceedingly agitated that afternoon, which Amelia found strange. She realized that she had asked a great deal of her, especially when Grace's friendship was more to her sister than herself, but surely that could not account for her odd demeanor.

Amelia leaned forward, as if that might possibly improve her eavesdropping. Something was brewing at Belgrave, and she was growing rather irritated that she seemed to be the only person left in the dark.

"You won't be able to hear them," Mr. Audley said.

She gave him a look that tried to be reproving.

"Oh, don't pretend you weren't trying. I certainly was."

"Very well." Amelia decided there was no point in protesting. "What do you suppose they are talking about?"

Mr. Audley shrugged. "Difficult to say. I would never presume to understand the female mind, or that of our esteemed host."

"You do not like the duke?" Because surely the implication was in his tone.

"I did not say that," he chided gently.

She pressed her lips together, wanting to say that he did not *have* to say it. But there was nothing to be gained in provocation, at least not at this moment, so instead she asked, "How long do you stay at Belgrave?"

"Eager to be rid of me, Lady Amelia?"

"Of course not." Which was more or less true. She did not mind him, on principle, although he had been rather inconvenient this afternoon. "I saw the servants moving trunks about. I thought perhaps they were yours."

"I imagine they belong to the dowager," he replied.

"Is she going somewhere?" Amelia knew she ought not to have sounded quite so excited, but there was only so much disinterest a young lady could feign.

"Ireland," he replied.

Before she could ask more, Thomas appeared in the doorway, looking decidedly more like himself than the last time she'd seen him.

"Amelia," he said, striding toward her.

"Your grace," she replied.

"How lovely to see you. I see that you have met our guest."

"Yes," she said. "Mr. Audley is quite diverting."

Thomas glanced over at the other gentleman, not, Amelia noted, with particular affection. "Quite."

There was an ominous silence, and then Amelia said, "I came to see Grace."

"Yes, of course," Thomas murmured. It was, after all, the ruse they'd concocted.

"Alas," Mr. Audley said, "I found her first."

Thomas gave him a look that would have quelled any man of Amelia's acquaintance, but Mr. Audley only smirked.

"I found *him*, actually," she put in. "I saw him in the hall. I thought he was you."

"Astounding, isn't it?" Mr. Audley murmured. He turned to Amelia. "We are nothing alike."

Amelia looked to Thomas.

"No," he said brusquely, "we are not."

"What do you think, Miss Eversleigh?" Mr. Audley asked.

Amelia turned toward the doorway. She had not realized that Grace had returned.

Mr. Audley rose to his feet, his eyes never leaving Grace. "Do the duke and I share any traits?"

At first Grace seemed not to know how to answer. "I'm afraid I do not know you well enough to be an accurate judge," she finally replied.

Mr. Audley smiled, and Amelia got the sense that they were sharing a moment she did not understand. "Well said, Miss Eversleigh," he said. "May I infer, then, that you know the duke quite well?"

"I have worked for his grandmother for five years," Grace said, her bearing stiff and formal. "During that time I have been fortunate enough to learn something of his character."

"Lady Amelia," Thomas cut in, "may I escort you home?"

"Of course," Amelia agreed, rather looking forward to the journey. She had not been expecting his company. It was a most delightful change of plans.

"So soon?" Mr. Audley murmured.

"My family will be expecting me," Amelia said.

"We will leave right now, then," Thomas said, offering her his arm. Amelia took it and stood.

"Er, your grace!"

They turned toward Grace, who was still standing near the doorway. She looked rather agitated. "If I might have a word with you," she said haltingly, "before you, er, depart. Please."

Thomas excused himself and followed Grace into the hall. They were still visible from the drawing room, although it was difficult—indeed impossible—to glean their conversation.

"Whatever can they be discussing?" Mr. Audley said, and she could tell from his tone that he knew exactly what they were discussing, and that he knew she did not know, and that he *absolutely* knew that raising the question would irritate her mightily.

"I am sure I have no idea," she bit off.

"Nor I," he said, breezy as always.

And then they heard: "Ireland!"

This was Thomas, his voice most uncharacteristically loud. Amelia would like to have known what was uttered next, but Thomas took Grace's arm and moved them both to the side, where they were completely out of view. And, apparently, out of earshot as well.

"We have our answer," Mr. Audley murmured.

"He can't be upset that his grandmother is leaving the country," Amelia said. "I would think he'd be planning a celebration."

"I rather think Miss Eversleigh has informed him that his grandmother intends that he accompany her."

"To Ireland?" Amelia drew back with surprise. "Oh, you must be mistaken."

He shrugged. "Perhaps. I am but a newcomer here."

"Aside from the fact that I cannot imagine why the dowager would wish to go to *Ireland*—not," she hastened to add, as she recalled that this was his birthplace, "that I wouldn't like to see your beautiful country, but it does not seem in character for the dowager, whom I have heard speak disparagingly of Northumberland, the Lake District, and indeed, all of Scotland." She paused, trying to imagine the dowager enjoying the rigors of travel. "Ireland seems a bit of a stretch for her."

He nodded graciously.

"But really, it makes no sense that she would wish for Wyndham to accompany her. They do not care for each other's company."

"How politely said, Lady Amelia. Does anyone care for their company?"

Her eyes widened in surprise. This was an even clearer declaration that he disliked Thomas. And said in his own house! It was really remarkably impolite.

And curious.

Just then, Thomas strode back into the room. "Amelia," he said rather briskly, "I am afraid I will not be able to see you home. I do apologize."

"Of course," she replied, shooting a look at Mr. Audley, although why she would do so, she wasn't quite sure.

"I shall make every arrangement for your comfort. Perhaps you would like to select a book from the library?"

"Can you read in a coach?" Mr. Audley queried.

"Can you not?" Amelia returned.

"I *can*. I can do almost anything in a coach. Or with a coach," he added with an odd smile.

Thomas took her arm with a rather surprising firmness and pulled her to her feet.

"It was lovely meeting you, Mr. Audley," Amelia said.

"Yes," he murmured, "it does seem that you are leaving."

"Amelia," Thomas said curtly, leading her away.

"Is something wrong?" she asked him once they had reached the hall. She looked about for Grace, but she had disappeared.

"Of course not," he said. "Merely matters to which I must attend."

Amelia was about to ask about the upcoming trip to Ireland, but for some reason she did not. She wasn't sure why; it was not a conscious decision, more of a feeling than anything else. Thomas seemed so distracted. She did not wish to upset him further.

And aside from that, she rather doubted he would answer her honestly if she did ask. He would not lie; that would be entirely out of his character. But he would brush off the query with something vague and condescending, and she would lose all the lovely feelings she had gained that morning.

"Might I take with me one of the atlases?" she asked. The trip home would be less than an hour, but she had so enjoyed looking at the maps. It was something they had done together, their heads bowed over the books, their foreheads nearly touching.

The outline of a continent, the pale blue shading of an ocean on the page—these would forever make her think of him.

As she was riding home, the carriage bumping gently over the ruts in the road, she turned the pages until she found Ireland. She rather liked the shape of it, all flat in the east, then seeming to reach out its arms toward the Atlantic in the west.

She would ask Thomas about the trip the next time she saw him. Surely he would not leave the country without telling her.

She closed her eyes, picturing his face, conveniently editing out his blackened eye. They had entered a new chapter in their relationship. Of this she was certain.

She still did not know why Thomas had been drinking the night before, but she told herself that she did not care. All that mattered was that it had led him to her, and perhaps her to herself.

She'd woken up. After years of sleepwalking, she'd woken up.

Chapter 13

Four days later

After his initial shock, Thomas realized that his grandmother had been right about one thing. A trip to Ireland was the only solution to their dilemma. The truth must come out, no matter how unpleasant. Mr. Audley might, with the proper encouragement, be willing to forgo his claim on the title (although Thomas doubted the dowager would allow that to happen). But Thomas knew that he could never find peace if he did not know who he really was. And he did not think he could continue in his position if he knew it rightly belonged to another.

Had his entire life been a lie? Had he never been the Duke of Wyndham, never been the heir to it, even? This would mean—well, truly, this was the only amusing part of it all—his father had never been the duke, either. It was almost enough to make him wish his father alive again, just to see his reaction.

Thomas wondered if they would have to change the inscription on his gravestone. Probably.

He wandered into the small saloon at the front of the house and poured himself a drink. He might actually enjoy erasing the title from his father's marker, he thought. It was good to know there might be some amusement in all this.

Thomas walked to the window and gazed outside. He came here quite frequently when he wished for solitude. He could get that in his office, of course, but there he was surrounded by ledgers and correspondence— reminders of tasks still incomplete. Here, he could simply think.

He supposed he disliked his cousin slightly less than he had before—in the four days since he'd found him in the drawing room with Amelia, their conversations had been perfectly civil—but he still found him hopelessly unserious. He knew that Audley was once a military officer, and as such must have had to exercise caution and judgment, but Thomas still had grave doubts about his ability to apply himself with the diligence necessary to run a dukedom.

Would he understand that the livelihoods and indeed the lives of hundreds of people depended upon him?

Would he feel the history in his position? The heritage? The unspoken covenant with the soil, the stones, the blood that had fed the ground for generations? Wyndham was more than a title one appended to one's name, it was . . .

It was . . .

Thomas sat down in his favorite leather chair, closing his eyes in anguish.

It was him. *He* was Wyndham, and he had no idea who he would be when it was all taken away. And it would. He was growing more certain of this by the day. Audley wasn't stupid. He would not lead them all the way to Ireland, for God's sake, if proof of his legitimacy was not waiting at their destination.

Audley had to know that he would still have been showered with privilege and money even if he'd declared his mother a dockside whore, known to his father for all of three minutes. Their grandmother was so desperately infatuated with the idea of her favorite son having produced a son of his own that she would have provided him with an income for life, regardless.

Audley's life would have been secure, and a great deal less complicated, if he was illegitimate.

Which meant that he wasn't. Somewhere in Ireland there was a church with proof of the marriage between Lord John Cavendish and Miss Louise Galbraith. And when they found it, Thomas knew he would still be Mr. Thomas Cavendish, gentleman of Lincolnshire, the grandson of a duke, but that would be as close as his connection went.

What would he do with himself? How would he fill his days?

Who would he be?

He looked down at his drink. He'd finished it some time ago, and he thought it was his third. What would Amelia say? He'd told her he did not overindulge in spirits, and he did not, as a normal matter of course. But life was anything but normal lately.

Perhaps this would be his new habit. Perhaps this was how he would fill his days—in the ignoble pursuit of oblivion. Pour enough brandy into him and he could forget that he did not know who he was or what he owned or how he was meant to act.

Or—he chuckled grimly at this—how others were meant to act with him. That would be amusing, actually, watching society scramble and stammer, with not a clue what to say. What macabre fun it would be to drop in at the Lincolnshire Dance and Assembly. London would be even worse.

And then there was Amelia. He supposed he would have to cry off, or at least insist that she do so, since as a gentleman he could not initiate the dissolution of the betrothal contract. But surely she would not want him. And certainly her family would not.

Amelia had been raised to be the Duchess of Wyndham, every bit as much as he had to be the duke. That was no longer a possibility, since he rather doubted that Audley was going to marry her. But there were many other titles in the land, and more than a handful of unmarried peers. Amelia could do far better than a penniless commoner with no useful skills.

No skills useful for anything other than owning large tracts of land and the occasional castle, that was.

Amelia.

He closed his eyes. He could see her face, the sharp curiosity in those hazel eyes, the light sprinkling of freckles across the bridge of her nose. He'd wanted to kiss her the other day, more than he'd realized at the time. He lay awake in bed, thinking about her, wondering if he wanted her now only because he could no longer have her.

He thought about peeling her dress from her body, of worshipping her with his hands, his lips, of making a conquest of her skin, counting the freckles she surely must hide beneath her clothing.

Amelia.

He poured another drink in her honor. It seemed only appropriate, since it was the ale that had brought them together the last time. This was fine brandy, potent and smooth, one of the last bottles he'd acquired before it became illegal to bring it in from France. He lifted his glass. She deserved a toast made with the very best.

And perhaps another, he decided, once he'd drained his glass. Surely Amelia was worth two glasses of brandy. But when he rose and crossed to the decanter, he heard voices in the hall.

It was Grace. She sounded happy.

Happy. It was baffling. Thomas could not even imagine such a simple, unfettered emotion.

And as for the other voice—it only took another second to place it. It was Audley, and he sounded as if he wanted to seduce her.

Bloody hell.

Grace fancied him. He'd seen it over the last few days, of course, how she blushed in his presence and laughed at his quips. He supposed she had a right to fall in love with whomever she wanted, but by God, *Audley*?

It felt like the worst sort of betrayal.

Unable to help himself, he moved toward the door. It was slightly ajar, just enough to listen without being seen.

"You can call me Jack," Audley said.

Thomas wanted to gag.

"No, I don't think so." But Grace sounded as if she was smiling, as if she didn't really mean it.

"I won't tell."

"Mmmmm . . . no."

"You did it once."

"That," Grace said, still obviously flirting, "was a mistake."

Thomas stepped into the hall. Some things simply could not be borne. *"Indeed."*

Grace gasped and looked at him with a rather satisfying level of shock.

"Where the devil did he come from?" Audley murmured.

"A pleasant conversation," Thomas drawled. "One of many, I assume."

"Were you eavesdropping?" Audley said. "For shame."

Thomas decided to ignore him. It was either that or strangle him, and he suspected that would be difficult to explain to the authorities.

"Your grace," Grace began, "I—"

Oh, for God's sake, if she could call Audley Jack, she could bloody well use his name again. "It's Thomas, or don't you recall?" he snapped. "You've used *my* name far more than once."

He felt a brief pang of remorse at her miserable expression, but that was quickly suppressed when Audley chimed in, in his usual glib manner.

"Is that so?" he said, gazing down at Grace. "In that case, I insist you call me Jack." He turned to Thomas and shrugged. "It's only fair."

Thomas held himself very still. Something ugly was growing within him, something furious and black. And every time Audley spoke, his tone was so droll, his smile so easy—it was as if none of this *mattered*. It fed the dark knot in his belly, it burned in his chest.

Audley turned back to Grace. "I shall call you Grace."

"You will not," Thomas snapped.

Audley lifted a brow but did not otherwise acknowledge him. "Does he always make these decisions for you?"

"This is my house," Thomas ground out. Damn it, he would not be ignored.

"Possibly not for long," Audley murmured.

It was his first directly confrontational comment, and for some reason Thomas actually found that funny. He looked at Grace, and at Audley, and it was suddenly clear how desperate Audley was to get her into his bed.

"Just so you know," Thomas said, unconsciously adopting Audley's tone, smile, his everything, "she doesn't come with the house."

Audley stiffened and his chin drew back. Ah, Thomas thought, a direct hit. Magnificent.

"Just what do you mean by that?" Audley bit off.

Thomas shrugged. "I think you know."

"Thomas," Grace said, trying to intercede.

He was reminded how bitterly he felt toward her. "Oh, we're back to Thomas, are we?"

And then Audley, in his usual fine fashion, turned to Grace and said, "I think he fancies you, Miss Eversleigh."

"Don't be ridiculous," Grace said dismissively.

And Thomas thought, Why not? Why *didn't* he fancy Grace? It would be a hell of a lot less complicated than this burgeoning desire for Amelia.

In any case, it amused him to have Audley think that he did, so he crossed his arms and stared down his nose at him.

Audley merely smiled, his very expression a dare. "I wouldn't wish to keep you from your responsibilities."

"Ah, now they are *my* responsibilities?"

"While the house is still yours."

"It's not just a house, Audley."

"Do you think I don't know that?" Something flashed in his eyes, something different and entirely new. It was fear, Thomas realized with a start. Audley was terrified of gaining the title.

As he damned well should be.

For the first time, Thomas began to feel a glimmer of respect for the other man. If he knew enough to be afraid . . .

Well, at the very least, it meant Audley wasn't a complete fool.

"Excuse me," Thomas said, because he no longer felt so steady. It was the brandy, yes, but also the encounter. No one was how they should be—not Grace, not Audley, and especially not himself.

He turned on his heel and left, shutting the door firmly behind him. He would still hear them if they spoke, but surely they would not be so foolish as to remain. They'd go somewhere else to laugh and flirt. Audley would try to kiss Grace, and maybe she would let him, and they would be happy, at least for this day.

Thomas sat in his chair, stared out the window, and wondered why he couldn't cry.

Later that night Thomas was sitting in his study, ostensibly for the purpose of going over his affairs. In truth, he'd been seeking privacy. He did not much enjoy the company of others these days, especially when the only "others" to enjoy were his grandmother, his new cousin, and Grace.

Several ledgers were open on his desk, their myriad columns filled with neat numbers, each carefully inked onto the page in his own hand. Belgrave's steward was paid to keep such records, of course, but Thomas liked to take care of his own set himself. Somehow the information felt different in his brain when it was he who had written the numbers down. He'd tried to give up the habit a few years back, since it seemed unnecessary to have two complete sets of records, but felt as if he couldn't see the forest for the trees.

A duke *had* to see the forest. Wyndham was a huge responsibility, with holdings across Britain. Would Audley see that? Would he respect it, or would he shuffle off the decisions to a variety of stewards and secretaries, as Thomas had seen so many of his contemporaries do, usually with disastrous results.

Could a man care for a heritage such as Wyndham if he had not been born to it? Thomas held it in reverence, but then again, he'd had a lifetime to develop his love for and knowledge of the land. Audley had arrived last week. Could he possibly understand what it all meant? Or was it something bred in the blood? Had he stepped foot into Belgrave and thought—*Aha, this is home*.

Unlikely. Not with their grandmother there to greet him.

Thomas rubbed his temples. It was worrisome. It could all fall apart. Not immediately; he had run the estate far too well for that. But given time, Audley could rip through the whole thing without even intending to.

"It won't be my problem," Thomas said aloud. He wouldn't be the duke. Hell, he probably wouldn't even stay in Lincolnshire. Wasn't there some sort of dispensation in his grandfather's will? Some sort of small house near Leeds he'd bought to parcel off to his younger son. He did not want to remain at hand to watch Audley assume his role. He'd take the other property and be done with them all.

He took a sip of the brandy on his desk—he was almost through with the bottle, which gave him some satisfaction. It hadn't been easy to obtain it, and he didn't particularly wish to leave it behind. But it did serve as a reminder of certain bodily functions, and so he pushed his chair back and stood. There was a chamber pot in the corner, but he'd recently refurbished this section of Belgrave with the latest in toileting technologies. He'd be damned if he was going to forgo the pleasure before getting shipped off to Leeds.

Off he went, moving down the hall. It was late; the house was settled and quiet. He took care of his business, pausing to admire the marvels of modern invention, then headed back to his study, where he fully intended to spend the night, or at least remain until he finished the brandy.

But on his way back he heard another person stirring about. He stopped and peered into the rose salon. A lighted candelabra sat on a table, illuminating the room with a flickering glow. Grace was in the far corner, shuffling about at the escritoire, opening and shutting drawers, a frustrated expression on her face.

He told himself he should apologize to her. His behavior that afternoon had been abominable. They had shared far too many years of friendship to allow it to end like this.

He said her name from the doorway, and she looked up, startled.

"Thomas," she said, "I did not realize you were still awake."

"It's not so late," he said.

She gave him a small smile. "No, I suppose not. The dowager is abed but not yet asleep."

"Your work is never done, is it?" he asked, entering the room.

"No," she said, with a resigned shrug. He'd seen her

make that motion countless times. And the expression that went along with it—a bit rueful, a bit wry. Truly, he did not know how she bore his grandmother. He put up with her because he had to.

Well, he supposed she had to put up with her, too. Employment opportunities for gently bred young ladies of little to no fortune were not exactly thick on the ground.

"I ran out of writing paper upstairs," she explained.

"For correspondence?"

"Your grandmother's," she affirmed. "I have no one with whom to correspond. I suppose once Elizabeth Willoughby marries and moves away . . . " She paused, looking thoughtful. "I shall miss her."

"Yes," he murmured, remembering what Amelia had told him. "You are good friends, aren't you?"

She nodded. "Ah, here we are." She pulled forth a small stack of paper, then looked up at him with a grimace. "I must go write your grandmother's letters now."

"She does not write them herself?" he asked with surprise.

"She thinks she does. But the truth is, her penmanship is dreadful. No one could possibly make out what she intends to say. Even I have difficulty with it. I end up improvising at least half in the copying."

He chuckled at that. Grace was such a good egg. He wondered why she'd never married. Were the gentlemen too intimidated by her position at Belgrave? Probably. He supposed he was at fault, too, so desperate to keep her on as his grandmother's companion that he had not done as he ought and provided her with a small dowry so she might rise from employment and find a husband.

"I must apologize, Grace," he said, walking toward her.

"For this afternoon? No, please, don't be silly. It's a terrible situation, and no one could fault you for—"

"For many things," he cut in. He should have given her the opportunity to find a husband. If nothing else, she wouldn't have been here when Audley had arrived.

"Please," she said, her face twisting into a miserable smile. "I cannot think of anything for which you need to make amends, but I assure you, if there were, I would accept your apology, with all graciousness."

"Thank you," he said. He supposed he felt better for that, but not much. And then, because one could always find refuge in the obvious, he said, "We depart for Liverpool in two days."

She nodded slowly. "I imagine you have much to do before we leave."

He thought about that. Not really. He'd spent the last four days under the assumption that he'd return to England with nothing, so he'd worked himself into a frenzy, making sure every last corner of the Wyndham estates was as it should be. He would not have anyone saying he'd sabotaged the new duke.

But he'd finished it all. There was a grain order to review, and his own personal packing to supervise, but other than that . . .

His days as the duke were over.

"Almost nothing," he told Grace, unable to keep the bite from his voice.

"Oh." She sounded surprised, not so much by his answer, but by the fact that he'd voiced it. "That must be a pleasant change."

He leaned forward. He could see that she was growing uncomfortable, and he'd had just enough to drink to enjoy that a bit. "I am practicing, you see," he said.

She swallowed. "Practicing?"

"To be a gentleman of leisure. Perhaps I should emulate your Mr. Audley."

"He is not my Mr. Audley," she immediately replied.

"He shall not worry," he continued, ignoring her protest. They both knew she was lying. "I have left all of the affairs in perfect order. Every contract has been reviewed and every last number in every last column has been tallied. If he runs the estate into the ground, it shall be on his own head."

"Thomas, stop," she said. "Don't talk this way. We don't know that he is the duke."

"Don't we?" Good Lord, which one of them was she trying to fool? "Come now, Grace, we both know what we will find in Ireland."

"We don't," she insisted, but her voice sounded wrong.

And he knew.

He took a step toward her. "Do you love him?"

She froze.

"Do you love him?" he repeated, losing patience. "Audley."

"I *know* who you're talking about," she snapped.

He almost laughed. "I imagine you do." And he thought to himself—they were doomed. The both of them. Amelia was lost to him, and Grace had gone and fallen in love with Audley, of all people. Nothing could happen there. He knew that he might have got away with marrying someone of Grace's status, but Audley never would. Once he became the duke, he'd have to marry some horse-faced girl whose birth was as high as his own. There would be skeptics and detractors aplenty. The new duke would need a brilliant marriage to prove to society that he was worthy of the title.

And besides, Audley was an irresponsible fool, clearly unworthy of a woman like Grace.

"How long have you been here?" he asked, trying to locate the answer through the fog in his brain.

"At Belgrave? Five years."

"And in all that time I haven't . . . " He shook his head. "I wonder why."

"Thomas." She eyed him warily. "What are you talking about?"

"Damned if I know." He laughed bitterly. "What's to become of us, Grace? We're doomed, you know. Both of us."

"I don't know what you're talking about."

He couldn't believe she'd had the nerve to pretend he hadn't been crystal clear. "Oh, come now, Grace, you're far too intelligent for that."

She looked to the door. "I should go."

But he was blocking her way.

"Thomas, I—"

And then he thought—why not? Amelia was as good as gone, and Grace—good, solid, dependable Grace—was right here. She was lovely, really, he'd always thought so, and a man could do far worse. Even a man without a farthing to his name.

He took her face in his hands and he kissed her. It was a desperate thing, born not of desire but of pain, and he kept kissing her, because he kept hoping that maybe it would turn into something else, that maybe if he tried hard enough, for long enough, something would spark between them and he would forget . . .

"Stop!" she pushed at his chest. "Why are you doing this?"

"I don't know," he said with a helpless shrug. It was the truth. "I'm here, you're here . . . "

"I'm leaving." But one of his hands was still on her arm. He should let go. He knew he should, but he couldn't. She might not have been the right woman, but maybe . . . maybe she wasn't entirely the wrong one. Maybe they could make a go of it, they two.

"Ah, Grace," he said. "I am not Wyndham any longer. We both know it." He felt himself shrugging, and then he held his hand toward her. It felt like he was finally allowing himself to surrender to the inevitable.

She stared at him curiously. "Thomas?"

And then—who knew where it had come from, but he said, "Why don't you marry me when this is all over?"

"What?" She looked horrified. "Oh, Thomas, you're mad."

But she did not pull away.

"What do you say, Gracie?" He touched her chin, tipping her up to look at him.

She didn't say yes, but she didn't say no. He knew she was thinking of Audley, but just then he didn't care. She felt like his only hope, his last shot at sanity.

He leaned down to kiss her again, pausing to remind himself of her beauty. That thick, dark hair, those gorgeous blue eyes—they should have had his heart pounding. If he pressed her against him, hard and demanding, would his body tighten with need?

But he didn't press her against him. He didn't want to. It felt wrong, and he felt dirty for even thinking of it, and when Grace turned her head to the side and whispered, "I can't," he did nothing to stop her. Instead, he rested his chin atop her head, holding her like he might a sister.

His heart twisted, and he whispered, "I know."

"Your grace?"

Thomas looked up from his desk the following morning, wondering just how much longer he might be addressed in that manner. His butler was standing in the doorway, waiting for acknowledgment.

"Lord Crowland is here to see you, sir," Penrith said. "With Lady Amelia."

"At this hour?" He blinked, glancing for the clock, which had gone unaccountably missing.

"It's half nine, sir," Penrith informed him. "And the clock is out for repair."

Thomas touched the bridge of his nose, which seemed to have single-handedly absorbed all of the ill-effects of the previous night's bottle of brandy. "Thought I was going mad there for a moment," he murmured. Although truly, the missing clock would have been the least of the symptoms.

"They are in the rose salon, sir."

Where he'd mauled Grace mere hours earlier. Lovely.

Thomas waited for Penrith to depart, then closed his eyes in mortification. Dear God, he'd kissed Grace. Hauled the poor girl into his arms and kissed her. What the devil had he been thinking?

And yet . . . he couldn't quite regret it. It seemed a sensible idea at the time. If he couldn't have Amelia . . .

Amelia.

Her name in his mind jolted him back to the present. Amelia was here. He could not keep her waiting.

He stood. She'd brought her father, never a good sign. Thomas got on well enough with Lord Crowland, but he could think of no reason why the man would pay a call so early in the morning. He could not even remember the last time the earl had been by.

Dear God, he hoped he hadn't brought the hounds. He had far too much of a headache for that.

It was not far to the rose salon, just down the hall. When he entered the room, he immediately saw Amelia, perched on a settee, looking as if she'd rather be somewhere else. She smiled, but it was really more of a grimace, and Thomas wondered if she was unwell.

"Lady Amelia," he said, though he really ought to have acknowledged her father first.

She stood, bobbing a little curtsy. "Your grace."

"Is something amiss?" he asked. He felt his head tilt, just the slightest little bit, as he looked into her eyes. They were back to green again, with little brown flecks at the edges. But she didn't look quite right.

When had he got to know her so well that he could recognize such subtleties in her appearance?

"I am quite well, your grace."

But he did not like that tone, all meek and proper. He wanted the other Amelia back, the one who had pored over dusty old atlases with him, her eyes shining with delight at her newfound knowledge. The one who had laughed with Harry Gladdish—at his expense!

Funny. He had never thought that a willingness to poke fun at him would be something he'd prize so highly in a wife, but there it was. He did not want to be placed on a pedestal. Not by her.

"Are you certain?" he asked, because he was growing concerned. "You look pale."

"Just the proper use of a bonnet," she said. "Perhaps you could tell your grandmother."

They shared a smile at that, and then Thomas turned to greet her father. "Lord Crowland. Forgive my in-attention. How may I be of service?"

Lord Crowland did not bother with niceties, or indeed even with a greeting. "I have lost my patience with you, Wyndham," he bit off.

Thomas glanced over at Amelia for explanation. But she was not quite looking at him.

"I am afraid I do not understand your meaning," Thomas said.

"Amelia tells me you leave for Ireland."

Amelia knew he was going to Ireland? Thomas blinked in surprise. This was news to him.

"I overheard you talking to Grace," she said, with a miserable swallow. "I didn't mean to. I'm sorry. I shouldn't have said. I didn't think he would be so angry."

"We have waited long enough," Crowland blustered. "You have kept my daughter dangling on a string for years, and now, finally, when we think you are about to deign to set a date, I hear that you are fleeing the country!"

"I do plan to return."

Crowland's face turned a bit purple. Perhaps dry wit had not been the best choice.

"What, sir," he snapped, "are your intentions?"

Thomas breathed in through his nose, long and deep, forcing his body to remain calm. "My intentions," he repeated. At what point was a man allowed to decide he'd had enough? That he was through with being polite, with trying to do the right thing? He considered the events of the last few days. All in all, he thought he'd done rather well. He hadn't killed anyone, and Lord knew, he'd been tempted.

"My intentions," Thomas said again. His hand flexed at his side, the only outward sign of his distress.

"Toward my daughter."

And really, that was enough. Thomas gave Lord Crowland an icy stare. "I hardly possess intentions toward anything else in your sphere."

Amelia gasped, and he should have felt remorse, but

he did not. For the past week he had been stretched, beaten, poked, prodded—he felt as if he might snap. One more little jab, and he was going to—

"Lady Amelia," came a new, highly unwelcome voice. "I did not realize you had graced us with your lovely presence."

Audley. Yes, of course he would be here. Thomas started to laugh.

Crowland eyed him with something approaching revulsion. Thomas, not Audley, who appeared just in from a ride, all windblown and roguishly handsome.

Or so Thomas assumed. It was difficult to know just what the ladies saw in the man.

"Er, Father," Amelia said hastily, "may I present Mr. Audley? He is a house guest at Belgrave. I made his acquaintance the other day when I was here visiting Grace."

"Where *is* Grace?" Thomas wondered aloud. Everyone else was in attendance. It seemed almost unkind to leave her out.

"Just down the hall, actually," Audley said, eyeing him curiously. "I was walking—"

"I'm sure you were," Thomas cut in. He turned back to Lord Crowland. "Right. You wished to know my intentions."

"This might not be the best time," Amelia said nervously. Thomas pushed down a sharp stab of remorse. She thought she was staving off some sort of repudiation, when the truth was far worse.

"No," he said, drawing the syllable out as if he were

actually pondering the matter. "This might be our only time."

Why was he keeping this a secret? What could he possibly have to gain? Why not just get the whole damned thing out in the open?

Grace arrived then. "You wished to see me, your grace?"

Thomas's brows rose with some surprise, and he looked about the room. "Was I *that* loud?"

"The footman heard you . . . " Her words trailed off, and she motioned toward the hall, where the eavesdropping servant presumably still loitered.

"Do come in, Miss Eversleigh," he said, sweeping his arm in welcome. "You might as well have a seat at this farce."

Grace's brow knitted with concern, but she came into the room, taking a spot near the window. Away from everyone else.

"I demand to know what is going on," Crowland said.

"Of course," Thomas said. "How rude of me. Where *are* my manners? We've had quite an exciting week at Belgrave. Quite beyond my wildest imaginings."

"Your meaning?" Crowland said curtly.

Thomas gave him a bland look. "Ah, yes. You probably should know—this man right here"—he flicked a wrist toward Audley—"is my cousin. He might even be the duke." Still looking at Lord Crowland, he shrugged insolently, almost enjoying himself. "We're not sure."

Chapter 14

Oh dear God.

Amelia stared at Thomas, and then at Mr. Audley, and then at Thomas, and then—

Everyone was looking at her now. Why was everyone looking at her? Had she spoken? Had she said it aloud?

"The trip to Ireland . . . " her father was saying.

"Is to determine his legitimacy," Thomas said. "It's going to be quite a party. Even my grandmother is going."

Amelia stared at him in horror. He was not himself. This was wrong. This was all wrong.

It could not be happening. She shut her eyes. Tight.

Please, someone say that this was not happening.

And then came her father's grim voice. "We will join you."

Her eyes flew open. "Father?"

"Stay out of this, Amelia," he said. He didn't even look at her when he said it.

"But—"

"I assure you," Thomas put in, and he wasn't looking at her, either, "we will make our determinations with all possible haste and report back to you immediately."

"My daughter's future hangs in the balance," her father returned hotly. "I will be there to examine the papers."

Thomas's voice turned to ice. "Do you think we try to deceive you?"

Amelia took a step toward them. Why wasn't anyone acknowledging her? Did they think her invisible? Meaningless in this horrible tableau?

"I only look out for my daughter's rights."

"Father, please." Amelia placed her hand on his arm. Someone had to talk to her. Someone had to listen. "Please, just a moment."

"I said stay out of this!" her father roared, and he threw back his arm. Amelia had not expected this rejection and she stumbled back, crashing into an end table.

Thomas was immediately at her side, taking her arm and helping her back to her feet. "Apologize to your daughter," he said, his tone deadly.

Her father looked stunned. "What the devil are you talking about?"

"Apologize to her!" Thomas roared.

"Your grace," Amelia said quickly, "please, do not judge my father too harshly. These are exceptional circumstances."

"No one knows that more clearly than I." As Thomas said this to her, his eyes never left her father's face. "Apologize to Amelia," he said, "or I will have you removed from the estate."

Amelia held her breath. They were all holding their breath, it seemed, except perhaps Thomas, who looked like an ancient warrior, demanding his due.

"I'm sorry," her father said, blinking in confusion. "Amelia"—he turned, finally looking at her—"you know I—"

"I know," she said, cutting him off. It was enough. She knew her father, knew his normally benign ways.

"Who is this man?" her father asked, motioning to Mr. Audley.

"He is the son of my father's elder brother."

"Charles?" Amelia gasped in dismay. The man her mother was to have married?

"John."

The one who'd died at sea. The dowager's favorite.

Her father nodded, pale and shaken. "Are you certain of this?"

Thomas only shrugged. "You may look at the portrait yourself."

"But his name—"

"Was Cavendish at birth," Mr. Audley said. "I went by Cavendish-Audley at school. You may check the records, should you wish."

"Here?" her father asked.

"In Enniskillen. I only came to England after serving in the army."

Amelia's father nodded approvingly. He'd always

wanted to join the military, she remembered. He couldn't, of course. He'd gained the earldom at the age of seventeen, with no male heirs behind him. Crowland could not risk losing the last earl before he'd had a chance to procreate. As it was, he'd had five daughters. Amelia wondered if he sometimes wished he'd just gone into the army. The outcome would have been the same, as far as the earldom was concerned.

"I am satisfied that he is a blood relation," Thomas said quietly. "All that remains is to determine whether he is also one by law."

"This is a disaster," her father muttered, and he walked over to the window to look out.

All eyes followed him—what else were they meant to look at, in such a silent room?

"I signed the contract in good faith," he said, still staring out over the lawn. "Twenty years ago, I signed the contract."

Amelia's eyes widened. She'd never heard her father speak this way. His voice was tense, barely controlled, like a string pulled taut and trembling, just waiting to snap.

Abruptly, he turned around. "Do you understand?" he demanded, and it was difficult to know just who he was yelling at until his eyes came to rest on Thomas's face.

"Your father came to me with his plans, and I agreed to them, believing you to be the rightful heir to the dukedom. She was to be a duchess. A duchess! Do you think I would have signed away my daughter had I known you were nothing but . . . but . . . "

Her father's face turned red and ugly as he tried to figure out just what Thomas was. Or would be, if Mr. Audley's claim was authenticated. Amelia felt sick. For herself. For Thomas.

"You may call me Mr. Cavendish, if you so desire," Thomas said, his voice terrifyingly calm. "If you think it might help you to accustom yourself to the idea."

But her father was not finished. "I will not allow my daughter to be cheated. If you do not prove to be the right and lawful Duke of Wyndham, you may consider the betrothal null and void."

No!

Amelia wanted to shout it. He couldn't just tear it all up. He couldn't *do* this to her. She looked frantically to Thomas. Surely he would say something. Something had happened between them. They were no longer strangers. He liked her. He cared for her. He would fight for her.

But no.

Her heart sank. Crushed under its own leaden weight.

Apparently he would not.

Because when her mind cleared enough for her to focus on his face, she saw that he was nodding. And he said, "As you wish."

"As you wish," she echoed, unable to believe it. But no one heard her. It was just a whisper. Just a horror-struck whisper from a woman no one seemed to notice.

They weren't looking at her. None of them. Not even Grace.

And then her father turned, and he looked at Mr. Audley, and he pointed his finger at him. "If that is the case," he said, "if you are the Duke of Wyndham, *you* will marry her."

Later that night, and every night for many weeks, Amelia relived that moment in her head. She saw her father move, turning, pointing. She saw his lips form the words. Heard his voice. Saw the shock on everyone's faces.

Saw the horror on Mr. Audley's.

And every time, when it all played out again, she said something different. Something clever, or something cutting. Maybe something witty, or something furious.

But always something.

In actuality, however, she said nothing. Not a word. Her own father was trying to foist her onto a man she did not know, in front of people she *did* know, and she said . . .

Nothing.

She did not even gasp. She felt her face freeze up like some hideous gargoyle, trapped in eternal torment. Her chin fell forward and her lips turned to stone in a hideous, shocked mask.

But she didn't make a sound. Her father was probably quite proud of her for that. No female hysterics from this quarter.

Mr. Audley appeared to have been similarly affected, but he regained his composure far more quickly, even if the first words out of his mouth were:

"Oh."

and:

"No."

Amelia thought she might be sick.

"Oh, you will," her father warned him, and she knew that tone. He did not use it often, but no one crossed him when he spoke like that. "You will marry her if I have to march you to the altar with my blunderbuss at your back."

"Father," she said, her voice cracking on the word, "you cannot do this."

But he paid her no mind. In fact, he took another furious step toward Mr. Audley. "My daughter is betrothed to the Duke of Wyndham," he hissed, "and the Duke of Wyndham she *will* marry."

"I am not the Duke of Wyndham," Mr. Audley said.

"Not yet," her father returned. "Perhaps not ever. But I will be present when the truth comes out. And I will make sure she marries the right man."

"This is madness," Mr. Audley exclaimed. He was visibly distressed now, and Amelia almost laughed at the horror of it. It was something to see, a man reduced to panic over the thought of marrying her.

She'd looked down at her arms, half expecting to see boils. Perhaps locusts would stream through the room.

"I do not even know her," Mr. Audley said.

To which her father replied, "That is hardly a concern."

"You are *mad!*" Mr. Audley cried out. "I am not going to marry her."

Amelia covered her mouth and nose with her hands,

taking a deep breath. She was unsteady. She did not want to cry. Above all else, she did not want that.

"My pardons, my lady," Mr. Audley mumbled in her direction. "It is not personal."

Amelia actually managed a nod. Not a graceful one, but maybe it was gracious. Why wasn't anyone saying anything? she remembered wondering. Why weren't they asking her opinion?

Why couldn't she seem to speak for herself?

It was like she was watching them all from far away. They wouldn't hear her. She could scream and shout, and no one would hear her.

She looked at Thomas. He was staring straight ahead, still as a stone.

She looked at Grace. Surely Grace would come to her aid. She was a woman. She knew what it meant to have one's life torn out from beneath.

And then it was back at Mr. Audley, who was still fumbling for any argument that would not leave him saddled with her. "I did not agree to this," he said. "I signed no contract."

"Neither did he," said her father, motioning toward Thomas with a tilt of his head. "His father did it."

"In his *name*," Mr. Audley practically yelled.

But her father did not even blink. "That is where you are wrong, Mr. Audley. It did not specify his name at all. My daughter, Amelia Honoria Rose, was to marry the seventh Duke of Wyndham."

"Really?" This, *finally*, from Thomas.

"Have you not looked at the papers?" Mr. Audley demanded of him.

"No," Thomas said. "I never saw the need."

"Good God," Mr. Audley swore, "I have fallen in with a band of bloody idiots."

Amelia saw no reason to contradict.

Mr. Audley looked directly at her father. "Sir," he said, "I will not marry your daughter."

"Oh, you will."

And that was when Amelia knew her heart was broken. Because it wasn't her father who said those words.

It was Thomas.

"What did you say?" Mr. Audley demanded.

Thomas strode across the room, stopping only when he was nearly nose-to-nose with Mr. Audley. "This woman has spent her entire life preparing to be the Duchess of Wyndham. I will not permit you to leave her life in shambles. Do you understand me?"

And all she could think was—*No.*

No. She didn't want to be the duchess. She didn't care one way or the other. She just wanted him. Thomas. The man she'd spent her whole life not knowing.

Until now.

Until he'd stood with her, looking down at some meaningless map, and explained to her why Africa was bigger than Greenland.

Until he'd told her that he liked her bossy.

Until he'd made her feel that she *mattered.* That her thoughts and opinions were worth something.

He had made her feel complete.

But here he was, demanding that she marry someone

else. And she didn't know how to stop it. Because if she spoke out, if she told them all what she wanted, and he rejected her again . . .

But Thomas wasn't asking *her* if she understood. He was asking Mr. Audley. And Mr. Audley said, "No."

Amelia took a gulp of air and looked up at the ceiling, trying to pretend that two men were not arguing over which of them had to marry her.

"No, I don't understand," Mr. Audley continued, his voice insultingly provoking. "Sorry."

She looked back. It was hard to look away. It was like a carriage accident, except it was her own life being trampled.

Thomas was looking at Mr. Audley with murder in his eyes. And then, almost conversationally, said, "I believe I will kill you."

"Thomas!" The cry sprang from her throat before she could stop to think, and she flew across the room, grabbing his arm to hold him back.

"You may steal my life away," Thomas growled, pulling on her arm like an angry, aggrieved animal. "You may steal my very name, but by God you will not steal hers."

So that was it. He thought he was doing the right thing. She wanted to cry with frustration. There would be no changing his mind. Thomas had spent his entire life doing the right thing. Never for himself. Always for Wyndham. And now he thought he was doing the right thing for her.

"She *has* a name," Mr. Audley retorted. "It's Willoughby. And for the love of God, she's the daughter of an earl. She'll find someone else."

"If you are the Duke of Wyndham," Thomas said furiously, "you will honor your commitments."

"If I'm the Duke of Wyndham, then you can't tell me what to do."

"Amelia," Thomas said with deadly calm, "release my arm."

Instead, she tightened her grip. "I don't think that's a good idea."

Her father chose that moment to intercede—*finally*. "Er, gentlemen, this is all hypothetical at this point. Perhaps we should wait until—"

"I wouldn't be the seventh duke, anyway," Mr. Audley muttered.

Her father looked somewhat irritated at the interruption. "I beg your pardon?"

"I wouldn't." Mr. Audley looked over at Thomas. "Would I? Because your father was the sixth duke. Except he wasn't. If I am." And then, if that weren't confusing enough: "Would he have been? If I was?"

"What the devil are you talking about?" Amelia's father demanded.

"Your father died before his own father," Thomas said to Mr. Audley. "If your parents were married, then *you* would have inherited upon the fifth duke's death, eliminating my father—and myself—from the succession entirely."

"Which makes me number six."

"Indeed," Thomas said tightly.

"Then I am not bound to honor the contract," Mr. Audley declared. "No court in the land would hold me to it. I doubt they'd do so even if I were the seventh duke."

"It is not to a legal court you must appeal," Thomas said quietly, "but to the court of your own moral responsibility."

Amelia swallowed. How like him that was, how upstanding and true. How did one argue with a man such as that? She felt her lips begin to tremble, and she looked to the door, measuring how many steps it would take to remove her from this place.

Mr. Audley stood stiffly, and when he spoke, his words were rigid as well. "I did not ask for this."

Thomas just shook his head. "Neither did I."

Amelia lurched back, choking down the cry of pain in her throat. No, he'd never asked for any of this. He'd never asked for the title, for the lands, for the responsibility.

He'd never asked for *her*.

She'd known it, of course. She'd always known he hadn't picked her, but she'd never thought it would hurt this much to hear him say it. She was just another of his many burdens, foisted onto him by virtue of his birth.

With privilege came responsibility. How true that was.

Amelia inched back, trying to get as far away from the center of the room as she could. She didn't want anyone to see her. Not like this, with eyes that threatened tears, hands that shook.

She wanted to fly away, to leave this room and—

And then she felt it. A hand in her own.

She looked down first, at the two hands entwined. And then she looked up, even though she knew it was Grace.

Amelia said nothing. She didn't trust her voice, didn't even trust her lips to mouth the words she wanted to say. But as her eyes met Grace's, she knew that the other woman saw what was in her heart.

She gripped Grace's hand and squeezed.

Never in her life had she needed a friend as much as she did in that moment.

Grace squeezed back.

And for the first time that afternoon, Amelia did not feel completely alone.

Chapter 15

Four days later, at sea

It was an uncommonly peaceful crossing, or so the captain told Thomas as dusk began to fall. Thomas was grateful for that; he'd not *quite* been made physically ill by the rise and fall of the Irish Sea, but it had been a close thing. A bit more wind or tide or whatever it was that made the small ship go up and down and his stomach would surely have protested, and in a most unpleasant manner.

He'd found that it was easier to remain on deck. Below, the air was thick, the quarters tight. Above, he could attempt to enjoy the tang of the salt air, the crisp sting of it on his skin. He could breathe.

Farther down the railing he could see Jack, leaning against the wood, gazing out at the sea. It could not have escaped him that this was the site of his father's death. Closer to the Irish coast, Thomas supposed, if his mother had managed to make it ashore.

What must it have been like, not to know one's father? Thomas rather thought that he'd prefer to have not known his, but by all accounts John Cavendish had been a much more amiable fellow than his younger brother Reginald.

Was Jack wondering what his life might have been, if not for a storm? He'd have been raised at Belgrave, certainly. Ireland would have been nothing but a familiar land—the spot where his mother was raised. He might have had the opportunity to visit from time to time, but it would not have been home.

He would have attended Eton, as all of the Cavendish boys did, and then gone on to Cambridge. He would have been enrolled at Peterhouse, because only the oldest of the colleges would do for the House of Wyndham, and his name would have been added to the long list of Cavendish Petreans inscribed on the wall of the library the family had donated hundreds of years earlier, back when the dukes had still been earls and the church was still Catholic.

It would not have mattered what he studied, or even if he did study. Jack would have been graduated no matter his marks. He would have been the Wyndham heir. Thomas was not sure what he would have had to do to get himself dismissed; he could not imagine that anything less than complete illiteracy would have done the trick.

A season in London would have followed, as it had for Thomas. Jack would have made merry there,

Thomas thought dryly. His was just the sort of wit that made a young unmarried ducal heir even more wildly attractive to the ladies. The army would certainly not have been permitted. And it went without saying that he would not have been out robbing coaches on the Lincoln Road.

What a difference a storm made.

As for Thomas, he had no idea where he might have ended up. Farther north, most likely, at some house provided by his mother's father. Would his father have been brought into business? Managing factories? It was difficult to imagine anything Reginald Cavendish would have detested more.

What might he have done with his life, had he not been born the only son of a duke? He could not imagine the freedom. From his earliest memories, his life had been mapped ahead of him. Every day he made dozens of decisions, but the important ones—the ones that mattered in his own life—had been made for him.

He supposed they had all turned out well. He'd liked Eton and loved Cambridge, and if he'd liked to have defended his country as Jack had—well, it did seem that His Majesty's army had acquitted itself just fine without him. Even Amelia . . .

He closed his eyes for a moment, allowing the pitch and roll of the boat to play games with his balance.

Even Amelia would have turned out to be an excellent choice. He felt like an idiot for having taken so long to know her.

All those decisions he'd not been allowed to make . . .

He wondered if he would have done a better job with them himself.

Probably not.

Off at the bow, he could see Grace and Amelia, sitting together on a built-in bench. They were sharing a cabin with the dowager, and since she had barricaded herself inside, they had elected to remain out. Lord Crowland had been given the other cabin. He and Jack would bunk below, with the crew.

Amelia didn't seem to notice that he was watching her, probably because the sun would have been in her eyes if she had looked his way. She'd taken off her bonnet and was holding it in her hands, the long ribbons flapping in the wind.

She was smiling.

He'd been missing that, he realized. He hadn't seen her smile on the journey to Liverpool. He supposed she had little reason to. None of them did. Even Jack, who had so much to gain, was growing ever more anxious as they drew closer to Irish soil.

He had his own demons waiting at the shore, Thomas suspected. There had to be a reason he'd never gone back.

He turned and looked west. Liverpool had long since disappeared over the horizon, and indeed, there was nothing to see but water, rippling below, a kaleidoscope of blue and green and gray. Strange how a lifetime of looking at maps did not prepare a man for the endless expanse of the sea.

So much water. It was difficult to fathom.

This was the longest sea voyage he'd ever taken. Strange, that. He'd never been to the Continent. The grand tours of his father's generation had been brought to a halt by war, and so any last educational flourishes he had made were on British soil. The army had been out of the question; ducal heirs were not permitted to risk their lives on foreign soil, no matter how patriotic or brave.

Another item that would have been different, had that other ship not gone down: he'd have been off fighting Napoleon; Jack would have been held at home.

His world was measured in degrees from Belgrave. He did not travel far from his center. And suddenly it felt so limited. So limiting.

When he turned back, Amelia was sitting alone, shading her eyes with her hand. Thomas looked about, but Grace was nowhere in sight. No one was about, save for Amelia and a young boy who was tying knots in ropes at the bow.

He had not spoken to her since that afternoon at Belgrave. No, that was not true. He was fairly certain they had exchanged a few *excuse me's* and perhaps a *good morning* or two.

But he had seen her. He'd watched her from afar. From near, too, when she was not looking.

What surprised him—what he had not expected—was how much it hurt, just to look at her. To see her so acutely unhappy. To know that he was, at least in part, the cause.

But what else could he have done? Stood up and said,

Er, actually I think I would like to marry her, after all, now that my future is completely uncertain? Oh yes, *that* would have met with a round of applause.

He had to do what was best. What was right.

Amelia would understand. She was a smart girl. Hadn't he spent the last week coming to the realization that she was far more intelligent than he'd thought? She was practical, too. Capable of getting things done.

He liked that about her.

Surely she saw that it was in her best interest to marry the Duke of Wyndham, whoever he might be. It was what had been planned. For her *and* for the dukedom.

And it wasn't as if she loved him.

Someone gave a shout—it sounded like the captain— and the young boy dropped his knots and scrambled away, leaving himself and Amelia quite alone on deck. He waited a moment, giving her the chance to leave, if she did not wish to risk being trapped into conversation with him. But she did not move, and so he walked toward her, offering her a deferential nod when he reached her side.

"Lady Amelia."

She looked up, and then down. "Your grace."

"May I join you?"

"Of course." She moved to the side, as far as she could while still remaining on the bench. "Grace had to go below."

"The dowager?"

Amelia nodded. "She wished for Grace to fan her."

Thomas could not imagine that the thick, heavy air belowdeck would be improved by pushing it about with a fan, but then again, he doubted his grandmother cared. She was most likely looking for someone to complain to. Or complain about.

"I should have accompanied her," Amelia said, not quite ruefully. "It would have been the kind thing to do, but . . . " She exhaled and shook her head. "I just couldn't."

Thomas waited for a moment, in case she wished to say anything more. She did not, which meant that he had no further excuse for his own silence.

"I came to apologize," he said. The words felt stiff on his tongue. He was not used to apologizing. He was not used to behaving in a manner that required apology.

She turned, her eyes finding his with startling directness. "For what?"

What a question. He had not expected her to force him to lay it out. "For what happened back at Belgrave," he said, hoping he would not have to go into more detail. There were certain memories one did not wish to keep in clarity. "It was not my intention to cause you distress."

She looked out over the length of the ship. He saw her swallow, and there was something melancholy in the motion. Something pensive, but not quite wistful.

She looked too resigned to be wistful. And he *hated* that he'd had any part in doing that to her.

"I . . . am sorry," he said, the words coming to him slowly. "I think that you might have been made to feel unwanted. It was not my intention. I would never wish you to feel that way."

She kept staring out, her profile toward him. He could see her lips press and purse, and there was something mesmerizing in the way she blinked. He'd never thought there could be so much detail in a woman's eyelashes, but hers were . . .

Lovely.

She was lovely. In every way. It was the perfect word to describe her. It seemed pale and undescriptive at first, but upon further reflection, it grew more and more intricate.

Beautiful was a daunting thing, dazzling . . . and lonely. But not lovely. Lovely was warm and welcoming. It glowed softly, sneaking its way into one's heart.

Amelia was lovely.

"It's growing dark," she said, changing the subject. This, he realized, was her way of accepting his apology. And he should have respected that. He should have held his tongue and said nothing more, because clearly that was what she wanted.

But he couldn't. He, who had never found cause to explain his actions to anyone, was gripped by a need to *tell* her, to explain every last word. He had to know, to feel it in his very soul that she understood. He had not wanted to give her up. He hadn't told her to marry Jack Audley because he wanted to. He'd done it because . . .

"You belong with the Duke of Wyndham," he said. "You do, just as much as I thought I *was* the Duke of Wyndham."

"You still are," she said softly, still staring ahead.

"No." He almost smiled. He had no idea why. "We both know that isn't true."

"I don't know anything of the sort," she said, finally turning to face him. Her eyes were fierce, protective. "Do you plan to give up your birthright based upon a painting? You could probably pull five men out of the rookeries of London who could pass for someone in one of the paintings at Belgrave. It is a resemblance. Nothing more."

"Jack Audley is my cousin," he said. He had not uttered the words many times; there was a strange relief in doing so. "All that remains to be seen is if his birth was legitimate."

"That is still quite a hurdle."

"One that I am sure will be easily reached. Church records . . . witnesses . . . there will be proof." He faced front then, presumably staring at the same spot on the horizon. He could see why she'd been mesmerized. The sun had dipped low enough so one could look in its direction without squinting, and the sky held the most amazing shades of pink and orange.

He could look at it forever. Part of him wanted to.

"I did not think you were a man to give up so easily," she said.

"Oh, I'm not giving up. I'm here, aren't I? But I must make plans. My future is not what I'd thought." Out of the corner of his eye he saw her begin to protest, so he added, with a smile, "Probably."

Her jaw tensed, then released. Then, after a few moments, she said, "I like the sea."

So did he, he realized, even with his queasy stomach. "You're not seasick?" he asked.

"Not at all. Are you?"

"A little," he admitted, which made her smile. He caught her eye. "You like when I am indisposed, don't you?"

Her lips pressed together a bit; she was embarrassed.

He loved that.

"I do," she confessed. "Well, not indisposed, exactly."

"Weak and helpless?" he suggested.

"Yes!" she replied, with enough enthusiasm that she immediately blushed.

He loved that, too. Pink suited her.

"I never *knew* you when you were proud and capable," she hastened to add.

It would have been so easy to pretend to misunderstand, to say something about how they had known each other all of their lives. But of course they had not. They had known the other's name, and their shared destiny, but that was all. And Thomas was finally coming to realize that it was not much.

Not enough.

"I'm more approachable when I'm sotted?" he tried to joke.

"Or seasick," she said kindly.

He laughed at that. "I'm lucky the weather is so fair. I'm told the seas are usually much less forgiving. The captain said that crossing from Liverpool to Dublin is often more difficult than the entire passage from the West Indies to England."

Her eyes lit with interest. "That can't be."

Thomas shrugged. "I only repeat what he told me."

She considered this for a moment, then said, "Do you know, this is the farthest I have ever been from home?"

He leaned a little closer. "Me, too."

"Really?" Her face showed her surprise.

"Where would I have gone?"

He watched with amusement as she considered this. Her face moved through a number of expressions, and then finally she said, "You are so fond of geography. I would have thought you would travel."

"I would like to have done." He watched the sunset. It was melting away too quickly for his tastes. "Too many responsibilities at home, I suppose."

"Will you travel if—" She cut herself off, and he did not need to be looking at her to picture the expression on her face precisely.

"If I am not the duke?" he finished for her.

She nodded.

"I expect so." He gave a little shrug. "I am not sure where."

Amelia turned to him suddenly. "I have always wanted to see Amsterdam."

"Really." He looked surprised. Maybe even intrigued. "Why is that?"

"All those lovely Dutch paintings, I think. And the canals."

"Most people travel to Venice for the canals."

She knew that, of course. Maybe that was part of the reason she'd never wanted to go there. "I want to see Amsterdam."

"I hope you shall," he said. He was quiet for just long

enough to make the moment noticeable. And then, softly: "Everybody should be able to realize at least one of their dreams."

Amelia turned. He was looking at her with the most gentle expression. It nearly broke her heart. What was left of it, at least. So she looked away. It was too hard otherwise. "Grace went below," she said.

"Yes, you'd said."

"Oh." How embarrassing. "Yes, of course. The fan." He did not reply, so she added, "There was something about soup, as well."

"Soup," he repeated, shaking his head.

"I could not decipher the message," Amelia admitted.

He gave her a rather dry half smile. "Now there is one responsibility I am not sorry to shed."

A little laugh rose in Amelia's throat. "Oh, I'm sorry," she said quickly, trying to force it down. "That was terribly rude of me."

"Not at all," he assured her. His face dipped closer to hers, his expression terribly conspiratorial. "Do you think Audley will have the nerve to send her away?"

"You didn't."

He held up his hands. "She's my grandmother."

"She is his, as well."

"Yes, but he doesn't know her, lucky chap." He leaned toward her. "I suggested the Outer Hebrides."

"Oh, stop."

"I did," he insisted. "Told Audley I was thinking of buying something there, just so I could maroon her."

This time she did laugh. "We should not be speaking of her this way."

"Why is it," he mused, "that everyone I know speaks of crotchety old ladies who, underneath their acerbic exteriors, have a heart of gold?"

She looked at him with amusement.

"Mine doesn't," he said, almost as if he could not quite believe the unfairness of it all.

She tried not to smile. "No." She gave up. She sputtered, then grinned. "She doesn't."

He looked at her, and their eyes caught each other's amusement, and they both burst out laughing.

"She's miserable," Thomas said.

"She doesn't like me," Amelia said.

"She doesn't like anyone."

"I think she likes Grace."

"No, she just dislikes her less than she dislikes everyone else. She doesn't even like Mr. Audley, even as she works so tirelessly to gain him the title."

"She doesn't like Mr. Audley?"

"He *detests* her."

She shook her head, then looked back out at the sunset, which was in its death throes over the horizon. "What a tangle."

"What an understatement."

"What a knot?" she offered, feeling very nautical.

She heard him let out a little snuff of amusement, and then he rose to his feet. She looked up; he was blotting out the last shafts of the sun. Indeed, he seemed to fill her entire vision.

"We could have been friends," she heard herself say.

"Could?"

"Would," she corrected, and she was smiling. It seemed the most amazing thing. How was it possible she had anything to smile about? "I think we would have been friends, if not for . . . If all this . . . "

"If everything were different?"

"Yes. No. Not everything. Just . . . some things." She began to feel lighter. Happier. And she had not the slightest clue why. "Maybe if we'd met in London."

"And we hadn't been betrothed?"

She nodded. "And you hadn't been a duke."

His brows rose.

"Dukes are very intimidating," she explained. "It would have been so much easier if you hadn't been one."

"And your mother had not been engaged to marry my uncle," he added.

"If we'd just *met*."

"No history between us."

"None."

His brows rose and he smiled. "If I'd seen you across a crowded room?"

"No, no, nothing like that." She shook her head. He was not getting this at all. She wasn't talking about romance. She couldn't bear to even think of it. But friendship . . . that was something else entirely. "Something far more ordinary," she said. "If you'd sat next to me on a bench."

"Like this one?"

"Perhaps in a park."

"Or a garden," he murmured.

"You would sit down next to me—"

"And ask your opinion of Mercator projections."

She laughed. "I would tell you that they are useful for navigation but that they distort area terribly."

"I would think—how nice, a woman who does not hide her intelligence."

"And I would think—how lovely, a man who does not assume I have none."

He smiled. "We would have been friends."

"Yes." She closed her eyes. Just for a moment. Not for long enough to allow her to dream. "Yes, we would."

He was quiet for a moment, and then he picked up her hand and kissed it. "You will make a spectacular duchess," he said softly.

She tried to smile, but it was difficult; the lump in her throat was blocking her way.

Then, softly—but not so softly that she was not intended to hear—he said, "My only regret is that you never were mine."

Chapter 16

The following day, at the Queen's Arms, Dublin

$\mathcal{D}$o you think," Thomas murmured, leaning down to speak his words in Amelia's ear, "that there are packets leaving directly from Dublin port, heading to the Outer Hebrides?"

She made a choking sound, followed by a very stern look, which amused him to no end. They were standing, along with the rest of their traveling party, in the front room of the Queen's Arms, where Thomas's secretary had arranged for their rooms on the way to Butlersbridge, the small village in County Cavan where Jack Audley had grown up. They had reached the port of Dublin in the late afternoon, but by the time they collected their belongings and made their way into town, it was well after dark. Thomas was tired and hungry, and he was fairly certain that Amelia, her father, Grace, and Jack were as well.

His grandmother, however, was having none of it.

"It is *not* too late!" she insisted, her shrill voice filling every corner of the room. They were now on minute three of her tantrum. Thomas suspected that the entire neighborhood had been made aware that she wished to press on toward Butlersbridge that evening.

"Ma'am," Grace said, in that calm, soothing way of hers, "it is past seven. We are all tired and hungry, and the roads are dark and unknown to us."

"Not to him," the dowager snapped, jerking her head toward Jack.

"I am tired and hungry," Jack snapped right back, "and thanks to you, I no longer travel the roads by moonlight."

Thomas bit back a smile. He might actually grow to like this fellow.

"Don't you wish to have this matter settled, once and for all?" the dowager demanded.

"Not really," Jack answered. "Certainly not as much as I want a slice of shepherd's pie and a tankard of ale."

"Hear hear," Thomas murmured, but only Amelia heard.

It was strange, but his mood had been improving the closer they got to their destination. He would have thought he'd grow more and more tortured; he was about to lose everything, after all, right down to his name. By his estimation, he ought to be snapping off heads by now.

But instead he felt almost cheerful.

Cheerful. It was the damnedest thing. He'd spent the

entire morning on deck with Amelia, swapping tales and laughing uproariously. It had been enough to make his stomach forget to be seasick.

Thank the Lord, he thought, for very large favors. It had been a close thing, the night before—keeping the three bites he'd eaten of supper in his belly, where it belonged.

He wondered if his odd amiability was because he had already accepted that Jack was the rightful duke. Once he had stopped fighting that, he just wanted to get the whole bloody mess over and done with. The waiting, truly, was the hardest part.

He'd gotten his affairs in order. He'd done everything required for a smooth transition. All that was left was to get it done. And then he could go off and do whatever it was he would have done had he not been tied to Belgrave.

Somewhere in the midst of his ponderings he realized that Jack was leaving, presumably to get that slice of shepherd's pie. "I do believe he has the right idea of it," Thomas murmured. "Supper sounds infinitely more appealing than a night on the roads."

His grandmother whipped her head around and glared at him.

"Not," Thomas added, "that I am attempting to delay the inevitable. Even soon-to-be-dispossessed dukes get hungry."

Lord Crowland laughed aloud at that. "He has you there, Augusta," he said jovially, and he wandered off to the taproom.

"I shall take my supper in my room," the dowager

announced. Or really, it was more of a bark. "Miss Eversleigh, you may attend to me."

Grace sighed wearily and started to follow.

"No," Thomas said.

"No?" the dowager echoed.

Thomas allowed himself a small smile. He truly *had* got all of his affairs in order. "Grace will dine with us," he told his grandmother. "In the dining room."

"She is my companion," the dowager hissed.

Oh, he was enjoying this. Far more than he'd thought. "Not anymore." He smiled genially at Grace, who was staring at him as if he'd lost his mind. "As I have not yet been removed from my position," he said, "I took the liberty of making a few last minute provisions."

"What the devil are you talking about?" the dowager demanded.

He ignored her. "Grace," he said, "you are officially relieved of your duties to my grandmother. When you return home, you will find a cottage deeded in your name, along with funds enough to provide an income for the rest of your life."

"Are you mad?" the dowager sputtered.

Grace just stared at him in shock.

"I should have done it long ago," he said. "I was too selfish. I couldn't bear the thought of living with her"— he jerked his head toward his grandmother—"without you there to act as a buffer."

"I don't know what to say," Grace whispered.

He shrugged modestly. "Normally, I'd advise 'Thank you,' but as I am the one thanking *you*, a mere 'You are a prince among men' would suffice."

Grace managed a wobbly smile and whispered, "You are a prince among men."

"It is always lovely to hear it," Thomas said. "Now, would you care to join the rest of us for supper?"

Grace turned toward the dowager, who was red-faced with rage.

"You grasping little whore," she spat. "Do you think I don't know what you are? Do you think I would allow you in my home again?"

Thomas was about to intercede, but then he realized that Grace was handling the situation with far more aplomb than he could ever have managed.

Her face calm and impassive, she said, "I was about to say that I would offer you my assistance for the rest of the journey, since I would never dream of leaving a post without giving proper and courteous notice, but I believe I have reconsidered." She turned to Amelia. "May I share your room this evening?"

"Of course," Amelia replied promptly. She linked her arm through Grace's. "Let us have some supper."

It was a magnificent exit, Thomas decided as he followed them, even if he could not see his grandmother's face. But he could well imagine it, red and sputtering. A cooler clime would do her good. Truly. He would have to take it up with the new duke.

"That was magnificent!" Amelia gushed, once they'd entered the dining room. "Oh, my goodness, Grace, you must be so thrilled."

Grace looked dazed. "I hardly know what to say."

"You needn't say anything," Thomas told her. "Just enjoy your supper."

"Oh, I shall." She turned to Amelia, looking as if she might burst out laughing at any moment. "I suspect this shall be the finest shepherd's pie I have ever tasted."

And then she did burst out laughing. They all did. They had their supper, the three of them, and they laughed and laughed and laughed.

And as Thomas drifted off to sleep that night, his ribs still aching from the laughter, it occurred to him that he could not recall a finer evening.

Amelia had enjoyed herself at supper as well. So much so, in fact, that the tension of the following morning hit her like a slap. She thought she'd risen early; Grace was still sleeping soundly when she slipped from the room to find breakfast. But when she reached the inn's private dining room, her father was already there, as was the dowager. There was no sneaking away; they had both seen her instantly, and besides, she was famished.

She supposed she could put up with her father's lectures (they had been coming with increasing frequency) and the dowager's venom (this had always been frequent) if it meant she could partake of whatever it was creating that heavenly, eggy aroma coming from the sideboard.

Eggs, probably.

She smiled. At least she could still amuse herself. That had to count for something.

"Good morning, Amelia," her father said as she sat down with her plate.

She dipped her chin in polite greeting. "Father." She then glanced over at the dowager. "Your grace."

The dowager pursed her lips and made a noise, but other than that did not acknowledge her.

"Did you sleep well?" her father inquired.

"Very well, thank you," she replied, though it was not quite true. She and Grace had shared a bed, and Grace moved around a lot.

"We depart in half an hour," the dowager said crisply.

Amelia had managed to fork one bite of eggs into her mouth, and took advantage of the time it took to chew to glance over at the doorway, which remained empty. "I don't think the others will be ready. Grace is still—"

"She is of no concern."

"You can't go anywhere without the two dukes," Lord Crowland pointed out.

"Is that supposed to be funny?" the dowager demanded.

Lord Crowland shrugged. "How else am I meant to refer to them?"

Amelia knew she ought to have been outraged. It was a most cavalier statement, all things considered. But her father was so offhand, and the dowager so offended—she decided it made far more sense to be amused.

"Sometimes I do not know why I work so hard to advance your entry into my family," the dowager said to Amelia, giving her a scathing glare.

Amelia swallowed, wishing she had a retort, because for once she rather thought she'd have been brave enough to say it. But nothing came to mind, at least nothing as fabulously cutting and witty as she would have liked, and so she clamped her mouth shut and stared at a spot on the wall over the dowager's shoulder.

"There is no call for such talk, Augusta," Lord Crowland said. And then, as she glared at him for his use of her name—he was one of the few who did, and it always infuriated her—he added, "A less equable man than I might take insult."

Fortunately, the chilly moment was broken by Thomas's arrival. "Good morning," he said smoothly, taking his seat at the table. He seemed not at all perturbed that no one returned his greeting. Amelia supposed that her father was too busy attempting to put the dowager in her place, and the dowager—well, she rarely returned anyone's greeting, so this was hardly out of character.

As for herself, she would have liked to have said something. Really, it was all very lovely now, not feeling so cowed in Thomas's presence. But when he sat—directly across from her—she'd looked up, and he'd looked up, and—

It wasn't that she was intimidated, exactly. It was just that she seemed to have forgotten how to breathe.

His eyes were *that* blue.

Except for the stripe, of course. She loved that stripe. She loved that he thought it was silly.

"Lady Amelia," he murmured.

She nodded her greeting, managing, "Duke," since *your grace* contained far too many syllables.

"I am leaving," the dowager abruptly announced, her chair scraping angrily across the floor as she rose to

her feet. She waited a moment, as if expecting someone to comment upon her departure. When no one did
(really, Amelia thought, did she honestly think anyone
would attempt to stop her?) the dowager added, "We
depart in thirty minutes." Then she turned the full
force of her glare on her. "You will ride with me in
the carriage."

Amelia wasn't sure why the dowager felt the need
to announce it. She'd been stuck with the dowager in
the carriage across England; why should Ireland be
any different? Still, something about her tone turned
the stomach, and as soon as the dowager was gone, she
let out a weary sigh.

"I think I might be seasick," she said, allowing herself to slump.

Her father gave her an impatient look, then rose to
refill his plate. But Thomas smiled. It was mostly with
his eyes, but still, she felt a kinship, warm and lovely,
and perhaps enough to banish the feeling of dread that
was beginning to pool in her heart.

"Seasick on land?" he murmured, his eyes smiling.

"My stomach feels sour."

"Turning?"

"Flipping," she affirmed.

"Strange, that," he said dryly, popping a piece of bacon
into his mouth and finishing off the bite before continuing. "My grandmother is capable of many things—I
cannot imagine that plague, famine, or pestilence would
be beyond her abilities. But seasickness . . . " He chuckled. "I'm almost impressed."

Amelia sighed, looking down at her food, which

was now only slightly more appetizing than a plate of worms. She pushed it away. "Do you know how long it will take to get to Butlersbridge?"

"Most of the day, I should think, especially if we stop for lunch."

Amelia glanced at the door through which the dowager had just exited. "She won't want to."

Thomas shrugged. "She won't have a choice."

Amelia's father returned to the table just then, his plate heaping full. "When you become duchess," he said to her, rolling his eyes as he sat, "your first order should be to banish her to the dower house."

When she became duchess. Amelia swallowed uncomfortably. It was still just awful, her own father so blithe about her future. He truly did not care which of the two men she married, so long as he was proven to be the rightful duke.

She looked at Thomas. He was busy eating. So she kept her eyes on him. And waited, and waited . . . until he finally noticed her attention and met her gaze. He gave a little shrug, which she was unable to interpret.

Somehow that made her feel even worse.

Mr. Audley was the next to arrive for breakfast, followed about ten minutes later by Grace, who appeared to have rushed down, all pink-cheeked and breathless.

"Is the food not to your liking?" Grace asked her, looking down at Amelia's barely touched plate as she took the seat recently vacated by the dowager.

"I'm not hungry," Amelia said, even as her stomach rumbled. There was a difference, she was coming to realize, between hunger and appetite. The former she had, the latter not at all.

Grace gave her a quizzical look, then ate her own breakfast, or at least as much of it as she could in the three minutes before the innkeeper arrived, looking somewhat pained.

"Er, her grace . . . " he began, wringing his hands. "She is in the carriage."

"Presumably abusing your men?" Thomas queried.

The innkeeper nodded miserably.

"Grace has not finished her meal," Mr. Audley said coolly.

"Please," Grace insisted, "let us not delay on my account. I'm quite satisfied. I—"

She coughed then, looking terribly embarrassed, and Amelia had the singular sensation of having been left out of a joke.

"I overfilled my dish," Grace finally finished, motioning toward her plate, which was still well over half full.

"Are you certain?" Thomas asked her. She nodded, but Amelia noticed that she shoveled several more forkfuls into her mouth as everyone rose to their feet.

The men went ahead to see to the horses, and Amelia waited while Grace wolfed down a bit more.

"Hungry?" she asked, now that it was just the two of them.

"Starving," Grace confirmed. She wiped her mouth with her serviette and followed Amelia out. "I didn't want to provoke the dowager."

Amelia turned, raising her brows.

"Further," Grace clarified, since they both knew that the dowager was always acting provoked about something or other. And sure enough, when they reached the carriage, the dowager was snapping away about this and that, apparently unsatisfied with the temperature of the hot brick that had been placed at her feet in the carriage.

A hot brick? Amelia nearly sagged. It was not a warm day, but nor was it the least bit chilly. They were going to roast in that carriage.

"She is in fine form today," Grace murmured.

"Amelia!" the dowager barked.

Amelia reached out and grabbed Grace's hand. Tightly. She had never in her life been so grateful for another person's presence. The thought of spending another day in the carriage with the dowager, without Grace as a buffer . . .

She couldn't bear it.

"Lady Amelia," the dowager repeated, "did you not hear me call your name?"

"I'm sorry, your grace," Amelia said, dragging Grace with her as she stepped forward. "I did not."

The dowager's eyes narrowed. She knew when she was being lied to. But she clearly had other priorities, because she flicked her head toward Grace and said, "*She* may ride with the driver."

Said with all the affection one might show to a mealworm.

Grace started to move, but Amelia yanked her back. "No," she said to the dowager.

"No?"

"No. I wish for her company."

"I do not."

Amelia thought of all the times she'd marveled at Thomas's cool reserve, at the way he could flay people with a stare. She took a breath, allowing some of that memory to seep into her, and then she turned it on the dowager.

"Oh, for heaven's sake," the dowager snapped, after Amelia had stared her down for several seconds. "Bring her up, then. But do not expect me to make conversation."

"I wouldn't dream of it," Amelia murmured, and she climbed up, Grace following behind.

Unfortunately for Amelia, and for Grace, and for Lord Crowland, who had decided to ride in the carriage after they'd stopped to water the horses, the dowager decided to make conversation after all.

Although *conversation* did imply a certain two-sidedness that Amelia was quite certain did not exist within the confines of their carriage.

There were many directives, and twice that complaints. But conversation was in short supply.

Amelia's father lasted only thirty minutes before he banged on the front wall, demanding to be let out.

Traitor, Amelia thought. He'd planned since her birth to place her in the dowager's household, and he could not manage more than a half an hour?

He made a rather feeble attempt at apology at lunch—not for attempting to force her to marry someone against her will, just for leaving the carriage that morning—but whatever sympathy she might have had for him vanished when he began to lecture her about her future and his decisions regarding thereof.

Her only respite came after lunch, when both the dowager and Grace nodded off. Amelia just stared out the window, watching Ireland roll by, listening to the clip-clop of the horses' hooves. And all the while she could not help but wonder how this had all come to pass. She was far too sensible to think herself dreaming, but really—how could one's life be so completely altered, almost overnight? It did not seem possible. Just last week she was Lady Amelia Willoughby, fiancée to the Duke of Wyndham. And now she was . . .

Dear heavens, it was almost comical. She was still Lady Amelia Willoughby, fiancée to the Duke of Wyndham.

But nothing was the same.

She was in love. With what was possibly the wrong man. And did *he* love her? She couldn't tell. He liked her, of that she felt sure. He admired her. But love?

No. Men like Thomas did not fall in love so quickly. And if they did—if *he* did—it would not be with someone like her, someone he'd known his entire life. If Thomas fell into an overnight sort of love, it would be with a beautiful stranger. He'd see her across a crowded room, he'd be struck by a powerful feeling, a knowledge that they shared a destiny. A passion.

That was how Thomas would fall in love.

If he fell in love.

She swallowed, hating the lump in her throat, hating the smell in the air, hating the way she could see the specks of dust floating through the late afternoon sunlight.

There was a lot to hate that afternoon.

Across from her, Grace began to stir. Amelia watched the process. It was actually rather fascinating to watch someone wake up; she didn't think she'd ever done so before. Finally Grace opened her eyes, and Amelia said quietly, "You fell asleep." She put a finger to her lips, motioning with her head toward the dowager.

Grace covered a yawn, then asked, "How much longer do you think we have until we get there?"

"I don't know. Perhaps an hour? Two?" Amelia sighed and leaned back, closing her eyes. She was tired. They were all tired, but she was feeling selfish just then and preferred to dwell upon her own exhaustion. Maybe she could nod off. Why was it that some people fell asleep so easily in carriages, and others—most notably herself—couldn't seem to do it anywhere but a bed? It didn't seem fair, and—

"What will you do?"

It was Grace's voice. And much as Amelia wanted to feign ignorance, she found that she could not do it. It didn't much matter, anyway, since the answer would be wholly unsatisfying. She opened her eyes. Grace looked as if she wished she had not asked.

"I don't know," Amelia said. She leaned back against the seat cushion and closed her eyes again. She liked traveling with her eyes closed. She felt the rhythm of the wheels better. It was soothing. Well, most of the time. Not today. Not on her way to some heretofore unknown village in Ireland, where her future would be decided by the contents of a church register.

Not today, after her father had lectured her for the entire luncheon meal, leaving her feeling rather like a recalcitrant child.

Not today, when—

"Do you know what the funniest part of it is?" Amelia asked, the words coming forth before she realized what she was saying.

"No."

"I keep thinking to myself, 'This isn't fair. I should have a choice. I should not have to be traded and bartered like some sort of commodity.' But then I think, 'How is this any different? I was given to Wyndham years ago. I never made a complaint.'"

She said this all to the darkness of her own eyelids. It was strangely more satisfying that way.

"You were just a baby," Grace said.

"I have had many years to lodge a complaint."

"Amelia—"

"I have no one to blame but myself."

"That's not true."

She finally opened her eyes. One of them, at least. "You're just saying that."

"No, I'm not. I would," Grace said, "but as it happens, I am telling the truth. It's not your fault. It's not anyone's fault, really. I wish it were. It would be so much easier that way."

"To have someone to blame?"

"Yes."

And then Amelia whispered, "I don't want to marry him."

"Thomas?"

Thomas? Whatever was she thinking? "No," Amelia said. "Mr. Audley."

Grace's lips parted with surprise. "Really?"

"You sound so shocked."

"No, of course not," Grace quickly replied. "It's just that he's so handsome."

Amelia gave a little shrug. "I suppose. Don't you find him a little *too* charming?"

"No."

Amelia looked at Grace with newfound interest. Her *no* had been a tad bit more defensive than she would have expected. "Grace Eversleigh," she said, lowering her voice as she darted a quick look toward the dowager, "do you fancy Mr. Audley?"

And then it was more than obvious that she did, because Grace stammered and spluttered, and made a noise that sounded rather like a toad.

Which amused Amelia to no end. "You *do*."

"It does not signify," Grace mumbled.

"Of course it signifies," Amelia replied pertly. "Does he fancy you? No, don't answer, I can see from your face that he does. Well. I certainly shall not marry him now."

"You should not refuse him on my account," Grace said.

"*What* did you just say?"

"I can't marry him if he's the duke."

Amelia wanted to swat her. How *dare* she give up on love? "Why not?"

"If he is the duke, he will need to marry someone suitable." Grace gave her a sharp look. "Of *your* rank."

"Oh, don't be silly. It's not as if you grew up in an orphanage."

"There will be scandal enough. He must not add to it with a sensational márriage."

"An actress would be sensational. You will merely be a week's worth of gossip." She waited for Grace to comment, but she looked so flustered, and so . . . so . . . *sad*. Amelia could hardly bear it. She thought of Grace, in love with Mr. Audley, and she thought of herself, drifting on the tide of other people's expectations.

This wasn't how she wanted to be.

This wasn't *who* she wanted to be.

"I do not know Mr. Audley's mind," she said, "or his intentions, but if he is prepared to dare everything for love, then you should be, too." She reached out and squeezed Grace's hand. "Be a woman of courage, Grace." She smiled then, as much for herself as for Grace.

And she whispered, "I shall be one, too."

Chapter 17

The journey to Butlersbridge proceeded much as Thomas had anticipated. Along with Jack and Lord Crowland, he rode horseback, the better to enjoy the fine weather. There was very little talk; they never quite managed to keep themselves in an even enough line to converse. Every now and then one of them would increase his pace or fall behind, and one horse would pass another. Perfunctory greetings would be exchanged.

Occasionally someone would comment on the weather.

Lord Crowland seemed rather interested in the native birds.

Thomas tried to enjoy the scenery. It was all very green, even more so than Lincolnshire, and he wondered about the annual rainfall. If precipitation here was higher, would that also translate into a better crop yield? Or would this be offset by—

Stop.

Agriculture, animal husbandry . . . it was all academic now. He owned no land, no animals save for his horse, and maybe not even that.

He had nothing.

No one.

Amelia . . .

Her face entered his mind, unbidden and yet very welcome. She was so much more than he'd anticipated. He did not love her—he *could* not love her, not now. But somehow . . . he missed her. Which was ridiculous, as she was just in the carriage, some twenty yards behind. *And* he'd seen her at their noontime picnic. *And* they'd breakfasted together.

He had no reason to miss her.

And yet he did.

He missed her laugh, the way it might sound at a particularly enjoyable dinner party. He missed the warm glow of her eyes, the way they would look in the early morning light.

If he ever got to see her in the early morning light.

Which he wouldn't.

But he missed it all the same.

He glanced over his shoulder, back at the carriage, half surprised to see that it looked exactly as it should, and not spitting flames through the windows.

His grandmother had been in fine form that afternoon. Now *there* was one thing he would not miss, once he was stripped of his title. The dowager Duchess of Wyndham had been more than an albatross on his back; she'd been a bloody Medusa, whose only purpose in life seemed to be to make his life as difficult as possible.

But his grandmother was not the only burden he'd be happy to shed. The endless paperwork. He'd not miss that. The lack of freedom. Everyone thought he could do as he pleased—all that money and power ought to lend a man utter control. But no, he was tied to Belgrave. Or he had been.

He thought of Amelia, her dreams of Amsterdam.

Well, hell. Come tomorrow, he could go to Amsterdam if he so desired. He could leave straight from Dublin. He could see Venice. The West Indies. There was nothing to stop him, no—

"Are you *happy*?"

"Me?" Thomas looked over at Jack in some surprise, then realized he'd been whistling. Whistling. He couldn't remember the last time he'd done so. "I suppose I am. It's a rather fine day, don't you think?"

"A fine day," Jack echoed.

"None of us is trapped in the carriage with that evil old hag," Crowland announced. "We should all be happy." Then he added, "Pardon," since the evil old hag was, after all, grandmother to both of his companions.

"Pardons unnecessary on my account," Thomas said, feeling rather jovial. "I agree with your assessment completely."

"Will I have to live with her?" Jack blurted out.

Thomas looked over and grinned. Was he only just now realizing the extent of his burdens? "The Outer Hebrides, my man, the Outer Hebrides."

"Why didn't you do it?" Jack demanded.

"Oh, believe me, I will, on the off chance I still possess any power over her tomorrow. And if I don't . . . " Thomas shrugged. "I'll need some sort of employment, won't I? I always wished to travel. Perhaps I shall be your scout. I'll find the oldest, coldest place on the island. I shall have a rollicking good time."

"For God's sake," Jack swore. "Stop talking like that."

Thomas regarded him curiously but he did not inquire. Not for the first time, he wondered just what, exactly, was going on in his cousin's head. Jack's face had taken on a haggard air, and his eyes were bleak.

He did not want to go home. No, he was *afraid* to go home.

Thomas felt a spark of something in his chest. Sympathy, he supposed, for a man he ought to despise. But there was nothing to say. Nothing to ask.

And so he didn't. For the rest of the journey he said nothing. Hours passed, and the air around him chilled with the night. They passed through charming little villages, through the larger, busier Cavan town, and then finally through Butlersbridge.

It ought to look sinister, Thomas thought. The shadows ought to be stretched and misshapen, and there should have been strange animal sounds, howling through the night.

This was where his life would be pulled out from beneath him. It did not seem right that it should appear so picturesque.

Jack was just a bit ahead, and he'd slowed down considerably. Thomas drew up alongside, then slowed his horse to keep an even pace. "Is this the road?" he asked quietly.

Jack nodded. "Just around the bend."

"They are not expecting you, are they?"

"No." Jack nudged his horse on into a trot, but Thomas held his to a walk, allowing Jack to go on ahead. There were some things a man needed to do alone.

At the very least, he could attempt to hold the dowager back while Jack made his homecoming.

He slowed as best as he could, positioning his mount so the carriage was forced to slow as well. At the end of the short drive he could see Jack dismount, climb the front steps, and knock on the door. A shaft of light streamed out when it was opened, but Thomas could not hear any words that were exchanged.

The carriage was parked to the side of the entryway, and the dowager was helped down by one of the grooms. She started to charge forward, but Thomas quickly slid from his saddle and grabbed her arm to hold her back.

"Let go of me," she snapped, attempting to break free.

"For the love of God, woman," Thomas shot back, "give him a moment with his relatives."

"*We* are his relatives."

"Have you not a single ounce of sensibility?"

"There are far greater matters at stake than—"

"There is *nothing* that cannot wait two more minutes. Nothing."

Her eyes narrowed. "I'm certain *you* think so."

Thomas swore, and not under his breath. "I have come this far, have I not? I have treated him with civility, and even lately with respect. I have listened to your vitriol and incessant complaining. I have ridden across two countries, slept in the bottom of a boat, and even—and this, I might add, was really the final insult—handed over my fiancée. I believe I have proven that I am prepared for whatever this place has to offer. But by all that is holy, I will not give up what shred of human decency I have managed to retain after growing up in a house with *you*."

Over her shoulder he could see Grace and Amelia, both open-mouthed, both staring.

"The man," he said through gritted teeth, "can have two bloody minutes with his family."

His grandmother stared at him for one long, icy second, and then said, "Do not curse in my presence."

Thomas was so dumbfounded by her complete lack of response to anything he'd said that he loosened his grip on her arm, and she wrenched away, hurrying over to the front steps, just behind Jack, who was embracing a woman Thomas imagined was his aunt.

"*Ahem,*" the dowager said, as only she could.

Thomas strode forward, ready to intercede if necessary.

"You must be the aunt," the dowager said to the woman on the steps.

Mrs. Audley just stared at her. "Yes," she finally replied. "And you are . . . ?"

"Aunt Mary," Jack cut in, "I am afraid I must introduce you to the dowager Duchess of Wyndham."

Mrs. Audley let go of him and curtsied, stepping aside as the dowager swept past her. "The *Duchess* of Wyndham?" she echoed. "Good heavens, Jack, couldn't you have sent notice?"

Jack's smile was grim. "It is better this way, I assure you." He turned to Thomas. "The Duke of Wyndham," he said, motioning with his arm. "Your grace—my aunt, Mrs. Audley."

Thomas bowed. "I am honored to make your acquaintance, Mrs. Audley."

She stammered something in response, clearly nonplussed by the arrival of a duke.

Jack completed the introductions, and the ladies were making their curtsies when Mrs. Audley pulled him aside. She spoke in a whisper, but her tone held enough panic that Thomas could hear every word.

"Jack, I haven't the rooms. We have nothing grand enough—"

"Please, Mrs. Audley," Thomas said, dipping his head in a gesture of respect, "do not put yourself out on my accord. It was unforgivable for us to arrive without notice. I would not expect you to go to any great lengths. Although perhaps your finest room for my grandmother." He tried not to sound too weary as he added, "It will be easier for everyone."

"Of course," Mrs. Audley said quickly. "Please, please, it's chilly. You must all come inside. Jack, I do need to tell you—"

"Where is your church?" the dowager demanded.

Thomas nearly groaned. Could she not wait until they were even shown in?

"Our church?" Mrs. Audley asked, looking to Jack in complete confusion. "At this hour?"

"I do not intend to worship," the dowager snapped. "I wish to inspect the records."

"Does Vicar Beveridge still preside?" Jack asked, clearly trying to cut the dowager off.

"Yes," his aunt replied, "but he will surely be abed. It's half nine, I should think, and he is an early riser. Perhaps in the morning. I—"

"This is a matter of dynastic importance," the dowager interrupted. "I don't care if it's after midnight. We—"

"I care," Jack cut in. "You are not going to pull the vicar out of bed. You have waited this long. You can bloody well wait until morning."

Thomas wanted to applaud.

"Jack!" Mrs. Audley gasped. She turned to the dowager. "I did not raise him to speak this way."

"No, you didn't," Jack said, but he glared at the dowager.

"You were his mother's sister, weren't you?" the dowager said to Mrs. Audley.

Who looked rather startled by the sudden change of topic. "I am."

"Were you present at her wedding?"

"I was not."

Jack turned to her in surprise. "You weren't?"

"No. I could not attend. I was in confinement. I never told you. It was a stillbirth." Her face softened. "Just one of the reasons I was so happy to have *you*."

"We shall make for the church in the morning," the

dowager declared. "First thing. We shall find the papers and be done with it."

"The papers?" Mrs. Audley echoed.

"Proof of the marriage," the dowager practically snarled. "Are you daft?"

That was too much. Thomas reached out and pulled her back, which was probably in her best interest, as Jack looked as if he might go for her throat.

"Louise was not married in the Butlersbridge church," Mrs. Audley said. "She was married at Maguiresbridge. In County Fermanagh, where we grew up."

"How far is that?" the dowager demanded, tugging at her arm.

Thomas held firm.

"Twenty miles, your grace," Mrs. Audley replied before turning back to her nephew. "Jack? What is this all about? Why do you need proof of your mother's marriage?"

Jack hesitated for a moment, then cleared his throat and said, "My father was her son," with a nod toward the dowager.

"Your father," Mrs. Audley gasped. "John Cavendish, you mean . . . "

Thomas stepped forward, feeling strangely prepared to take charge of the rapidly deteriorating situation. "May I intercede?"

Jack nodded in his direction. "Please do."

"Mrs. Audley," Thomas said, "if there is proof of your sister's marriage, then your nephew is the true Duke of Wyndham."

"The true Duke of—" Mrs. Audley covered her mouth in shock. "No. It's not possible. I remember him. Mr. Cavendish. He was—" She waved her arms in the air, as if trying to describe him with gestures. Finally, after several attempts at a more verbal explanation, she said, "He would not have kept such a thing from us."

"He was not the heir at the time," Thomas told her.

"Oh, my heavens. But if Jack is the duke, then you—"

"Are not," he finished wryly. He glanced over at Amelia and Grace, who were watching the entire exchange from just inside the front door. "I am sure you can imagine our eagerness to have this settled."

Mrs. Audley could only stare at him in shock.

Thomas knew just how she felt.

Amelia wasn't sure what time it was. Certainly after midnight. She and Grace had been shown to their room several hours earlier, and even though she had long since washed her face and donned her nightclothes, she was still awake.

For a long time she'd lain beneath her blankets, pretending there was some kind of music to Grace's even, sleep-lulled breathing. Then she'd moved to the window, deciding that if she couldn't sleep, she might as well have something better to look at than the ceiling. The moon was nearly full, its light rendering the stars a bit less twinkly.

Amelia sighed. She had enough trouble picking out the constellations as it was.

Somewhat apathetically, she located the Big Dipper.

Then the wind blew a cloud over it.

"Oh, it figures," she muttered.

Grace began to snore.

Amelia sat on the wide window ledge, letting her head lean up against the glass. She'd done this when she was younger and couldn't sleep—go to the window, count the stars and the flowers. Sometimes she even climbed out, before her father had the majestic oak outside her window pruned back.

That had been fun.

She wanted that again. Fun. Tonight. She wanted to banish this grim despondency, this horrible sense of dread. She wanted to go outside, to feel the wind on her face. She wanted to sing to herself where no one could hear. She wanted to stretch her legs, still cramped from so much time in the carriage.

She hopped down from her perch and donned her coat, tiptoeing past Grace, who was mumbling in her sleep. (But sadly, nothing she could make out. She certainly would have stayed and listened, had Grace been making any sense.)

The house was quiet, which she'd expected, given the hour. She had some experience sneaking through sleeping households, although her past exploits had been limited to pranks on her sisters—or revenge for their pranks on her. She kept her footsteps light, her breathing even, and before she knew it, she was in the hall, pushing open the front door and slipping out into the night.

The air was crisp and tingling with dew, but it felt

glorious. Hugging her coat close, she moved across the lawn toward the trees. Her feet were freezing—she hadn't wanted to risk the noise her shoes would have made—but she didn't care. She'd happily sneeze tomorrow if it meant freedom tonight.

Freedom.

Grinning and laughing, she broke into a run.

Thomas couldn't sleep.

This did not surprise him. Indeed, after he'd bathed the dust from his body, he changed into a fresh shirt and breeches. A nightshirt would be of no use this night.

He'd been shown to a very fine bedchamber, second only to the one given to his grandmother. The room was not overly large, nor were the furnishings obviously new or expensive, but it was all of fine quality, lovingly cared-for and warm and welcoming. There were miniatures on the desk, placed artfully in the corner where they could be gazed upon while one was writing one's correspondence. There had been miniatures on the mantel in the drawing room, too, lovingly displayed in a row. The frames were a bit worn, the paint rubbed down where they'd been picked up and admired.

These miniatures—these people in the miniatures—they were loved.

Thomas had tried to imagine a similar display at Belgrave and almost laughed. Of course, portraits of all the Cavendishes had been painted, most more than once. But the paintings hung in the gallery, formal documents of grandeur and wealth. He never looked at them. Why would he? There was no one he wished to see, no one whose smile or good humor he wished to recall.

He wandered to the desk and picked up one of the little portraits. It looked like Jack, perhaps a decade younger.

He was smiling.

Thomas found *himself* smiling, although he was not certain why. He liked this place. Cloverhill, it was called. A sweet name. Fitting.

This would have been a nice place to grow up.

To learn to be a man.

He set the miniature down and moved to the nearby window, leaning both hands against the sill. He was tired. And restless. It was a noxious combination.

He wanted this done.

He wanted to move forward, to find out—no, to *know* who he was.

And who he wasn't.

He stood there for several minutes, staring out over the tidy lawn. There was nothing to see, not in the dead of night, and yet he could not seem to make himself move. And then—

His eyes caught a flash of movement, and he drew closer to the glass. Someone was outside.

Amelia.

It couldn't be, and yet it indisputably was she. No one else had hair of that color.

What the devil was she doing? She wasn't running off; she was far too sensible for that, and besides, she was not carrying a bag. No, she seemed to have decided to take a stroll.

At four in the morning.

Which was decidedly *not* sensible.

"Daft woman," he muttered, grabbing a robe to throw over his thin shirt as he dashed out of his room. Was this what his life might have been, had he managed to marry her? Chasing her down in the middle of the night?

Less than a minute later he exited through the front door, which he noted had been left an inch ajar. He strode across the drive and onto the lawn where he'd seen her last, but nothing.

She was gone.

Oh, for the love of—he did *not* want to yell out her name. He'd wake the entire household.

He moved forward. Where the devil was she? She couldn't have gone far. More than that, she *wouldn't* have gone far. Not Amelia.

"Amelia?" he whispered.

Nothing.

"Amelia?" It was as loud as he dared.

And then suddenly there she was, sitting up in the grass. "Thomas?"

"Were you *lying down*?"

Her hair was down, hanging down her back in a simple braid. He didn't know that he'd ever seen her this way. He couldn't imagine when he could have done. "I was looking at the stars," she said.

He looked up. He couldn't not, after such a statement.

"I was waiting for the clouds to pass," she explained.

"*Why?*"

"Why?" she echoed, looking at him as if *he* was the one who'd just made an incomprehensible statement.

"It is the middle of the night."

"Yes, I know." She tucked her feet under her, then pushed down against the ground with her hands and stood. "But it's my last chance."

"For what?"

She gave a helpless shrug. "I don't know."

He started to say something, to scold her, shake his head at her foolishness. But then she smiled.

She looked so beautiful he almost felt struck.

"Amelia." He didn't know why he was saying her name. He had nothing specific to tell her. But she was there, standing before him, and he had never wanted a woman—no, he had never wanted *anything*—more than he wanted her.

On a damp lawn, in the middle of Ireland, in the middle of the night, he wanted her.

Completely.

He hadn't let himself think about it. He desired her; he'd long since given up pretending he didn't. But he had not let himself dream it, not let himself see it in his mind—his hands on her shoulders, sliding down her back. Her dress, falling away beneath his hungry fingers, exposing her perfect—

"You need to go inside," he said hoarsely.

She shook her head.

He took a long, haggard breath. Did she know what she risked, remaining out here with him? It was taking all his strength—more than he'd ever dreamed he possessed—to keep himself rooted to his spot, two proper paces away from her. Close . . . so close, and yet not within his reach.

"I want to be outside," she said.

He met her eyes, which was a mistake, because everything she was feeling—every hurt, and wrong, and insecurity—he saw them, hovering in her amazing eyes.

It tore through him.

"I was upstairs," she continued, "and it was stuffy, and hot. Only it wasn't hot, but it felt like it should be."

It was the damnedest thing, but he understood.

"I'm tired of feeling trapped," she said sadly. "My whole life, I've been told where to be, what to say, who to talk to . . ."

"Who to marry," he said softly.

She gave a small nod. "I just wanted to feel free. If only for an hour."

He looked at her hand. It would be so easy to reach out, to take it in his. Just one step forward. That was all it would take. One step, and she would be in his arms.

But he said, "You need to go inside." Because it was what he was supposed to say. It was what she was supposed to do.

He could not kiss her. Not now. Not here. Not when he had absolutely no faith in his ability to break it off.

To end a kiss with a kiss. He didn't think he could do it.

"I don't want to marry him," she said.

Something within him curled and tightened. He'd known this; she'd made it more than clear. But still . . . now . . . when she stood there in the moonlight . . .

They were impossible words. Impossible to bear. Impossible to ignore.

I don't want him to have you.

But he didn't say it. He could not let himself say it. Because he knew, come morning when all was revealed, Jack Audley would almost certainly be proven as the Duke of Wyndham. And if he said it, if he said to her, right now—*be with me* . . .

She would do it.

He could see it in her eyes.

Maybe she even thought she loved him. And why wouldn't she? She had been told her entire life that she was supposed to love him, to obey him, to be grateful for his attentions and for the luck that had bound her to him so many years ago.

But she didn't really know him. Right now he wasn't even sure he knew himself. How could he ask her to be with him when he had nothing to offer?

She deserved more.

"Amelia," he whispered, because he had to say *something*. She was waiting for it, for his reply.

She shook her head. "I don't want to do it."

"Your father—" he said, his voice choked.

"He wants me to be a duchess."

"He wants what's best for you."

"He doesn't know."

"*You* don't know."

The look she gave him was devastating. "Don't say that. Say anything else, but don't say I don't know my own mind."

"Amelia . . . "

"*No.*"

It was a horrible sound. Just that one syllable. But it came from deep within her. And he felt it all. Her pain, her anger, her frustration—they sliced through him with startling precision.

"I'm sorry," he said, because he did not know what else to say. And he was sorry. He wasn't sure what for, but this horrible aching feeling in his chest—it had to be sorrow.

Or maybe regret.

That she wasn't his.

That she would never be his.

That he could not set aside the one little piece of him that knew how to be upstanding and true. That he could not say *to hell with it all* and just take her, right here, right now.

That, much to his surprise, it turned out that it wasn't the Duke of Wyndham who always did the right thing.

It was Thomas Cavendish.

The one piece of himself he would never lose.

Chapter 18

*I*t was ironic, Amelia had thought more than once during the journey to Cloverhill that she had recently become so enamored of cartography. Because she was only just now coming to realize how thoroughly her own life had been mapped out by others. Even with all her plans torn asunder, her new map, with whatever routes her life was meant to take, was being drawn by others.

Her father.

The dowager.

Even Thomas.

Everyone, it seemed, had a hand in her future except for her. But not tonight.

"It's late," she said softly.

His eyes widened, and she could see his confusion.

"But not too late," she whispered. She looked up. The clouds had blown off. She hadn't felt the wind—she hadn't felt anything except for him, and he hadn't even touched her. But somehow the sky was clear. The stars were out.

That was important. She didn't know why, but it was.

"Thomas," she whispered, and her heart was skipping. Pounding.

Breaking.

"Thom—"

"Don't," he said, his voice hoarse. "Don't say my name."

Why?

It was on the tip of her tongue, desperate to be voiced, but she didn't ask. Somehow she knew she shouldn't. Whatever the answer was, she didn't want to hear it. Not now, not when he was staring down at her with such a hot, sad intensity.

"No one is here," she whispered. It was true. Everyone was asleep. And she wasn't sure why she was saying something so obvious. Maybe she just wanted him to know . . . without saying it so clearly. If he leaned down, if he kissed her . . .

She would welcome it.

He shook his head. "Someone is always here."

But he was wrong. It was the middle of the night. Everyone was asleep. They were alone, and she wanted . . . she wanted . . .

"Kiss me."

His eyes flared, and for a moment it almost looked as if he were in pain. "Amelia, don't."

"Please." She smiled, as cheekily as she could manage. "You owe it to me."

"I—" First he looked surprised, then amused. "I owe it to you?"

"For twenty years of engagement. You owe me a kiss."

He slid into a reluctant smile. "For twenty years of engagement, I should think I'd owe you several."

She wet her lips. They'd gone dry from the fast rush of her breath. "One will suffice."

"No," he said softly, "it wouldn't. It would never be enough."

She stopped breathing. He was going to do it. He was going to kiss her. He was going to kiss her, and by God, she would kiss him back.

She stepped forward.

"Don't," he said, but his voice was not firm.

She reached out, her hand coming within inches of his.

"Amelia, *don't*," he said roughly.

Oh no. He was not going to push her away. She would not let him. He was not going to say it was for her own good, or that he knew best, or that anyone knew best except for her. This was her life, and her night, and as God was her witness, he was her man.

She launched herself at him.

On him, really.

"Am—"

It might have been her name he'd been trying to say. Or it might have been a grunt of surprise. She didn't know. She didn't care. She was much too far gone to worry over such trivialities. She had his face in her hands and she was kissing him. Clumsily, perhaps, but with all the crazy energy that was burning through her.

She loved him.

She *loved* him. Maybe she hadn't told him, and maybe she'd never be given the opportunity to do so, but she loved him. And right now she was going to kiss him.

Because that's what a woman in love did.

"Thomas," she said, because she *would* say his name. She'd say it over and over if he'd only let her.

"Amelia . . . " He put his hands on her shoulders, preparing to push her away.

She could not allow it. She threw her arms around him, pressing the length of her body against his. Her hands sank into his hair, pulling him toward her as her lips pressed against his. "Thomas," she moaned, the word sinking into his skin. "Thomas, please . . . "

But he didn't move. He stood stiffly, with no reaction to her onslaught, and then . . .

Something softened. First it was in his chest, as if he'd finally allowed himself to breathe. And then one of his hands moved . . . slowly, almost shaking . . . to the small of her back.

She shivered. She moaned against him. She let one of her hands sink into his hair. And then she begged.

"Please."

If he rejected her now . . . She didn't think she could bear it.

"I need you," she whispered.

He went very still. So still that she thought she'd lost him. But then he exploded with passionate energy. His arms wrapped around her with stunning speed, and he wasn't just kissing her back . . .

Dear God, it felt as if he were devouring her.

And she wanted to let him.

"Oh, yes," she sighed, and she sank more deeply into him. This was what she'd wanted. She'd wanted him, yes, but more than that, she'd wanted *this*. The power, the knowledge that *she* had started something. *She* had kissed *him*.

And he wanted it. He wanted *her*.

It made her shiver. It made her melt inside. It made her want to knock him to the ground and straddle him and—

Good God, what had become of her?

Whoever she was, whoever she'd been just hours earlier—that woman was gone, replaced by some wanton spirit who had not spent twenty-one years of life learning to be a proper lady. When she'd kissed him—no, when she threw herself at him, praying he wouldn't push her away—it had been a thing of her emotions. She was angry, and desperate, and sad, and wistful, and she'd wanted, just for once, to feel as if she were in control.

But now—emotion was gone. Her body had taken over, fueled by a need she'd only barely tasted before now. It was as if she'd been gripped from within. Something was tensing, twisting. It was deep inside of her, in places she'd never discussed, never even acknowledged.

And he—Thomas—only made it worse.

And better.

No, worse.

"Please," she begged, wishing she knew what she was asking for. Then she moaned, because he was making it better again. His lips were on her throat, and his hands were everywhere—in her hair, stroking her back, cupping her bottom.

She wanted him closer. Most of all, she wanted *more*. She wanted his heat, his strength. She wanted his skin, burning against hers. She wanted to arch her back, to spread her legs.

She wanted to *move*. In ways she'd never dreamed possible.

Squirming in his embrace, she tried to shrug off her coat, but it only made it to the crook of her elbows before he groaned, "You'll be cold."

She struggled to free her right arm from its sleeve. "You can keep me warm."

He pulled back, just enough so she could see his haggard expression. "Amelia . . . "

She heard the old Thomas in his voice. The one who always did the right thing. "Don't stop," she begged him. "Not tonight."

Thomas took her face in his hands, holding her so their noses were a few inches apart. His eyes caught hers, tortured and bleak. "I don't want to," he said, his voice ragged.

But I have to.

They both knew what he'd left unspoken.

"I . . . I can't . . . " He stopped, taking a shudder-

ing breath as he forced himself to step back. "I can't
. . . do something . . . that will . . . " He was choosing
his words carefully. Either that or he could not manage
normal rational thought. "If I do this . . . Amelia . . . "
He raked his hand through his hair, his nails biting into
his scalp. He wanted the pain. Right now he needed it.
Something, *anything,* that might ground him, keep him
from falling apart.

From losing the last bit of himself.

"I can't do something that will decide your future,"
he made himself say. He looked up, half hoping she'd
turned away, but no, there she was, staring at him, her
eyes wide, her lips parted. He could see her breath
in the damp night, each puff whispering through the
air.

It was torture. His body was screaming for her. His
mind . . .

His heart.

No.

He did not love her. He *could not* love her. There
could be no god so cruel as to inflict this upon him.

He forced himself to breathe. It was not easy, especially when his eyes slid from her face . . . lower . . .
along her neck . . .

The small tie at the bodice of her nightgown was par-
tially undone.

He swallowed. He'd seen far more of her, on numer-
ous occasions. Evening dresses were almost always
lower cut. And yet he could not take his eyes off the
little strings, the single loop that had flopped down
onto the swell of her breast.

If he pulled it . . .

If he reached out and took it between his fingers, would her gown fall open? Would the fabric slide away?

"Go inside," he said raggedly. "Please."

"Thom—"

"I can't leave you alone out here, and I can't— I can't—" He drew a long breath. It did nothing to calm his blood.

But she did not move.

"Go inside, Amelia. If not for yourself, then do it for me."

He saw her mouth his name. She did not understand.

He tried to breathe; it was difficult. He hurt with desire. "It is taking everything I have not to take you right now."

Her eyes widened, flaring with warmth. It was tempting, so tempting, but—

"Don't let me become the brute who ruined you, one night before . . . before . . . "

She licked her lips. It was a nervous gesture, but his blood burned.

"Amelia, *go.*"

And she must have heard the desperation in his voice, because she went, leaving him alone on the lawn, rock hard and cursing himself for a fool.

A noble fool, perhaps. An honest one. But still, a fool.

Several hours later Thomas was still wandering the halls of Cloverhill. He'd waited for nearly an hour after

Amelia left to go back inside. He told himself that he liked the cold night air; it felt good in his lungs, prickling at his skin. He told himself he didn't mind that his feet were freezing, surely turning into prunes in the damp grass.

It was all ballocks, of course. He knew that if he didn't give Amelia ample time (and then some) to get back to her room—the one she thankfully shared with Grace—he would go after her. And if he touched her again, if he even so much as sensed her presence before morning, he would not be able to stop himself this time.

A man had only so much strength.

He'd gone back up to his own room, where he'd warmed his freezing feet by the fire, and then, far too restless to remain in place, he donned his shoes and moved quietly downstairs, in search of something— anything—that might distract him until morning.

The house was still quiet, of course. Not even the sound of servants, up to perform their morning chores. But then he thought he heard something. A soft thump, or maybe the scrape of a chair against floor. And when he looked more closely down the hall, he saw a bit of light, flickering onto the floor through an open doorway.

Curious, he moved down the hall and peered inside. Jack sat alone, his face gaunt and exhausted. He looked, Thomas thought, like he himself felt.

"Can't sleep?" Thomas asked.

Jack looked up. His face remained oddly devoid of expression. "No."

"Nor I," Thomas said, walking in.

Jack held up a bottle of brandy. It was more than three-quarters full, attesting to a need for solace, not for oblivion. "It's good. I think my uncle was saving it," he said. He looked down at the bottle and blinked. "Not for this, I imagine."

There was a set of snifters near the window, so Thomas walked over and took one. It seemed somehow entirely unstrange that he should be here now, drinking brandy with the man who would, within hours, steal everything but his soul.

He sat across from Jack and set the snifter down on the small, low table that sat between the two wingback chairs. Jack reached forward and poured him a generous dose.

Thomas took it and drank. It was good. Warm and mellow, and as close to what he needed as any spirit could strive for. He took another sip and leaned forward, resting his forearms on his thighs as he stared out the window, which he noted with a thankful prayer did not face the lawn where he had been kissing Amelia. "It will be dawn soon," he said.

Jack turned in the same direction, watching the window. "Has anyone awakened?" he asked.

"Not that I've heard."

They sat in silence for several moments. Thomas nursed his brandy slowly. He'd drunk far too much lately. He supposed he'd had as good an excuse as any—better than most, really. But he did not like the man he was becoming. Grace . . . He would never have kissed her had it not been for drink.

Already he would lose his name, his rank, his every last possession. He did not need to surrender his dignity and good judgment as well.

He sat back, comfortable in the silence as he watched Jack. He was coming to realize that his newfound cousin was more of a man than he'd initially judged him to be. Jack would take his responsibilities seriously. He would make mistakes, but then so had he. Maybe the dukedom would not thrive and grow under Jack's stewardship, but nor would it be run into the ground.

It was enough. It had to be enough.

Thomas watched as Jack picked up the bottle of brandy and started to pour himself another glass. But just as the first drops were splashing down, he stopped, abruptly righting the bottle. He looked up, his eyes finding Thomas's with unexpected clarity. "Do you ever feel as if you are on display?"

Thomas wanted to laugh. Instead, he did not move a muscle. "All the time."

"How do you bear it?"

He thought about that for a moment. "I don't know anything else."

Jack closed his eyes and rubbed his forehead. It almost looked, Thomas thought, as if he were trying to obliterate a memory.

"It's going to be hideous today," Jack said.

Thomas nodded slowly. It was an apt description.

"It's going to be a bloody circus."

"Indeed."

They sat there, doing nothing, and then they both looked up at precisely the same moment. Their eyes met, and then Thomas glanced to the side, over at the window.

Outside.

"Shall we?" Jack asked.

"Before anyone—"

"Right now."

Thomas set down his half-drunk glass of brandy and stood. He looked over at Jack, and for the first time he felt their kinship. "Lead the way."

And it was strange, but as they mounted their horses and rode off, Thomas finally recognized the lightness in his chest.

It was freedom.

He did not particularly want to give up Wyndham. It was . . .

Him. Wyndham. It was him. That's who he was.

But this was wonderful. Sneaking off, tearing through the dawn as it rose over the roads . . .

He was discovering that maybe there was more to him than his name. And maybe, when all was said and done, he'd still be whole.

Chapter 19

Thomas found the ride to Maguiresbridge surprisingly pleasant. Not that he'd expected the countryside to be anything but picturesque, but the circumstances of the day did not lend themselves toward an amiable outlook. As for Jack—he seemed uninclined toward conversation, but he did occasionally provide bits and pieces of the local history.

Jack had enjoyed growing up here, Thomas realized. No, more than that, he'd loved it. His aunt was a lovely woman; there was no other way to describe her. Thomas was quite sure that she would have made a wonderful mother. Certainly Cloverhill would have been a far more enjoyable place to be a child than Belgrave.

Ah, irony. By all rights, Jack had been robbed of his inheritance. And yet Thomas was beginning to feel that he had been the one cheated. Not that he'd likely have had a more pleasant childhood were he not the

Wyndham heir; his father would have been even more bitterly tempered living in the North, known to all as a factory owner's son-in-law.

Still, it did make him wonder. Not of what might have been, but of what could be. He had made it a mission not to emulate his father, but he had never given much thought to what sort of father he himself might someday prove to be.

Would his home be adorned with miniatures, the painted frames worn down by too much handling?

Of course, that presupposed that he had a home, which was very much still up in the air.

A small village came into view, and Jack slowed, then stopped, staring into the distance. Thomas looked at him curiously; he didn't think that Jack had meant to pause.

"Is this it?" he asked.

Jack gave a nod, and together they rode forward.

Thomas looked around as they approached the village. It was a tidy little place, with storefronts and homes tucked up next to each other along a cobbled street. A thatched roof here, daub and wattle there . . . it was no different than any other small village in the British Isles.

"The church is that way," Jack said, motioning with his head.

Thomas followed him along what he presumed was the high street until they reached the church. It was a simple gray stone building, with narrow arched windows. It looked ancient, and he could not help but think it would be a rather nice place to be married.

It was, however, deserted. "It does not look as if anyone is about," he said.

Jack glanced over at a smaller building, to the left of the church. "The register will likely be at the rectory."

Thomas nodded, and they dismounted, tying their horses to a hitching post before making their way to the front of the rectory. They knocked several times before they heard footsteps moving toward them from within.

The door opened, revealing a woman of middling years. Thomas assumed she was the housekeeper.

"Good day, ma'am," Jack said, offering her a polite bow. "I am Jack Audley, and this is—"

"Thomas Cavendish," Thomas interrupted, ignoring Jack's look of surprise. It seemed grasping to introduce himself with his full title during the last few minutes of its legitimacy.

Jack looked as if he wanted to roll his eyes, but instead he turned back to the housekeeper and said, "We would like to see the parish register."

She stared at them for a moment and then jerked her head toward the rear. "It's in the back room," she said. "The vicar's office."

"Er, is the vicar present?" Jack asked.

Thomas elbowed him hard in the ribs. Good God, was he *asking* for company?

But if the housekeeper found their request the least bit intriguing, she did not show it. "No vicar just now," she said, sounding bored. "The position is vacant." She walked over to the sofa and sat down, telling them over her shoulder, "We're supposed to get someone new soon. They send someone from Enniskillen every Sunday to deliver a sermon."

She then picked up a plate of toast and turned her back on them completely. Thomas took that as permission to enter the office, and walked in, Jack a few paces behind.

There were several shelves against the wall that stood opposite the fireplace, so Thomas started there. Several Bibles, books of sermons, poetry . . . "Do you know what a parish register looks like?" he asked. He tried to recall if he'd ever seen the register at his parish church, back near Belgrave. He supposed he must have, but it could not have been particularly distinctive, else he would have remembered it.

Jack didn't answer, and Thomas did not feel like pressing further, so he set to work inspecting the shelves.

Moral Rectitude and the Modern Man. No, thank you.

History of Fermanagh. He'd pass on that as well. Lovely as the county was, he'd had enough of it.

Account of the Voyages by James Cook. He smiled. Amelia would like that one.

He closed his eyes and took a breath, allowing himself a moment to think of her. He'd been trying not to. All through the morning, he'd kept his mind focused on the landscape, his reins, the bit of mud stuck to the back of Jack's left boot.

But not Amelia.

Certainly not her eyes, which were not at all the color

of the leaves on the trees. The bark, maybe. With the leaves, together. Green and brown. A mix. He liked that.

Nor had he not been thinking of her smile. Or the exact shape of her mouth when she'd stood across from him the night before, breathless in her desire for him.

He wanted her. Dear God, he wanted her.

But he did not love her.

He could not. It was untenable.

He returned to the work at hand with grim purpose, pulling every book without an embossed title off the shelf so he could open it and look inside. Finally he reached a section with nothing but ledgers. He pulled one out, and his heart began to pound when he realized that the words before him were recordings of births. Deaths. Marriages.

He was looking at one of the church registers. The dates were wrong, though. Jack's parents would have married in 1790, and these were all far too recent.

Thomas looked over his shoulder to say something to Jack, but he was standing stiffly by the fire, his shoulders drawn up toward his ears. He looked frozen, and Thomas realized why he had not heard him moving about the room, looking for the register.

Jack had not moved since they had entered.

Thomas wanted to say something. He wanted to stride across the room and shake some bloody sense into him because what the *devil* was he complaining about? *He*, not Jack, was the one whose life would be ruined at the end of the day. *He* was losing his name, his home, his fortune.

His fiancée.

Jack would walk out of this room one of the richest and most powerful men in the world. He, on the other hand, would have nothing. His friends, he supposed, but they were few in number. Acquaintances he had in abundance, but friends—there was Grace, Harry Gladdish . . . possibly Amelia. He found it difficult to believe that she would wish to see him after all was said and done. She would find it too awkward. And if she ended up marrying Jack . . .

Then he would find it too awkward.

He closed his eyes, forcing himself to refocus on the matter at hand. *He* was the one who had told Amelia that she must marry the Duke of Wyndham, whoever that might turn out to be. He couldn't bloody well complain because she followed his instructions.

Thomas put the parish register back on the shelf and pulled out another, checking the dates that led each entry. This one was a bit older than the first, concluding at the very end of the eighteenth century. He tried another, and then a fourth, and this time, when he looked down at the careful, elegant handwriting, he found the dates he was looking for.

He swallowed and looked at Jack. "This may be it."

Jack turned. The corners of his mouth were pinched, and his eyes looked haunted.

Thomas looked down at the book and realized that his hands were trembling. He swallowed. He had made it through the day up to this point with surprising purpose. He'd been a perfect stoic, prepared to do what was right for Wyndham.

But now he was scared.

Still, he pulled from his reserves and managed an ironic smile. Because if he could not behave like a man, then what was left of him? At the end of the day, he had his dignity and his soul. That was all.

He looked up at Jack. Into his eyes. "Shall we?"

"You can do it," Jack said.

"You don't want to look with me?"

"I trust you."

Thomas's lips parted, not quite in surprise—because, really, why wouldn't Jack trust him? It wasn't as if he could alter the pages right there in front of him. But still, even if he was terrified by the outcome, wouldn't he want to see? Wouldn't he want to read the pages himself? Thomas could not imagine coming all this way and not looking down as each page was turned.

"No," Thomas said. Why should he have to do this alone? "I won't do it without you."

For a moment Jack just stood there unmoving, and then, cursing under his breath, he went over to join him at the desk.

"You're too bloody noble," Jack bit off.

"Not for long," Thomas muttered. He set the book on the desk, opening it to the first page of records. Jack stood beside him, and together they looked down at the tight, sensible penmanship of the Maguiresbridge vicar, circa 1786.

Thomas swallowed nervously. His throat felt tight. But he had to do this. It was his duty. To Wyndham.

Wasn't that his entire life? Duty to Wyndham?

He almost laughed. If ever anyone had accused him of taking duty too far . . .

This had to be it.

Looking down, he turned the pages until he found the correct year. "Do you know what month your parents would have married in?" he asked Jack.

"No."

It was no matter, Thomas decided. It was a small parish. There were not many weddings.

Patrick Colville and Emily Kendrick, 20 March, 1790
William Figley and Margaret Plowright, 22 May, 1790

He moved his fingers along the page, sliding them around the edge. Breath held, he turned the page.

And there they were.

John Augustus Cavendish and Louise Henrietta Galbraith, married 12 June, 1790, witnessed by one Henry Wickham and Philip Galbraith.

Thomas closed his eyes.

So this was it. It was gone. Everything that had defined him, everything he possessed . . .

Gone. All of it.

And what was left?

He opened his eyes, looking down at his hands. His body. His skin and his blood and his muscle and bone.

Was it enough?

Even Amelia was lost to him. She'd marry Jack or some other, similarly titled fellow, and live out her days as some other man's bride.

It stung. It burned. Thomas could not believe how much it burned.

"Who is Philip?" he whispered, looking down at the register. Because Galbraith—it was Jack's mother's name.

"What?"

Thomas looked over. Jack had his face in his hands.

"Philip Galbraith. He was a witness."

Jack looked up. And then down. At the register. "My mother's brother."

"Does he still live?" Thomas didn't know why he was asking. The proof of the marriage was right there in his hands, and he would not contest it.

"I don't know. He did the last I knew. It has been five years."

Thomas swallowed and looked up, staring off into space. His body felt strange, almost weightless, as if his blood had changed into something thinner. His skin was tingling and—

"Tear it out."

Thomas turned to Jack in shock. He could not have heard correctly. "What did you say?"

"Tear it out."

"Are you mad?"

Jack shook his head. "You are the duke."

Thomas looked down at the register, and it was then, with great sadness, that he truly accepted his fate. "No," he said softly, "I'm not."

"No." Jack grabbed him by the shoulders. His eyes were wild, panicked. "You are what Wyndham needs. What everyone needs."

"Stop, you—"

"Listen to me," Jack implored. "You are born and bred to the job. I will ruin everything. Do you understand? I cannot do it. I *cannot* do it."

Jack was scared. It was a good sign, Thomas told himself. Only a stupid man—or an exceedingly shallow one—would see nothing but the riches and prestige. If Jack saw enough to be terrified, then he was man enough for the position.

And so he just shook his head, holding Jack's gaze with his own. "I may be bred to it, but you were born to it. And I cannot take what is yours."

"I don't want it!" Jack burst out.

"It is not yours to accept or deny," Thomas said. "Don't you understand? It is not a possession. It is who you are."

"Oh, for God's sake," Jack swore. His hands were shaking. His whole body was shaking. "I am *giving* it to you. On a bloody silver platter. You stay the duke, and I shall leave you alone. I'll even be *your* scout in the Outer Hebrides. Anything. Just tear the page out."

"If you didn't want the title, why didn't you just say that your parents hadn't been married at the outset?" Thomas shot back. "I asked you if your parents were married. You could have said no."

"I didn't *know* that I was in line to inherit when you questioned my legitimacy."

Thomas stared down at the register. Just one book—
no, just one page of one book. That was all that stood
between him and everything that was familiar, everything he thought was true.

It was tempting. He could taste it in his mouth—
desire, greed. Fear, too. A galling dose of it.

He could tear out that page and no one would be the
wiser. The pages weren't even numbered. If they removed it carefully enough, no one would realize it was
gone.

Life would be normal. He would return to Belgrave
precisely as he'd left, with all the same possessions, responsibilities, and commitments.

Including Amelia.

She should have been his duchess by now. He should
never have dragged his feet.

If he tore out that page . . .

"Do you hear that?" Jack hissed.

Thomas perked up, his ear instinctively tilting toward
the window.

Horses.

"They're here," Thomas said.

It was now or never.

He stared at the register.

And stared.

"I can't do it," he whispered.

And then—it happened so fast—Jack pushed by him,
knocking him aside. Thomas just managed to snap his
face back when he saw Jack with his hands on the register . . . ripping it apart.

Thomas hurled himself forward, landing hard on Jack as he tried to grab the torn page from his fingers, but Jack slid out from his grasp, launching himself toward the fire.

"Jack, no!" Thomas yelled, but Jack was too quick, and even as he caught hold of his arm, Jack managed to hurl the paper into the fire.

Thomas staggered back, horrified by the sight of it. The center caught the flame first, bursting a hole through the middle of the page. Then the corners began to curl, blackening until they crumbled.

Soot. Ashes.

Dust.

"God in heaven," Thomas whispered. "What have you done?"

Amelia had thought that she'd never again have to ponder the words *worst day* and *of my life* in the same sentence. After the scene in the Belgrave drawing room, when two men had nearly come to blows over which one of them would be forced to marry her—well, one didn't generally think such depths of humiliation could be achieved twice in one lifetime.

Her father, however, had apparently not been informed of this.

"Papa, stop," she pleaded, digging in her heels— quite literally—as he attempted to drag her through the door of the Maguiresbridge rectory.

"I'd think you'd be a bit more eager to have an answer," he said impatiently. "God knows I am."

It had been a dreadful morning. When the dowager discovered that the two men had ridden off to the church without her, she went—and Amelia did not think this an exaggeration—berserk. Even more chilling was the speed with which she recovered. (Under a minute, by Amelia's estimation.) The dowager's rage was now channeled into icy purpose, and frankly, Amelia found this even more frightening than her fury. As soon as she found out that Grace did not intend to accompany them to Maguiresbridge, she latched herself to Grace's arm and hissed, "Do not leave me alone with that woman."

Grace had tried to explain that Amelia wouldn't be alone, but Amelia was having none of that and refused to leave without her. And as Lord Crowland would not go without Amelia, and they needed Mrs. Audley to direct them to the proper church . . .

It was a crowded carriage that made its way to County Fermanagh.

Amelia was wedged in on the rear-facing seat with Grace and Mrs. Audley, which would have been no trouble whatsoever except that she was facing the dowager, who kept demanding that poor Mrs. Audley update her on their progress. Which meant that Mrs. Audley had to twist, jostling into Grace, who jostled into Amelia, who was already overly tense and apprehensive.

And then, as soon as they arrived, her father had grabbed her by the arm and hissed one last lecture in her ear about fathers and daughters and the rules governing the relations thereof, not to mention three full sentences about dynastic legacies, family fortunes, and responsibilities to the Crown.

All in her ear, and all in under a minute. If she hadn't been forced to endure the same set of directives so many times in the past week, she would not have understood a word of it.

She'd tried to tell him that Thomas and Jack deserved their privacy, that they should not have to discover their fates with an audience, but she supposed the point was now moot. The dowager had charged ahead, and Amelia could hear her bellowing, "Where is it?"

Amelia twisted, facing Grace and Mrs. Audley, who were following several horrified paces behind. But before she could say anything, her father yanked hard on her arm, and she went stumbling over the threshold behind him.

A woman stood in the center of the room, teacup in hand, the expression on her face somewhere between startled and alarmed. The housekeeper, probably, although Amelia could not inquire. Her father was still dragging her along behind him, determined not to allow the dowager to reach Thomas and Jack too far ahead of him.

"Move," he growled at her, but a strange, almost preternatural panic had begun to set in, and she did not want to go into that back room.

"Father . . . " she tried to say, but the second syllable died on her tongue.

Thomas.

There he was, standing in front of her now that her father had hauled her through the doorway. He was standing very still, utterly expressionless, his eyes focused at a spot in the wall that held no window, no painting—nothing at all, save for his attention.

Amelia choked back a cry. He had lost the title. He didn't have to say a word. He did not even have to look at her. She could see it in his face.

"How dare you leave without me?" the dowager demanded. "Where is it? I demand to see the register."

But no one spoke. Thomas remained unmoving, stiff and proud, like the duke they'd all thought he was, and Jack—good heavens, he looked positively ill. His color was high, and it was clear to Amelia that he was breathing far too fast.

"What did you find?" the dowager practically screamed.

Amelia stared at Thomas. He did not speak.

"He is Wyndham," Jack finally said. "As he should be."

Amelia gasped, hoping, *praying* that she'd been wrong about the look on Thomas's face. She did not care about the title or the riches or the land. She just wanted *him,* but he was too bloody proud to give himself to her if he was nothing more than Mr. Thomas Cavendish, gentleman of Lincolnshire.

The dowager turned sharply toward Thomas. "Is this true?"

Thomas said nothing.

The dowager repeated her question, grabbing Thomas's arm with enough ferocity to make Amelia wince.

"There is no record of a marriage," Jack insisted.

Thomas said nothing.

"Thomas is the duke," Jack said again, but he sounded scared. Desperate. "Why aren't you listening? Why isn't anyone listening to me?"

Amelia held her breath.

"He lies," Thomas said in a low voice.

Amelia swallowed, because her only other option was to cry.

"No," Jack burst out, "I'm telling you—"

"Oh, for God's sake," Thomas snapped. "Do you think no one will find you out? There will be witnesses. Do you really think there won't be any witnesses to the wedding? For God's sake, you can't rewrite the past." He looked at the fire. "Or burn it, as the case may be."

Amelia stared at him, and then she realized—*he could have lied.*

He could have lied. But he didn't.

If he'd lied—

"He tore the page from the register," Thomas said, his voice a strange, detached monotone. "He threw it into the fire."

As one, the room turned, mesmerized by the flames crackling in the fireplace. But there was nothing to see, not even those dark sooty swirls that rose into the air when paper burned. No evidence at all of Jack's crime. If Thomas had lied—

No one would have known. He could have kept it all. He could have kept his title. His money.

He could have kept *her.*

"It's yours," Thomas said, turning to Jack. And then he bowed. To Jack. Who looked aghast.

Thomas turned, facing the rest of the room. "I am—" He cleared his throat, and when he continued, his voice was even and proud. "I am Mr. Cavendish," he said, "and I bid you all a good day."

And then he left. He brushed past them all and walked right out the door.

He didn't look at Amelia.

And as she stood there in silence, it occurred to her—he hadn't looked at her at all. Not even once. He had stood in place, staring at the wall, at Jack, at his grandmother, even at Grace.

But he'd never looked at her.

It was a strange thing in which to take comfort. But she did.

Chapter 20

Thomas had no idea where he intended to go. When he moved through the rectory, brushing past the house-keeper, who'd gone from disinterest to unabashed eavesdropping; when he walked down the front steps and into the bright Irish sunlight; when he stood there for a moment, blinking, disoriented, he only had one thought—

Away.

He had to get away.

He did not want to see his grandmother. He did not want to see the new Duke of Wyndham.

He did not want Amelia to see *him*.

And so he hopped on his horse and rode. He rode all the way to Butlersbridge, since it was the only place he knew. He passed the drive to Cloverhill—he was not ready to go back *there*, not when the rest of them would be returning so soon—and continued on until he saw a public house on his right. It looked reputable enough, so he dismounted and went in.

And that was where Amelia found him, five hours later.

"We've been looking for you," she said, her tone trying to be bright and cheerful.

Thomas closed his eyes for a moment, rubbing one finger along the bridge of his nose before he replied. "It appears you have found me."

She sucked in her lips, her eyes resting on the half-empty tankard of ale that sat before him.

"I am not drunk, if that is what you are wondering."

"I would not fault you if you were."

"A tolerant woman." He sat back in his chair, his posture lazy and loose. "What a pity I did not marry you."

Not drunk, perhaps, but he'd had enough alcohol to have become a little bit mean.

She did not reply. Which was probably for the best. If she'd given him the set-down he so richly deserved, he'd have had to respond in kind. Because that was the sort of mood he was in. And then he'd have to dislike himself even more than he did right now.

Frankly, he found the whole proposition rather tiresome.

She did not deserve his foul mood, but then again, he *had* attempted to remove himself from social interaction. She was the one who had hunted him down, all the way to the Derragarra Inn.

She sat in the chair across from him, regarding him with an even expression. And then it occurred to him—

"What are you doing here?"

"I believe I said I was looking for you."

He looked around. They were in a pub, for God's sake. Men were drinking. "You came without a chaperone?"

She gave a little shrug. "I doubt anyone has noticed I've gone missing. There is quite a bit of excitement at Cloverhill."

"All are feting the new duke?" he asked, dry and wry.

She cocked her head to the side, a tiny acknowledgment of his sarcasm. "All are feting his upcoming marriage."

He looked up sharply at that.

"*Not* to me," she put in hastily, raising a hand as if to ward off the query.

"Yes," he murmured. "All that feting would be a bit awkward without the bride."

Her mouth clamped together, betraying her impatience with him. But she kept her temper, saying, "He is marrying Grace."

"Is he now?" He smiled at that. For real. "That's good. That's a good thing."

"They seem to love each other very much."

He looked up at her. She was sitting very quietly. It wasn't just her voice, though; it was her demeanor, her aspect. Her hair was pulled back loosely, with a few misbehaving tendrils tucked behind her ears, and her mouth—she wasn't smiling, but she wasn't frowning, either. Considering all that had transpired that day, she was remarkably serene and composed. And maybe a little happy. If not for herself, then for Jack and Grace.

"The proposal was very romantic," she informed him.

"You witnessed it?"

She grinned. "We all did."

"Even my grandmother?"

"Oh, yes."

He chuckled, despite his determination to remain cross. "I am sorry I missed it."

"I am sorry you missed it, too."

There was something in her voice . . . And when he looked up, there was something in her eyes, too. But he didn't want to see it. He didn't want to know it. He did not want her pity or her sympathy or whatever it was when a woman's face held that awful expression—a little bit maternal, a little bit sad, as if she wanted to fix his problems for him, make it all go away with a kiss and a *There, there.*

Was it too much to ask for a few bloody moments to wallow in his own miseries?

And they *were* his own. It wasn't the sort of thing that could ever be classified as a shared experience.

Ah, yes, I am the man formerly known as the Duke of Wyndham.

It was going to be bloody brilliant at parties.

"I think Mr. Audley is scared," Amelia said.

"He should be."

She nodded a bit at that, her expression thoughtful. "I suppose so. He will have a great deal to learn. You always seemed terribly busy whenever I was at Belgrave."

He took a drink of his ale, not because he wanted it—it was his third tankard, and he rather thought he'd had enough. But if she thought he was planning to drink himself stupid, perhaps she'd leave.

It would be easier without her.

Today. Here. He was Mr. Thomas Cavendish, gentleman of Lincolnshire, and right now it would be easier without her.

But she did not take the hint, and if anything, she seemed to be settling more deeply into her seat as she said, "Grace will help him, I'm sure. She knows so much about Belgrave."

"She's a good woman."

"Yes, she is." She looked down at her fingers, idly tracing the scratches and grooves in the table, then glanced back up. "I did not know her very well before this trip."

He found that an odd statement. "You have known her your entire life."

"But not well," she clarified. "She was always Elizabeth's friend, not mine."

"I imagine Grace would disagree with that assessment."

Her brows rose, just enough to exhibit her disdain. "It is easy to see that you don't have siblings."

"Meaning?"

"It's impossible for one to have friendships in equal measure with two siblings. One must always be the primary friend."

"How complicated it must be," he said in a dry voice, "befriending the Willoughby sisters."

"Five times more complicated than befriending *you*."

"But not nearly as difficult."

She looked at him with a cool expression. "At the moment, I would have to concur."

"Ouch." He smiled, but without much humor. *Much* being a bit of an overstatement.

She did not respond, which for some reason needled him. And so—even though he *knew* he was being an ass—he leaned over, peering down at her hands.

She pulled them back immediately. "What are your doing?"

"Checking for claws," he replied, his very voice a smirk.

She stood. Abruptly. "You are not yourself."

It was enough to make him laugh. "You've only just realized?"

"I'm not talking about your name," she shot back.

"Oh, it must be my charming attitude and aspect, then."

Her lips pinched. "You are not usually so sarcastic."

Good Lord. What did she expect from him? "Pray have a bit of sympathy, Lady Amelia. Am I permitted at least a few hours to mourn the loss of everything I hold dear?"

She sat, but her movements were gingerly, and she did not look comfortable in her position. "Forgive me." Her jaw clenched, and she swallowed before she said, "I should be more understanding."

He let out an aggravated breath, rubbing his hand over his eye and forehead. Damn, he was tired. He hadn't slept the night before, not a wink, and at least an hour of his wakefulness had been spent in the rather uncomfortable state of wanting *her*. And now she was acting like *this*?

"Don't beg my forgiveness," he said, exhausted by the whole thing.

She opened her mouth, then shut it. He suspected she'd been about to apologize for apologizing.

He took another drink.

Again, she did not take the hint. "What will you do?"

"This afternoon?" he murmured, knowing full well that wasn't what she meant.

She gave him a peeved look.

"I don't know," he said irritably. "It's only been a few hours."

"Well, yes, but you've been thinking about it for over a week. And on the boat you seemed quite certain that this would be the outcome."

"It's not the same."

"But—"

"For God's sake, Amelia, will you let well enough alone?"

She drew back, and he instantly regretted his outburst. But not enough to apologize for it.

"I should go," she said, her voice flat.

He certainly wasn't going to stop her. Hadn't he been *trying* to be rid of her? She would walk out that door, and he'd finally have some peace and quiet, and he wouldn't have to just sit here, trying so hard not to look at her face.

At her mouth.

At that little spot on her lips that she liked to touch with her tongue when she was nervous.

But as she rose to her feet, something grabbed him from the inside—that annoying little kernel of integrity that refused to make its exit along with the rest of his identity.

Bloody hell.

"Do you have an escort?" he asked.

"I don't need one," she replied, clearly unimpressed with his tone.

He stood, his chair scraping loudly against the floor. "I will escort you back."

"I believe I said—"

He took her arm, a bit more roughly than he'd intended. "You are an unmarried woman, alone in a foreign land."

She gave him a look of some disbelief. "I have a mount, Thomas. It is not as if I will be walking the roads alone."

"I will escort you," he repeated.

"Will you be civil?"

"Civility seems to be the one thing I cannot lose," he said dryly. "Else I'd have been happy to leave you be."

For a moment he thought she might argue, but her innate good sense took hold. "Very well," she said, with an impatient breath. "You may feel free to deposit me at the end of the lane, should you wish."

"Is that a dare, Lady Amelia?"

She turned to him with eyes so sad he almost felt punched. "When did you start calling me *lady* again?"

He stared at her for several moments before finally answering, soft and low, "When I ceased to be a lord."

She made no comment, but he saw her throat work. Bloody hell, she had better not cry. He could not *do* this if she cried.

"Let us return, then," she said, and she pulled her arm free and stepped quickly in front of him. He heard the catch in her voice, though, and as she walked to the door, he could see that her gait was not right.

She looked too stiff and she was not holding her hands the way she usually did. Her arm did not sway in that tiny, graceful movement he so adored.

Except he hadn't realized he adored it.

He had not even *known* that he knew the rhythms of her walk until he saw that she wasn't doing it.

And it was so damned frustrating that now, in the middle of all of this rot, when he wanted to do nothing but sit and be sorry for himself, he hurt for *her*.

"Amelia," he said once they exited the inn. His voice sounded abrupt, but he hadn't meant to call out to her. It had just . . . happened.

She stopped. Her fingers went up to her face and back down again before she turned.

"I'm sorry," he said.

She did not ask why, but the question hung in the air nonetheless.

"For being so rude. You were undeserving of it."

She looked up and then to the side before finally meeting his gaze. "You behaved far better than most men would have done in your situation."

Somehow he managed a smile. "If you happen to meet someone else—in my situation, that is—kindly give him my direction."

A tiny, mortified giggle escaped her lips. "I'm so sorry," she got out. Barely.

"Oh, don't be. If anyone deserves to laugh, it is you."

"No," she said immediately. "No. I could never—"

"That's not what I meant," he said, cutting her off before she could say something that might make him feel even more of a clod. "Merely that you've had your life overturned as well."

He helped her up to her saddle, trying not to allow his hands to linger at her waist. Or to notice that she smelled like roses.

"It's not far back to Cloverhill," she said once they were on their way.

He nodded.

"Oh yes, of course you must know that. You'd have ridden past, on the way back from Maguiresbridge."

He nodded again.

She nodded, too, then faced front, her eyes focused securely on the road ahead of her. She was quite a good rider, he noted. He did not know how she'd fare under less sedate conditions, but her posture and seat were perfect.

He wondered if her spine would soften, if her shoulders might slouch just a bit if she actually turned and looked at him.

But she didn't. Every time he glanced in her direction, he saw her profile. Until finally they reached the turnoff to Cloverhill.

"The end of the drive, I believe you specified," he murmured.

"Are you coming in?" she asked. Her voice wasn't tentative, but there was something heartbreakingly careful about it.

"No."

She nodded. "I understand."

He doubted that she did, but there seemed no reason to say it.

"Are you coming back at all?" she asked.

"No." He hadn't thought about it until this moment, but no, he did not wish to journey back to England with their traveling party. "I will make my own way back to Belgrave," he told her. And after that, he could not say. He supposed he'd remain in residence for a week or so to show Jack what was what. Collect his belongings. Surely some of it was his and not the dukedom's. It would be rather hard to swallow if he did not even own his own boots.

Why that was more depressing than the loss of the entire bloody castle, he'd never know.

"Good-bye, then," she said, and she smiled a bit. But just a bit. In its own way, her smile was the saddest thing he'd ever seen.

"Good-bye, Amelia."

She paused for a moment, then nudged her mount to the left, preparing to set off down the drive.

"Wait!" he called out.

She turned in her seat, her eyes shining hopeful. A bit of her hair caught the breeze, lifting through the air in a sinuous arc before she impatiently jabbed at it, shoving it behind her ear.

"I must beg a favor," he said. It was true, actually, although that did not quite explain the relief he felt when she brought her mount back to his side.

"Of course," she said.

"I need to write a short letter. To the duke." He cleared his throat. It was difficult to guess just how long it would take before that rolled off his tongue. "Will you be my messenger?"

"Yes, but I would be happy just to pass along a message. So you don't have to go to the trouble of . . . " Her hand worked awkwardly through the air. "Well, to the trouble of writing it, I suppose."

"If you pass along my words, they will know you have seen me."

Her lips parted but she did not reply.

"You have your reputation to consider," he said quietly.

She swallowed, and he knew what she was thinking. They had never had to worry about her reputation before.

"Of course," she said, her voice clipped.

"Will you meet me right here?" he asked. "Just after sundown."

"No."

He blinked in surprise.

"You might be late, and I don't wish to wait for you on a public road."

"I won't be late," he told her.

"I will meet you at the gazebo."

"There is a gazebo?"

"Mrs. Audley showed it to me earlier." She explained to him how to get there, then added, "It is not far from the house. But you won't be seen, if that is your concern."

He nodded. "Thank you. I appreciate your assistance."

She rode away then, and he waited, watching her as she grew smaller and smaller in the distance. He waited until she went around the slight curve in the drive, taking her out of his vision. And then he waited some more.

And then, finally, when he knew in his heart that she'd got down from her horse and made her way inside, he turned and rode off.

But not until then.

Chapter 21

Sundown came late this time of year, and as Mrs. Audley kept country hours, it was well past supper by the time Amelia made her way to the gazebo. As she'd expected, no one made note of her departure. Her father had retired to his room directly after the meal; he was still rather cross over Jack's proposal to Grace. The dowager had not even bothered to come down in the first place.

After their meal, Mrs. Audley invited Amelia to join her in the drawing room with Jack and Grace, but Amelia declined. She had spent an hour in the same place with the same three people before supper, and the entire conversation consisted of tales of Jack's exploits in his younger days. Which were indeed amusing. But perhaps more so if one were in love with him, which she was not. No one was surprised when she said she was tired and would prefer to read in bed.

She took a book from the small library, climbed the stairs, reclined upon her bed for a minute to give the covers a properly rumpled look, then stole her way outside. If Grace went back to the room while she was out—which Amelia highly doubted; she'd been hanging on Mrs. Audley's every word—it would appear that she had wandered out for just a moment. To the library, for another book. Or maybe to find something to eat. There was no reason anyone might suspect that she was planning to meet Thomas. Everyone had expressed their curiosity, of course, as to his whereabouts, but it was understood that he would wish for some time to himself.

The sun was sinking along the horizon as she made her way to the gazebo, and already the air was getting that flat quality to it—the colors less vivid, the shadows gone. She told herself that their meeting meant nothing, that she was simply doing him a favor, collecting his letter so she might leave it on a table in the front hall and then feign surprise with all the rest when it was discovered. And it probably *was* nothing. She was not going to be throwing herself at him again; her last attempt at passion had surely fulfilled whatever quota of mortification she was due for her lifetime. And Thomas had given her no indication that he wished to pursue their romance further. Not now that he'd lost Wyndham.

He was so bloody proud. She supposed that was what came of living one's life as one of the twenty or so most powerful men in the land. She could tear her heart from her chest and hand it to him, tell him she'd love him until the day she died, and he would still refuse to marry her.

For her own good.

That was the worst of it. He'd say it was for her own good, that she deserved more.

As if she'd ever valued him for his title and riches. If this had all happened just last month, before they'd spoken, before they kissed . . .

She wouldn't have cared.

Oh, she'd be embarrassed, she supposed, the next time she went to London. But there would be plenty who'd say she made a lucky escape, not to have married him before he lost the title. And she knew her worth. She was the reasonably attractive, intelligent (but not—*oh, thank you, Mother*—too intelligent), well-dowered daughter of an earl. She'd not remain on the shelf for long.

It would all have been perfectly acceptable if she hadn't gone and fallen in love with him.

Him. Not the title, not the castle. Him.

But he would never understand that.

She hurried across the lawn, hugging her arms to her body to ward off the evening chill. She'd taken the long way around so she would not pass by the drawing room window. It occurred to her that she was getting quite experienced at sneaking around this house.

There had to be something funny in that.

Or at the very least, ironic.

Or maybe just sad.

She could see the gazebo in the distance, its white paint visible in the dimming light. It would only be another minute before—

"Amelia."

"Oh!" She jumped a foot. "Dear heavens, Thomas, you gave me a fright."

He smiled lopsidedly. "You weren't expecting me?"

"Not *here*." The gazebo was still many yards away.

"My apologies. I saw you and it seemed impolite not to make myself known."

"No, of course, I'm just—" She took a breath, patting her chest with her hand. "My heart is still racing."

There was a moment of silence, and then another.

And then one more.

It was awful. Awkward and empty and all those things she'd thought were normal back before she truly knew him. When he was the duke, and she was his lucky fiancée. And they never had anything to say to each other.

"Here you are." He thrust a piece of paper at her, folded over and sealed with wax. Then he gave her his signet ring. "I was going to use it on the wax," he said, "but then I realized . . . "

She looked down at the ring, emblazoned with the Wyndham crest. "It would have been funny, actually."

"Painfully so."

She touched the wax. It was smooth where it had been pressed down with a plain, flat stamp. She looked up and tried to smile. "Perhaps I shall get you a new one. For your birthday."

"A new ring?"

Oh dear, that had come out wrong. "No, of course not." She cleared her throat, embarrassed now, then mumbled, "That would be too presumptuous."

He waited, then cocked his head forward to indicate that he was still wondering what she'd meant.

"A stamp. For sealing wax," she explained, and she hated the cadence of her voice. Only four words, but she sounded all babblish. Silly and nervous. "You'll still need to send letters."

He seemed intrigued. "What shall you choose as the design?"

"I don't know." She looked down at the ring again, then put it in her pocket for safekeeping. "Have you a motto?"

He shook his head.

"Do you want a motto?"

"Do you want to give me one?"

She chuckled. "Oh, you should not tempt me."

"Meaning?"

"Meaning that given time, I could come up with something far more clever than *Mors ærumnarum requies*."

His brow furrowed as he attempted to translate.

"Death is rest from afflictions," she informed him.

He laughed.

"The Willoughby heraldic motto," she said, rolling her eyes. "Since the time of the Plantagenets."

"I'm so sorry."

"On the other hand, we do live to very old ages."

And then, because she was finally enjoying herself, she added, "Crippled, arthritic, and wheezing, I'm sure."

"Don't forget gout."

"You're so kind to remind me." She rolled her eyes, then gave him a curious look. "What *is* the Cavendish motto?"

"*Sola nobilitus virtas.*"

Sola nobili— She gave up. "My Latin is rusty."

"Virtue is the only nobility."

"Oh." She winced. "That is ironic."

"Isn't it, though?"

She didn't know what to say after that. And neither, apparently, did he. She smiled awkwardly. "Right. Well." She held up the missive. "I shall take good care of this."

"Thank you."

"Good-bye, then."

"Good-bye."

She turned to go, then stopped and turned back around, holding the letter about level with her shoulder. "Should I assume this means that you do not plan to rejoin us at Cloverhill?"

"No. I would not be good company."

She gave him a little nod, her lips in an awkward, close-mouthed smile. Her arm came back down, and she knew she should leave. And she started to, she really did, or at least she thought about starting to, but then—

"It's all in there," he said.

"I beg your pardon?" She sounded a bit breathless, but maybe he did not notice.

"The letter," he explained. "I laid out my intentions. For Jack."

"Of course." She nodded, trying not think about how jerky the movement felt. "I'm sure you were very thorough."

"Conscientious in all things," he murmured.

"Your new motto?" She was holding her breath, delighted to have found a new avenue of conversation. She did not want to say good-bye. If she walked away now, it was all done, wasn't it?

He smiled politely and dipped his chin at her. "I shall look forward to your gift."

"Then I will see you again?" Oh, *blast*. Blast blast *blast*. She had not meant that to come out as a question. It was supposed to be a statement, dry and sophisticated and definitely not uttered in that tiny little pathetically hopeful voice.

"I'm sure you will."

She nodded.

He nodded.

They stood there. Looking at each other.

And then—

From her lips—

In the most unbelievably stupid—

"I love you!"

Oh God.

Oh God oh God oh God oh God. Where had that come from? She wasn't supposed to say that. And it wasn't supposed to sound so desperate. And he wasn't supposed to be staring at her as if she'd grown horns. And she wasn't supposed to be shaking and she *was* supposed to be breathing and oh dear God she was going to cry because she was such a wretch and—

She threw up her hands. Shook them. "I have to go!"

She ran. *Oh bloody bloody.* She'd dropped the letter.

She ran back. "Sorry." Scooped it up. Looked at him.

Oh, that was a mistake. Because now she was talking again, as if her mouth had done *anything* but make a fool of her this evening. "I'm so sorry. I shouldn't have said that. I didn't, well, I shouldn't have. And I'm—I'm—" She opened her mouth, but her throat had closed up, and she thought she might have stopped breathing, but then, finally, like some horrifying belch, it came out—

"I really have to go!"

"Amelia, wait." He put his hand on her arm.

She froze, closing her eyes at the agony of it.

"You—"

"I shouldn't have said it," she blurted out. She had to cut him off before he said anything. Because she knew he wasn't going to say that he loved her in return, and nothing else would be bearable.

"Amelia, you—"

"No!" she cried. "Don't say anything. Please, you'll only make it worse. I'm sorry. I've put you in a terrible position, and—"

"*Stop.*" He put his hands on her shoulders, his grip firm and warm, and she wanted so much to let her head sigh to the side, so she could rest her cheek against him.

But she didn't.

"Amelia," he said. He looked as if he was searching for words. Which could not be a good sign. If he loved her . . . if he wanted her to know this . . . wouldn't he know what to say?

"It has been a most unusual day," he said haltingly. "And—" He cleared his throat. "Many things have happened, and it would not be surprising if you *thought* that—"

"You think I just came to this conclusion this afternoon?"

"I don't—"

But she could not even begin to tolerate his condescension. "Did you ever wonder why I fought so hard against having to marry Mr. Audley?"

"Actually," he said rather quietly, "you did not say much."

"Because I was dumbfounded! Thunderstruck. How do you think you would feel if your father suddenly demanded you marry someone you'd never met, and *then* your fiancé, with whom you *thought* you were finally forming a friendship, turned and demanded the same thing?"

"It was for your own good, Amelia."

"No, it was not!" She shook him off, practically screaming the words. "Would it really be for my own good to be forced into marriage with a man who is in love with Grace Eversleigh? I'd only just stopped thinking I was going to get that with you!"

There was an awful silence.

She had not just said that. Please, please, she didn't just say that.

His face went slack with surprise. "You thought I was in love with Grace?"

"She certainly knew you better than I did," she muttered.

"No, I wouldn't—I mean, I didn't, except—"

"Except what?"

"Nothing." But he looked guilty. Of something.

"Tell me."

"Amelia—"

"Tell me!"

And she must have looked a complete virago, ready to go for his throat, because he shot back with, "I asked her to marry me."

"What?"

"It did not mean anything."

"You asked someone to marry you and it did not mean anything?"

"It's not how it sounded."

"When did you do this?"

"Before we left for Ireland," he admitted.

"Before we—" Her mouth dropped open in outrage. "You were still engaged to me. You can't ask someone to marry you when you are promised to another."

It was the most unbelievably un-Thomas action she could have ever imagined.

"Amelia—"

"No." She shook her head. She did not want to hear his excuses. "How could you do this? You always do the right thing. Always. Even when it's a bloody nuisance, you always—"

"I didn't think I would be engaged to you for very much longer," he cut in. "I just said to her that if Audley turned out to be the duke, that perhaps we ought make a go of it when it was all over and done with."

"Make a *go*?" she echoed.

"I didn't say it like that," he muttered.

"Oh, my God."

"Amelia . . ."

She blinked, trying to take it all in. "But you wouldn't marry me," she whispered.

"What are you talking about?"

She looked up, finally able to focus on his face. Sharply, on his eyes, and for once she did not care how blue they were. "You said you would not marry me if you lost the title. But you would marry Grace?"

"It's not the same thing," he said. But he looked embarrassed.

"Why? How? How is it different?"

"Because you deserved more."

Her eyes widened. "I think you just insulted Grace."

"Damn it," he muttered, raking his hand through his hair. "You're twisting my words."

"I think you are doing a fine job of twisting them yourself."

He took a deep breath, clearly trying to calm his temper. "Your whole life you have expected to marry a duke."

"What does that matter?"

"What does that *matter*?" For a moment he looked incapable of words. "You have no idea what your life might be, stripped of your connections and your money."

"I don't need that," she protested.

But he continued as if he had not heard her. "I have nothing, Amelia. I have no money, no property—"

"You have yourself."

He gave a self-mocking snort. "I don't even know who that is."

"I do," she whispered.

"You're not being realistic."

"You're not being fair."

"Amelia, you—"

"No," she cut in angrily. "I don't want to hear it. I can't believe the level of your insult."

"My insult?"

"Am I really such a hothouse flower that you don't think I could withstand the tiniest of hardships?"

"It won't be tiny."

"But Grace could do it."

His expression grew stony, and he did not reply.

"What did she say?" Amelia asked, her words almost a sneer.

"What?"

Her voice grew in volume. "What did Grace say?"

He stared at her as if he'd never seen her before.

"You asked her to marry you," she ground out. "What did she say?"

"She refused," he finally replied, his voice clipped.

"Did you kiss her?"

"Amelia . . . "

"Did you?"

"Why does it matter?"

"Did you kiss her?"

"Yes!" he exploded. "Yes, for the love of God, I kissed her, but it was nothing. Nothing! I tried, believe me I tried to feel something, but it was nothing like *this*." He grabbed her then, and his lips came down on hers so fast and so hard that she did not have time to breathe. And then it didn't matter. His hands were on her, pressing her against him—hard—and she could feel his arousal against her, and she wanted him.

She wanted this.

She tore at his clothing, wanting nothing so much as the heat of his skin against hers. His lips were on her neck, and his hand was under her skirt, moving up her leg.

She was panting with desire. His thumb was on the soft flesh of her inner thigh, pressing, stroking, and she wasn't sure she could stand. She clutched at his shoulders for support, sighing his name, moaning it, begging him over and over again for more.

And his hand moved even higher, until it was at the crook of her leg, where it met her hip, so close . . . so close to . . .

He touched her.

She went stiff, and then she sagged against him, instinctively softening herself as he touched her. "Thomas," she moaned, and before she knew it, he'd laid her on the ground, and he was kissing her, and he was touching her, and she had no idea what to do, had no thought at all except that she wanted this. She wanted everything he was doing and more.

His fingers continued to tickle, and then he slipped one inside of her in the most wicked caress of all. She arched beneath him, gasping at the shock and pleasure of it. He'd slipped inside so easily. Had her body been waiting for this? Preparing itself for this very moment, when he would settle himself between her thighs and touch her?

She was breathing faster, harder, and she wanted him closer. Her blood was pounding through her body, and all she could do was grab at him, clutch his back, his hair, his buttocks—anything to pull him against her, to feel the mounting pressure of his body on hers.

His mouth moved to her chest, to the flat plane of skin left exposed by her dress. She shivered as he found the neckline of her dress, his lips tracing it around . . . down . . . from her collarbone to the gentle swell of her breast. He took the fabric between his teeth and began to tug, gently at first, and then with greater vigor when it did not give. Finally, with a muffled curse, he brought his hand down and grabbed at the fabric that gathered over her shoulder, giving it a yank until it slid over her arm. Her breast slid free, and she barely had a chance to gasp before his mouth closed over the tip.

A soft shriek escaped her lips, and she did not know whether to pull back or push forward, and in the end it did not matter, because he was holding her securely in place, and judging from his growls of pleasure, she was not going anywhere. His hand—the one that had been delivering such sweet torture—had curved around her backside and was pulling her relentlessly against his desire. And his other hand—it slid along the soft, sensitive skin of her arm, stretching her up, and up, until their hands were both over their heads.

Their fingers entwined.

I love you, she wanted to cry.

But she didn't. She couldn't speak, couldn't allow herself to utter a word. He would stop if she did. She didn't know how she knew it, or why she was so certain, but she knew it was true. If she did anything to break the spell, to bring him back to reality, he would stop. And she could not bear it if that happened.

She felt his hands move between their bodies, fumbling with the fastenings of his breeches, and then there he was. Hard and hot, pressing her, then stretching her, and she was not sure if this was going to work, and then she was no longer so certain she was going to like it, and then—

He thrust forward with a primal grunt, and she could not help it—she let out a tiny scream of pain.

He froze instantly.

As did she.

He pushed himself up so that his head drew back, and she got the impression that he was only just now seeing her. The haze of passion had been pricked, and now—oh, it was everything she'd feared . . .

He regretted it.

"Oh my God," he whispered. "Oh my God."

* * *

What had he done?

It was a bloody stupid question, and an even stupider time to ask it, as he was lying atop Amelia, buried to the hilt, and they were in a field. A *field*. He'd taken her virginity without even a care to her comfort. Her dress was bunched around her waist, there were leaves in her hair, and good God—he hadn't even managed to take off his boots.

"I'm so sorry," he whispered.

She shook her head, but he could not tell from her expression what she meant.

He would marry her now. There could be no question. He had ruined her in the most debasing way possible. Had he even whispered her name? In the entire time he'd been making love to her—had he said her name? Had he been aware of anything besides his own unrelenting desire?

"I'm sorry," he said again, but words could never be enough. He moved to withdraw, so that he could help her, comfort her.

"No!" she cried, grabbing his shoulders. "*Please.* Don't go."

He stared down at her, unable to believe her words. He knew that this had not been rape. She had wanted it, too. She had moaned for him, clutched his shoulders, gasping his name in her desire. But surely now she would wish to end it. To wait for something more civilized. In a bed. As a wife.

"Stay," she whispered, touching his cheek.

"Amelia," he said raggedly, and he prayed she could hear all of his thoughts in that single word, because he did not think he could give voice to them.

"It's done," she said softly. But then her eyes grew fierce. "And I will *never* regret it."

He tried to say something; he made *some* sort of noise, but it came from deep within, from some elemental spot where he had no words.

"Shhh." She touched her finger to his lips. "It's done," she said again. And then she smiled, her expression the culmination of a million years of womanly experience. "Now make it good."

His pulse quickened, and then her hand crept up the back of his leg until it reached the bare skin of his buttocks.

He gasped.

She squeezed. "Make it *wonderful*."

And he did. If the first part of his lovemaking had been all frenetic thrusts and mindless passion, now he was a man with a purpose. Every kiss was pure artistry, every touch designed to bring her to the heights of pleasure. If something made her gasp with delight, he did it again . . . and again.

He whispered her name . . . over and over again, against her skin, into her hair, as his lips teased her breast. He would make this good for her. He would make it *wonderful*. He would not rest until he'd brought her to the heights of ecstasy, until she shattered in his arms.

This was not about him. For the first time in weeks, something was *not* about him. It was not about his name or who he was or anything other than what he could do to bring her pleasure.

It was for her. Amelia. It was all for her, and maybe it always would be, for the rest of his days.

And maybe he wouldn't mind that.

Maybe it was a good thing. A very good thing.

He looked down at her, his breath catching as he saw her lips part in a tiny sigh of desire. He'd never seen anything so beautiful. Nothing compared, not the most brilliant of diamonds, the most spectacular of sunsets. Nothing compared to her face in that moment.

And then it was clear.

He loved her.

This girl—no, this woman—whom he'd politely ignored for years had reached inside him and stolen his heart.

And suddenly he didn't know how he'd ever thought he could allow her to marry Jack.

He didn't know how he thought he could live apart from her.

Or how he could live just one more day without knowing that she would one day be his wife. Bear his children. Grow old with him.

"Thomas?"

Her whisper brought him back, and he realized he'd stopped moving. She was gazing up at him with a mix of curiosity and need, and her eyes . . . her expression . . . He couldn't explain what it did to him, or rather how, but he was happy.

Not content, not satisfied, not amused.

Happy.

Lovesick, champagne in the veins, want-to-shout-it-to-the-world happy.

"Why are you smiling?" she asked, and then she was smiling, too, because it was infectious. It had to be. He could not keep it inside.

"I love you," he said, and he knew his face must belie the surprise and wonder he was feeling.

She looked instantly cautious. "Thomas . . . "

It was imperative that she understood. "I'm not saying it because you said it, and I'm not saying it because I obviously have to marry you now, I'm saying it because . . . because . . . "

She went very still beneath him.

He whispered the last: "I'm saying it because it is true."

Tears formed in her eyes, and he bent down to gently kiss them away. "I love you," he whispered. And then he could not stop his sly smile. "But for once in my life, I'm not going to do the right thing."

Her eyes widened with alarm. "What do you mean?"

He kissed her cheek, then her ear, then the graceful edge of her jaw. "The right thing, I think, would be to stop this madness right now. Not that you're not properly ruined, but I really ought to get your father's permission before continuing."

"Continuing *this*?" she choked out.

He repeated his kisses on the other side of her face. "I would never be so crude. I meant the courtship. In the general sense."

Her mouth opened and closed a few times, then finally slid into something that wasn't sure if it ought to be a smile.

"But that would be cruel," he murmured.

"Cruel?" she echoed.

"Mmm. Not to continue with *this*." He pushed forward. Just a tiny bit, but enough to make her squeak in surprise.

He nuzzled her neck, increasing the rhythm between them. "To start something, and not finish it—that doesn't seem like the right thing, does it?"

"No," she answered, but her voice was strained and her breaths were growing ragged.

So he continued. He loved her with his body just as he loved her with his heart. And when he felt her shudder beneath him, he finally let go, exploding inside of her with a force that left him spent, exhausted . . . and complete.

Maybe it wasn't the right way to seduce the woman he loved, but it had certainly been good.

Chapter 22

In the end, Thomas did do the right thing.

Almost.

Amelia had expected that he would seek out her father the next day and formally ask for her hand in marriage. Instead, he asked her to deliver the note and his ring as planned, adding that he would see her in a fortnight in England.

He loved her, he said. He loved her more than he could ever say, but he needed to return on his own.

Amelia understood.

And so it came to pass that she was sitting in the Burges Park drawing room almost three weeks later, in the company of her mother, all four of her sisters, and two of her father's dogs, when the butler appeared in the doorway and announced:

"Mr. Thomas Cavendish, my lady."

"Who?" was Lady Crowland's immediate reply.

"It's Wyndham!" Elizabeth hissed.

"He's not Wyndham any longer," Milly corrected.

Amelia looked down at her book—some dreadful etiquette guide her mother had termed "improving"—and smiled.

"Why on earth would he come here?" Lady Crowland asked.

"Perhaps he is still engaged to Amelia," Milly suggested.

Her mother turned to her with utter horror. "Don't we *know*?"

"I don't think we do," Milly replied.

Amelia kept her eyes on her book.

"Amelia," Lady Crowland said sharply. "What *is* the status of your betrothal?"

Amelia tried to answer with a shrug and a blank look, but it became quickly apparent that this was not going to suffice, so she said, "I am not certain."

"How is that possible?" Milly asked.

"I did not break it off," Amelia said.

"Did he?"

"Er . . ." Amelia paused, unsure of where to direct her reply, as the query had come from five different sources. Her mother, she finally decided, and she turned in her direction and said, "No. Not formally."

"What a muddle. What a *muddle*." Lady Crowland brought her hand to her head, looking much aggrieved. "You shall have to end it, then. He will not do so; he is far too much of a gentleman for that. But surely he would never expect you to marry him *now*."

Amelia bit her lip.

"He is most likely here to provide you with the opportunity to end it. Yes, that must be it." Lady Crowland turned to the butler and said, "Show him in, Granville. And the rest of you—" She waved a hand in the general direction of her daughters, which was not easy, as they were scattered about the room. "We shall greet him and then discreetly make our regrets and leave."

"A mass exodus is meant to be discreet?" Milly asked.

Lady Crowland gave her a look, then turned to Amelia, exclaiming, "Oh! Do you think your father should be here?"

"I do," Amelia said, feeling remarkably serene, all things considered. "I really do."

"Milly," Lady Crowland said, "go find your father."

Milly's mouth fell open. "I can't leave *now*."

Lady Crowland let out a dramatic sigh. "Oh, for heaven's sake, was a mother ever so beleaguered?" She turned to Elizabeth.

"Oh, no," Elizabeth said instantly. "I don't want to miss a thing."

"You two," Lady Crowland said, waving her hand toward her two youngest. "Go find your father, and no complaining about it." She put her hand to her head. "This is going to give me a megrim, I'm sure." When her daughters did not move quickly enough, she added, "There is nothing to see here! Wyndham—"

"Cavendish," Milly corrected.

Lady Crowland rolled her eyes. "Whoever heard of such a thing? Long-lost cousin, indeed." And then, with remarkable verbal agility, she turned back to the two younger girls hovering near the doorway. "Go!"

They went, but not before skidding into Thomas, who had just been shown in. He was holding a rather large, flat package, which, at Lady Crowland's direction, he set down against the wall.

"Lady Crowland," he said, executing a deep bow.

Amelia felt an elbow in her ribs. Elizabeth's.

"He doesn't look devastated," Elizabeth whispered. "Didn't he just lose everything?"

"Maybe not everything," Amelia murmured. But Elizabeth did not hear; she was too busy trying not to appear as if she were gawking, which of course she was.

Thomas turned to the three Willoughby sisters. "Lady Elizabeth," he said politely, "Lady Amelia, Lady Millicent."

They all bobbed their curtsies, and he returned the gesture with an elegant tilt of his head.

Lady Crowland cleared her throat. "What a pleasant surprise this is, your, er . . . "

"Mr. Cavendish," he said with gentle humor. "I have had a few weeks to become accustomed to it."

"And of course it is your name," Milly put in.

"Millicent!" her mother scolded.

"No, no," Thomas said with a wry smile. "She is correct. Thomas Cavendish has been my name since birth."

There was an awkward moment, then Lady Crowland said, "You appear to be in good health."

"Very good, my lady. And you?"

"As well as can be expected." She sighed, tapping her chest a few times. "Children can be so exhausting."

"I hope to find that out for myself someday," Thomas said.

Lady Crowland colored at that, stammering, "Well, of course we all hope to be blessed by children, don't we?"

"I can't recall the last time she referred to me as a blessing," Milly muttered.

Amelia ignored her. She was far too happy just to gaze at Thomas from across the room. She'd missed him, but she hadn't realized just how much until she could finally *see* him, with her own eyes. Only now she wanted to touch him. She wanted to throw her arms around him and burrow into his embrace. She wanted to kiss him, to smell him, to be near him.

She sighed. Apparently quite loudly. Milly kicked her, and it was then that she realized everyone was looking at her.

Amelia just grinned. She couldn't help it.

Her mother gave her an odd look, then turned to Thomas and said, "I expect you would like a few moments of privacy with Amelia."

"I would like that above all things," he said smoothly, "although I also—"

"Cavendish!"

Amelia looked to the door. Her father had arrived.

"Lord Crowland," Thomas greeted him.

"Was wondering when you'd return. Not that I blamed you for deserting us in Ireland. Very well, I suppose we have matters to take care of." He glanced about the room, as if only then noticing the flock of Willoughby women standing stiffly throughout. "Hmmph. Perhaps in my office?"

Amelia fully expected him to agree. Thomas would never make a formal proposal of marriage without first securing permission from her father. Or at least trying to. She did not know what Thomas would do if her father did not agree, but she had every faith that they would be married.

It would just be so much easier if her family made no protest.

But Thomas surprised her. Indeed, he surprised everyone when he said, "There is no need to retire to another room. I have nothing to say that cannot be said in front of everyone."

"I *love* when people say that," Milly remarked.

"Milly!" Elizabeth hissed.

"He can't hear me."

"I can, actually," Thomas murmured.

Amelia had to cover her mouth to stifle her laughter.

"Are you done?" Lord Crowland demanded, giving his three eldest an annoyed glance.

They did not reply; there was only so much insubordination one could safely demonstrate in such a setting.

"Very well, then," Lord Crowland said, turning to Thomas. "What is it you need to tell me?"

"First of all," Thomas replied, "I wish to formally dissolve the betrothal contract."

Elizabeth gasped, and even Milly looked aghast at this public declaration.

Amelia just smiled. She had no idea what he had planned, but she trusted him.

"Consider it done," Lord Crowland said. "Although I rather thought it was already null."

Thomas tipped his head ever so slightly. "It's good to make things clear, though, wouldn't you agree?"

Lord Crowland blinked a few times, unsure of what he was getting at.

"I would like to make one more thing clear," Thomas said.

And then he turned.

Looked Amelia in the eyes.

Walked across the room.

Took her hands.

The room fell away, and there was just him . . . and her . . . and joy. Amelia felt herself start to laugh— silent and giddy—with far too much happiness than she could ever keep inside.

"Amelia," he said, and his eyes never left hers.

She started to nod, even though he hadn't asked her anything. But she couldn't help it. He had only to whisper her name and she wanted to shout. *Yes! Yes!*

He dropped to one knee. "Amelia Willoughby," he said, a little louder now, "will you do me the very great honor of becoming my wife?"

She kept nodding. She couldn't stop.

"I ask *you*," he continued, "because this time it is *your* choice."

"Yes," she whispered. And then she shouted it. "*Yes! Yes!*"

He slipped a ring on her shaking finger. She had not even noticed that he'd been holding one, so intent had she been on his face.

"I love you," he said. Right there, in front of everyone.

"I love you, too." Her voice shook, but the words were true.

He stood then, still holding her hand, and turned to her father. "I do hope you will give us your blessing."

His tone was light, but the intention was clear. They would marry with or without it.

"Can you provide for her?" Lord Crowland asked bluntly.

"I have reached a settlement with the new duke. She shall want for nothing."

"You won't have a title," Lady Crowland pointed out, but not unkindly. It was more of a reminder, a gentle check that her daughter had thought things through.

"I don't need one," Amelia answered. And later, when she thought about it, she supposed that all of her love for him must have been shining in her face because her mother grew misty, mumbling some sort of nonsense about dust as she dabbed at her eyes.

"Well, then," Lord Crowland said, looking very much as if he'd rather be out with his hounds. "I suppose it's settled." Then, as an afterthought: "Again."

"I should have married you sooner," Thomas said to Amelia, bringing one of her hands to his lips.

"No, you shouldn't have done. I might not have fallen in love with you if you'd been my husband."

"Care to explain that?" he asked, his smile amused.

"Not really," she said, feeling very cheeky.

"Oh, I almost forgot," he said quite suddenly. "I brought you a gift."

She grinned despite herself; she'd never been so sophisticated that she could hide her excitement for gifts.

He strode to the opposite side of the room, past her entire family, who were still watching the tableau with some disbelief, and picked up the large flat package he'd brought in earlier.

"Over here," he directed, setting it down on a nearby table.

Amelia hastened to his side, as did the rest of the Willoughbys. "What is it?" she asked, beaming up at him.

"Open it," he urged. "But carefully. It's delicate."

She did, untying the string and then gingerly peeling off the paper.

"What is *that*?" Milly demanded.

"Do you like it?" Thomas asked.

Amelia nodded, overwhelmed. "I love it."

"What *is* it?" Milly persisted.

It was a map. A heart-shaped map.

"A cordiform projection," Thomas told her.

She looked up at him excitedly. "It does not distort area. Look how small Greenland is."

He smiled. "I will confess that I purchased it more for its heart-shaped properties."

She turned toward her family. "Is this not the most romantic gift you have ever seen?"

They stared at her as if she'd gone mad.

"A map," Lady Crowland said. "Isn't that interesting?"

Elizabeth cleared her throat. "May I see the ring?"

Amelia thrust out her arm, letting her sisters ooh and ahh over her new diamond while she gazed up at her new—that was to say, her new old—fiancé.

"Is this where I am meant to make a clever comment about your having found the map of my heart?" he asked.

"Can you do it without making me cry?"

He pondered that. "I don't think so."

"Very well, say it, anyway."

He did.

And she cried.

"Well, *that's* a love match," Milly declared.

They nodded. It was, indeed.

Epilogue

Windsor Castle
July 1823

"Are we done?"

The king was bored. George IV never enjoyed his meetings with the Lord Chamberlain. They were always so ill-timed. He did not know how Montrose did it, but they always seemed to interfere with a planned meal.

"There is just one more thing, Majesty." The Duke of Montrose—his Lord Chamberlain for over two years now—shuffled a few papers, looked down, then looked up. "The Earl of Crowland has died."

George blinked. "That's a pity."

"He was in possession of five daughters."

"No sons?"

"Not a one. There is no heir. The title has reverted to you, Majesty."

"This was recent?"

"Earlier this month."

"Ah, well." George yawned. "We shall have to give the widow ample time to grieve before we reabsorb the property."

"Very kind of you as always, Majesty."

"There is little point in— Wait a moment." George's brow furrowed. "Crowland, you say? Wasn't he involved in that dreadful Wyndham matter?"

"His daughter was engaged to the duke. Er, the first one." Montrose cleared his throat. "But there is the matter of the earldom. With Crowland available—"

"How is Wyndham?" George cut in.

"Er, which one?"

George had a good laugh at that. "The new one. The real one. Eh, the other one, too. He was a good sort. We always liked him. He quite dropped out of sight, didn't he?"

"I believe he is recently returned from Amsterdam."

"What the devil was he doing there?"

"I do not know, Majesty."

"He married the Crowland girl, though, didn't he? After the whole mess with the title."

"He did."

"What a strange girl she must be," George mused. "Surely she could have done better."

"My wife informs me it was a love match," Montrose said.

George chuckled. It was so difficult to find proper amusement these days. This was a fine tale.

Montrose cleared his throat. "We do need to settle

the matter of the empty earldom. It can certainly sit, but—"

"Give it to Cavendish," George said with a wave.

Montrose stared at him in shock. "To . . ."

"To Cavendish. The former Wyndham. The Lord knows he deserves it after all he's been through."

"I don't believe his wife was the eldest daughter. The precedent—"

George had another laugh over that. "We daresay there is no precedent for any of this. We shall wait six months. Give the family time to grieve before the transfer."

"Are you certain, Majesty?"

"This amuses us, James."

Montrose nodded. The king only rarely used his Christian name. "He shall be most grateful, I'm sure."

"Well, it isn't a dukedom," George said with a chuckle. "But still . . ."

Seven months later, at Crowland House, London

"Oh, I do not think I can call you Lord Crowland," Amelia said, taking a sip of her tea. "It makes me feel as if I am talking to my father."

Thomas just shook his head. It had only been a month since they were called down to Windsor, and just a week since the news had been made public. He'd only just got used to not turning every time someone said *Wyndham*.

A footman entered the room, bearing a large tray. "The newspapers, sir," he intoned.

"Oh, it's a Wednesday, isn't it?" Amelia exclaimed, immediately moving toward the tray.

"You are addicted to that gossip rag," Thomas accused.

"I can't help it. It's so delicious."

Thomas picked up the *Times* and looked for political notes. He supposed he'd be back in the Lords now. He would need to be better informed.

"Oooh," Amelia murmured, positively buried in her news sheet.

Thomas looked up. "What?"

She waved him off. "Nothing you would be interested in. Oh!"

"Now what?"

This time she ignored him entirely.

He turned back to the paper, but he'd only got three sentences in when Amelia shrieked.

"What *is* it?" he demanded.

She waved her gossip rag in the air. "We're here! We're here!"

"Let me see that," he said, snatching it out of her hand. He looked down and read:

From Wyndham to Cavendish to Crowland. . .

This Author offers a point to whomever correctly identifies the man married to the former Lady Amelia Willoughby. And indeed, after five years amongst the untitled masses, surely the new earl would take Mr. Shakespeare to task. That which we call a gentleman with a title, estate, and thirty thousand per year smells infinitely sweeter than a mere mister.

Surely the new Lady Crowland would agree. Or would she? Despite her longstanding engagement with the man who once was Wyndham, she married the fellow when he had barely a farthing to his name.

If that isn't a love match, This Author shall eat her quill . . .

LADY WHISTLEDOWN'S SOCIETY PAPERS, 4 FEBRUARY 1824

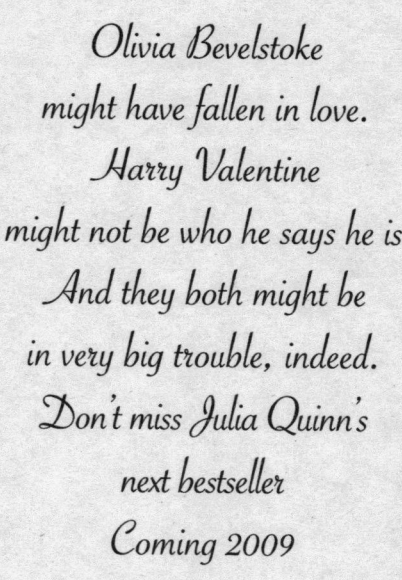

Olivia Bevelstoke
might have fallen in love.
Harry Valentine
might not be who he says he is.
And they both might be
in very big trouble, indeed.
Don't miss Julia Quinn's
next bestseller
Coming 2009
from

Avon Books

Want more *Bridgertons?*

YOU GOT IT!

JQE 0207